DISCARD

I STOOD BACK AND WATCHED HIS MOVEMENTS. Daniel had that way about him that could shut me down in an instant. I rubbed my hands together and jumped up and down to generate some heat. Most Minnesotans have thick blood, but how could Daniel even stand to be outside in only short sleeves? I kicked the gravel a couple of times and worked up my courage again. "Tell me . . . I mean . . . why did you come back? Why now, after all this time?"

Daniel looked up at me. His dark eyes searched my face. There was something different about those too-familiar eyes. Maybe it was the way the orange light from the streetlamp illuminated his pupils. Maybe it was the way he stared without blinking. His eyes made him look . . . hungry.

ALSO BY BREE DESPAIN

The Lost Saint: A Dark Divine Novel
(Available January 2011)

OTHER EGMONT USA BOOKS YOU MAY ENJOY

Candor
by Pam Bachorz

Dangerous Neighbors
by Beth Kephart

Raised by Wolves
by Jennifer Lynn Barnes

Shadow Hills
by Anastasia Hopcus

Siren
by Tricia Rayburn

The Dark Divine

BREE DESPAIN

EGMONT
USA

New York

For Brick,
Because you brought home that laptop all those years ago and
said, "You'd better start writing."
I.L.Y.R.U.T.T.M.A.B.A.
Always,
Bree

EGMONT
We bring stories to life

First published by Egmont USA, 2010
This paperback edition published by Egmont USA, 2010
443 Park Avenue South, Suite 806
New York, NY 10016

1 3 5 7 9 8 6 4 2

www.egmontusa.com
www.breedespain.com

THE LIBRARY OF CONGRESS HAS CATALOGED THE HARDCOVER EDITION AS FOLLOWS
Despain, Bree
The Dark Divine / Bree Despain
p. cm.
Summary: Grace Divine, almost seventeen, learns a dark secret when her childhood friend—
practically a brother—returns, upsetting her pastor-father and the rest of her family, around
the time strange things are happening in and near their small Minnesota town.
ISBN 978-1-60684-057-3 (hardcover) — ISBN 978-1-60684-065-8 (reinforced library binding)
— eBook ISBN 978-1-60684-117-4
[1. Interpersonal relations—Fiction. 2. Supernatural—Fiction. 3. Family life—Minnesota—
Fiction. 4. Christian life—Fiction. 5. High schools—Fiction.
6. Schools—Fiction. 7. Minnesota—Fiction.] I. Title.
PZ7.D4518Dar 2010
[Fic]—dc22
2009018680

Paperback ISBN 978-1-60684-154-9

Book design by JDRIFT DESIGN

Printed in the United States of America

CPSIA tracking label information:
Random House Production • 1745 Broadway • New York, NY 10019

Sacrifice

Blood fills my mouth. Fire sears my veins. I choke back a howl. The silver knife slips—the choice is mine.

I am death or life. I am salvation or destruction. Angel or demon.

I am grace.

I plunge in the knife.

This is my sacrifice—

I *am* the monster.

CHAPTER ONE

Prodigal

"Grace! You have *got* to see the new guy." April bounded up to me in the junior hallway. Sometimes she reminded me of the cocker spaniel I used to own—she trembled in excitement over just about anything.

"Hottest guy ever?" I almost dropped my backpack. Stupid combination locker.

"No way. This guy is totally nasty. He got kicked out of his last two schools, *and* Brett Johnson says he's on parole." April grinned. "Besides, everybody knows Jude is the hottest guy ever." She jabbed me in the side.

I did drop my backpack. My box of pastels dumped out at my feet. "*I* wouldn't know." I grumbled and squatted to pick up my shattered pastels. "Jude's my brother, remember?"

April rolled her eyes. "He did ask about me at lunch, right?"

"Yeah"—I picked through the chalk bits—"he said, 'How's April?' and I said, 'She's fine,' and then he gave me half of his turkey sandwich." I swear, if she had a disloyal bone in her body, I'd worry April was only my friend to get close to my brother—like half the other girls in this school.

"Hurry up," she said, glancing over her shoulder.

"You could help." I waved a broken pastel at her. "I just bought these on my way back from the café."

April crouched and picked up a blue one. "What's with these anyway? I thought you were working with charcoal."

"I can't get it to look right." I plucked the piece of chalk from her fingers and stuck it back in the box. "I'm starting over."

"But it's due tomorrow."

"I can't turn it in if it isn't right."

"I don't think it looks that bad," April said. "Besides, the new guy seems to like it."

"What?"

April bounced up. She grabbed my arm. "Come on. You have to see this." She sprang toward the art room, pulling me with her.

I clung to my pastels. "You are so weird."

April laughed and quickened her pace.

"Here she comes," Lynn Bishop called as we rounded the corner to the art department. A group of students congregated in front of the doorway. They parted to either side as we approached. Jenny Wilson glanced at me and whispered something to Lynn.

"What's the big deal?" I asked.

April pointed. "That is."

I stopped and stared at him. This guy more than pushed the limits of Holy Trinity's dress code in a holey Wolfsbane T-shirt and black, dingy jeans, shredded at the knees. His shaggy, dyed-black hair hid his face, and he held a large sheet of paper in his pale white hands. It was *my* charcoal drawing, and he was sitting in my seat.

I left the group of bystanders and strode up to the table. "Excuse me, you're in my spot."

"Then you must be Grace," he said without looking up. Something about his raspy voice made my arm hairs stand on end.

I stepped back. "How'd you know my name?"

He pointed at the masking tape name tag on the supply bucket I'd left out during lunch. "Grace Divine." He snorted. "Your parents must have some God complex. I bet your dad is a minister."

"Pastor. But that's none of your business."

He held my drawing in front of him. "Grace Divine. They must expect great things from you."

"They do. Now move."

"This drawing is anything but great," he said. "You've got these branches all wrong, and that knot should be turned up, not down." He picked up one of my charcoals between his thin fingers and drew on the paper.

I was ticked off by his audacity, but what I couldn't believe was the ease with which he wove thick and thin black lines into striking charcoal branches. The same tree I'd been agonizing over all week came to life on the paper. He used the side of his pinky to smudge the coal on the trunk—a major "don't" in Barlow's class, but the rough blending had just the right effect for the tree's bark. I watched him shade along the bottom of the branches, but then he began to fix the knot in the lowest one. How could he have known what that knot was supposed to look like?

"Stop it," I said. "That's mine. Give it back." I grabbed at the paper but he pulled it away. "Hand it over!"

"Kiss me," he said.

I heard April yelp.

"What?" I asked.

He leaned over the drawing. His face was still obscured by his shaggy hair, but a black stone pendant slipped out of his shirt. "Kiss me, and I'll give it back."

I grabbed his hand that held the charcoal. "Who the hell do you think you are?"

"So you don't recognize me?" He looked up and pushed his hair out of his face. His cheeks were pale and hollow, but it was his eyes that made me gasp. The same dark eyes I used to call "mud pies."

"Daniel?" I let go of his hand. The charcoal pencil plinked onto the table. A million questions slammed against one another in my brain. "Does Jude know you're here?"

Daniel wrapped his fingers around the black pendant that hung from his neck. His lips parted as if to speak.

Mr. Barlow came up to us, his arms crossed in front of his barrel-like chest. "I told you to report to the counselors' office before joining this class," he said to Daniel. "If you cannot respect me, young man, then perhaps you do not belong here."

"I was just leaving." Daniel shoved back his chair and slumped past me, his dyed hair veiling his eyes. "See you later, Gracie."

I looked at the charcoal drawing he left behind. The black lines laced together into the silhouette of a lone, familiar tree. I brushed past Mr. Barlow and the group of students in the doorway. "Daniel!" I shouted. But the hallway was deserted.

Daniel was good at disappearing. It's what he did best.

DINNER

I listened to forks and knives clinking on plates and dreaded my turn in the infamous Divine family daily ritual—the "so what did you do today?" part of dinner.

Dad went first. He was quite excited about the parish-sponsored charity drive. I'm sure it was a nice change for him. He'd been holed up studying in his private office so much lately that Jude and I joked that he must be trying to start his own religion. Mom told us about her new intern at the clinic, and that Baby James had learned the words *peas*, *apple*, and *turtle* at day care. Charity reported that she got an A on her science test.

"I got most of my friends to donate coats to the clothing drive," Jude announced when he finished cutting Baby James's meat loaf into bite-sized pieces.

I wasn't surprised. Some people in Rose Crest tried to claim that Jude's goodness was just an act, but he really was that kind of person. I mean, who else would give up the freedom of senior year to do independent study at the parish three afternoons a week? Or fail to make the varsity hockey team with all his friends because he wasn't willing to be aggressive enough. Sometimes it was hard being his younger sister, but it was nearly impossible *not* to love Jude.

I hated the thought of what my news might do to him.

"That's great," Dad said to Jude.

"Yeah." He grinned. "Yesterday, I told everyone I was donating a coat and encouraged them to help out."

"Which coat are you giving away?" Mom asked.

"The red one."

"Your North Face? But that one's practically like new."

"Because I've barely worn it in the last three years. It seems selfish to keep it in my closet when someone else could use it."

"Jude's right," Dad said. "We need good-quality clothing. It's not even Thanksgiving yet, and they're already predicting another record-breaking winter."

"Yes!" Charity cheered. Mom grumbled. She never did understand why Minnesotans *rooted* for record-breaking cold.

I was moving my mashed potatoes around my plate with my fork when Dad turned to me and asked the question I was so not looking forward to. "You've been particularly quiet this evening, Grace. How was your day?"

I put down my fork. The hunk of meat loaf in my mouth felt like Styrofoam when I swallowed. "I saw Daniel today."

Mom glanced up from trying to prevent James from chucking his food across the table. The look that said, *We don't mention that name in our house,* passed over her eyes.

We discussed just about everything around our kitchen table: death, teen pregnancy, politics, and even religious injustice in the Sudan—but there was one topic we never talked about anymore: Daniel.

Dad wiped his mouth with his napkin. "Grace and

Jude, I could use both of you at the parish tomorrow afternoon. We've had a great response to the charity drive. I can't even get into my office, it's packed so full of canned corn." He gave a slight chuckle.

I cleared my throat. "I talked to him."

Dad's laugh strangled off, almost like he was choking.

"Whoa," Charity said, her fork paused halfway to her mouth. "Way to go with the revelations, Grace."

Jude slid back his chair. "May I be excused?" he asked, and put his napkin on the table. He didn't wait for a response and walked out of the kitchen.

I glanced at Mom. *Now look what you did*, her eyes seemed to say.

"Peas!" James shouted. He threw a handful of them at my face.

"I'm sorry," I whispered, and left the table.

LATER

I found Jude sitting on the front porch, wrapped in the blue afghan from the couch. His breath made white puffs in front of his face.

"It's freezing, Jude. Come inside."

"I'm fine."

I knew that he wasn't. Few things ever upset Jude. He didn't like the way some girls at school would say cruel stuff and then try to pass it off as "just kidding." He hated it when people used the Lord's name in vain, and he absolutely couldn't tolerate anyone who claimed the Wild would never win the Stanley Cup. But Jude didn't scream or yell when he was mad. He got real quiet and folded into himself.

I rubbed my arms for warmth and sat next to him on the steps. "I'm sorry I spoke to Daniel. I didn't mean to make you mad."

Jude massaged the parallel scars that scraped across the back of his left hand. It was something he did a lot. I wondered if he was even conscious of it. "I'm not mad," he finally said. "I'm worried."

"About Daniel?"

"About you." Jude looked into my eyes. We had the same Roman nose and dark brown hair, but the resemblance in our violet eyes always felt a bit eerie—especially now, when I saw how much pain was reflected in his gaze. "I know the way you feel about him. . . ."

"Felt. That was more than three years ago. I was just a kid then."

"You're still a child."

I wanted to say something snide, like *So are you*, because he was barely a year older than me. But I knew he wasn't trying to be mean when he said it. I just wished Jude would realize that I was nearly seventeen; I'd been dating and driving for almost a year.

Cold air seeped through my thin cotton sweater. I was about to go inside when Jude took my hand in his.

"Gracie, will you promise me something?"

"What?"

"If you see Daniel again, promise me you won't talk to him?"

"But—"

"Listen to me," he said. "Daniel is dangerous. He isn't the person he used to be. You have to promise to stay away from him."

I twisted my fingers in the yarn of the blanket.

"I'm serious, Grace. You have to promise."

"Okay, fine. I will."

Jude squeezed my hand and looked off into the distance. It seemed like he was staring a million miles away, but I knew his gaze rested on the weathered walnut tree—the one I'd been trying to draw in art class—that separated our yard from the neighbor's. I wondered if he was thinking about that night, three years ago, when he last saw Daniel—the last time any of us saw him.

"What happened?" I whispered. It had been a long time since I'd had the nerve to ask that question. My family acted like it was nothing. But *nothing* wasn't bad enough to explain why Charity and I were sent away to our grandparents for three weeks. Families don't stop talking about something that was *nothing*. *Nothing* didn't explain the thin white scar—like the ones on his hand—above my brother's left eye.

"You're not supposed to say bad things about the dead," Jude mumbled.

I shook my head. "Daniel isn't dead."

"He is to me." Jude's face was blank. I'd never heard him talk like that before.

I sucked in a breath of frigid air and stared at him, wishing I could read the thoughts behind his stony eyes. "You know you can tell me anything?"

"No, Gracie. I really can't."

His words stung. I pulled my hand out of his grasp. I didn't know how else to respond.

Jude stood up. "Leave it alone," he said softly as he draped the afghan around my shoulders. He went up the steps, and I heard the screen door click shut. The television's blue light flickered through the front window.

A large black dog padded across the deserted street. It stopped under the walnut tree and looked up in my direction. The dog's tongue lolled out in a pant. Its eyes fixed on me, glinting with blue light. My shoulders collapsed with a shiver, and I shifted my gaze up to the tree.

It had snowed before Halloween, but that had all melted away a few days later, and it probably wouldn't snow again until Christmas. In the meantime, everything in the yard was crusty and brown and yellow, except for the walnut tree, which creaked in the wind. It was white as ash and stood like a wavering ghost in the light of the full moon.

Daniel had been right about my drawing. The branches *were* all wrong, and the knot in the lowest one should have been turned up. Mr. Barlow had asked us to illustrate something that reminded us of our childhood. All I could see was that old tree when I looked at my piece of paper. But in the past three years, I had made it a point to avert my eyes when I passed it. It hurt to think about it—to think about Daniel. Now, as I sat on the porch, watching that old tree sway in the moonlight, it seemed to stir my memories until I couldn't help remembering.

The afghan slipped off my shoulders as I stood. I glanced back at the front-room window and then to the tree. The dog was gone. It may sound weird, but I was glad that dog wasn't watching as I went around to the side of the porch and crouched between the barberry bushes. I braved a nasty scratch on my hand as I felt under the porch for something I wasn't even sure was there anymore. My fingertips brushed something cold. I reached farther in and slid it out.

The metal lunch box felt like an ice block in my bare hands. It was spotted with rust, but I could still make out the faded Mickey Mouse logo as I wiped years' worth of grime off the lid. It came from a time that seemed so long ago. It used to be a treasure box where Jude, Daniel, and I kept our special things like pogs, and baseball cards, and that strange long tooth we found in the woods behind the house. But now it was a small metal coffin—a box that held the memories I wished would die.

I opened the lid and pulled out a tattered leather

sketchbook. I flipped through the musty pages until I found the last sketch. It was of a face I had drawn over and over again because I could never get it right. He had hair so blond it was almost white then, not shaggy and black and unwashed. He had a dimple in his chin and a wry, almost devious smile. But it was his eyes that always eluded me. I could never capture their deepness with my simple pencil strokes. His eyes were so dark, so deep. Like the rich mud we used to sink our toes into at the lake—they were mud-pie eyes.

MEMORIES

"You want it? Come and get it." Daniel tucked the bottle of turpentine behind his back and lunged sideways like he was going to run away.

I crossed my arms and leaned against the trunk of the tree. I'd already chased him through the house, across the front yard, and around the walnut tree a couple of times—all because he'd sneaked into the kitchen while I was working and stole my bottle of paint remover without saying a word. "Give it back, now."

"Kiss me," Daniel said.

"What?"

"Kiss me, and I'll give it back." He fingered the moon-shaped knot in the lowest branch of the tree and flashed me a devious grin. "You know you want to."

My cheeks flamed. I wanted to kiss him with all the

longing in my eleven-and-a-half-year-old heart, and I knew he knew it. Daniel and Jude had been best friends since they were two, and I—only a year younger—had trailed behind them since I was old enough to walk. Jude never minded when I wanted to tag along. Daniel hated it—but then again, only a girl could play Queen Amidala to Daniel's Anakin and Jude's Obi-Wan Kenobi. And despite all Daniel's teasing, he was my first real crush.

"I'll tell," I said lamely.

"No, you won't." Daniel leaned forward, still grinning. "Now kiss me."

"*Daniel!*" his mother shrieked from the open window of his house. "You better come clean up this paint."

Daniel shot straight up, his eyes wide with panic. He looked at the bottle in his hand. "Please, Gracie? I need it."

"You could have asked in the first place."

"*Get in here, boy!*" his father roared out the window.

Daniel's hands shook. "Please?"

I nodded, and he ran toward his house. I hid behind the tree and listened to his father yell at him. I don't remember what Daniel's father said. It wasn't his words that ripped me open; it was the sound of his voice—getting deeper and more like a vicious snarl as he went on. I sank into the grass, with my knees pulled to my chest, and wished I could do something to help.

That was almost five and a half years before I saw him in Barlow's class today. It was two years and seven months before he disappeared. But only one year before he came to live with us. One year before he became our brother.

CHAPTER TWO

Promises, Promises

My mother had this weird rule about secrets. When I was four, she sat me down and explained that I was never to keep one. A few minutes later I marched up to Jude and told him my parents got him a Lego castle for his birthday. Jude started to cry, and Mom sat me back down and told me that a surprise was something everyone would eventually know, and a secret was something no one else was ever supposed to find out. She looked me right in the eyes and told me in this real serious tone that secrets were wrong and no one had the right to ask me to keep one.

I wish she'd set the same rule for promises.

The problem with promises is that once you've made one, it's bound to be broken. It's like an unspoken cosmic rule. If Dad says, "Promise you won't be late for curfew," the car is fated to break down, or your watch will magically stop working, and your parents refuse to get you a cell phone so you can't just call and tell them you're running behind.

Seriously, no one should have the right to ask you to keep a promise—especially if they don't consider all the facts.

It was completely unfair of Jude to make me promise not to have anything to do with Daniel. He didn't take into account that Daniel was back in our school now. He didn't have the same memories that I had. I didn't intend to speak to Daniel again, but the only problem was—because Jude had made me *promise* not to—I was afraid of what I might do.

That fear gripped the breath in my chest as I stood outside the art-department door. My sweating palm slipped on the knob as I tried to turn it. Finally, I pushed the door open and looked to the table in the front row.

"Hey, Grace," someone said.

It was April. She sat in the seat next to my empty chair. She snapped her gum as she unpacked her pastels. "Did you catch that documentary on Edward Hopper we were supposed to watch last night? My DVR totally had a meltdown."

"No. I guess I missed it." I scanned the room for Daniel. Lynn Bishop sat in the back row, gossiping with Melissa Harris. Mr. Barlow worked on his latest "prorecycling" sculpture at his desk, and a few students trickled into the classroom before the bell.

"Oh, crap. Do you think there's going to be a quiz?" April asked.

"This is art class. We paint pictures while listening to classic rock." I checked the room one last time. "I doubt there are going to be quizzes."

"Boy, you're crabby today."

"Sorry." I got my supply bucket out from the cubbies and sat in the seat next to her. "I guess I've got a lot on my mind."

My tree drawing sat on top of the bucket. I told myself to hate it. I told myself to rip it up and throw it away. Instead, I picked it up and traced the perfect lines, my finger just above the paper so I wouldn't smudge the charcoal.

"I don't get why you even care about him," April said for the sixth time since yesterday. "I mean, I thought you said that Daniel guy was hot."

I stared down at the drawing. "He used to be."

The tardy bell rang. A few seconds later the door creaked open. I looked up and expected to see Daniel. The same way I used to expect to run into him at the mall or see him slip around a corner downtown after he disappeared.

But it was Pete Bradshaw who came through the door. He was an office aide fourth period. He waved to April and me as he delivered a note to Mr. Barlow.

"Now *he's* cute," April whispered, and waved back. "I can't believe he's your chem lab partner."

I was about to wave also, but then I got this sinking feeling in the pit of my stomach. Pete dropped the note on Barlow's desk and came over to us.

"We missed you last night," he said to me.

"Last night?"

"The library. We had a study group for the chemistry test." Pete rapped his knuckles on the table. "You were supposed to bring the donuts this time."

"I was?" That sinking feeling got deeper. I'd sat out on the porch last night, thinking about Daniel, until I was practically a Popsicle, and had forgotten all about our study group—and the test. "I'm sorry. Something came up." I fingered the drawing.

"I'm just glad you're okay." Pete grinned and pulled a roll of papers from his back pocket. "You can borrow my notes during lunch if you want."

"Thanks." I blushed. "I'll need them."

"More painting, less talking," Mr. Barlow bellowed.

"Later." Pete winked and left the room.

"He is *so* going to ask you to the Christmas dance," April whispered.

"No way." I looked at my drawing and couldn't remember what I'd planned on doing next. "Pete doesn't like me like that."

"What, are you blind?" April said a little too loudly.

Mr. Barlow glared at her.

"Pastels are far superior to charcoals," April said, trying to cover. She glanced at the teacher's desk and then whispered, "Pete is so into you. Lynn said that Misty told her that Brett Johnson said that Pete thinks you're hot and he wants to ask you out."

"Really?"

"Really." She waggled her eyebrows. "You are *so* lucky."

"Yeah. Lucky." I looked down at Pete's notes and then at the drawing. I knew I should feel lucky. Pete was what April called a "triple threat"—a cute senior, a hockey player, *and* a total brain. Not to mention, one of Jude's best friends. But it seemed strange to feel lucky that someone liked me. Luck shouldn't have anything to do with it.

Twenty minutes later, there was still no sign of Daniel when Barlow got up from his desk and stood in front of the class. He stroked his handlebar mustache, which draped over his jowls. "I think we'll try something new today," he said. "Something to challenge your minds along with your creativity. How about we have a pop quiz on Edward Hopper?"

There was a collective groan from the class.

"Oh, crap," April whispered.

"*Oh, crap,*" I whispered back.

THE LUNCH BREAK

Mr. Barlow cleared his throat over and over again in irritation as he handed back our quizzes. He returned to his sculpture and twisted a wire around an empty Pepsi can with melodramatic jerks. When the lunch bell rang, he cleared out of the art room with the rest of the students.

April and I stayed behind. AP art was a two-period class with a lunch break in the middle. But April and I were the only juniors, so we usually kept working through lunch to show Mr. Barlow that we were serious enough to be in his advanced class—except on the days Jude invited us to eat with him and his friends at the Rose Crest Café (the off-campus lunchtime haven for popular seniors).

April sat next to me, perfecting the shading on her pastel drawing of roller skates while I tried to study Pete's notes. But the more I tried to concentrate, the more the words on the pages jumbled into an unintelligible mess. That sinking feeling I had before seemed to churn inside me until it turned into trembling anger and I couldn't think about anything else. How dare Daniel show up after all this time and then disappear again. No explanations. No apologies. No closure.

I knew there could be a million reasons why he hadn't shown up today, but I was sick and tired of excusing his behavior. Like when he'd steal food out of my sack lunches, or whenever his teasing got too intense, or when he'd forget to return my art supplies—I'd chalk it up to all the stuff he'd been through in his life and let it slide. But I wouldn't excuse how he'd crept back into my life just long enough to cause me to disappoint my parents, upset my brother, ditch out on Pete, bomb a quiz, and potentially fail my chemistry test. I felt so stupid, wasting my time thinking about him, and now he didn't even have the decency to show up. Now I really wanted to see him one more time. Just long enough to tell him off . . . or smack his face . . . or something worse.

Daniel's tree drawing sat on the table taunting me. I hated the way it seemed so perfect, with its smooth, entangled lines that I never could have drawn myself. I picked up the drawing, marched over to the wastebasket, and unceremoniously chucked it in.

"Good riddance," I said to the trash can.

"Okay, now I know you're insane," April said. "That's due in like an hour."

"It wasn't mine anyway—not anymore."

CHAPTER THREE
Tabula Rasa

WHAT HAPPENED AFTER LUNCH

When art class started up again, I pulled out a crisp new piece of drawing paper and shot off a sketch of my favorite childhood teddy bear. It wasn't exactly up to par with my usual work—actually it wasn't up to par with my usual work when I was nine—but Mr. Barlow had a "no tolerance" policy for not finishing an assignment. I figured shoddy work was better than no work, and slipped it under the stack of drawings on Barlow's desk before leaving class.

April hung back to discuss her portfolio, and I ambled off to my chemistry test with only slightly less foreboding. My stomach felt better once I decided to forget I'd ever seen Daniel, but as far as the test? Well, my mother was *not* going to be happy. I'd managed to go over Pete's notes a couple of times before lunch ended, but even if I'd had a full night of studying, I'd be lucky to pull a C. I'm not a bad student. I have a 3.8 GPA, but I'm most definitely right-brained.

AP chem was my mom's idea. Dad loved it when I worked on my paintings at the kitchen counter. He said it reminded him of his days in art school before he decided to join the clergy like his father and grandfather. But Mom wanted me to "keep my options open"—which meant she wanted me to become a psychologist, or a nurse like her.

I slipped into my seat next to Pete Bradshaw and drew in a deep breath, preparing to let out a languid sigh to prove I wasn't nervous, and was caught off guard by the clean, spicy scent of my chem lab partner. Pete had gym fifth period, and his hair was still damp from the shower. I'd noticed his scent of citrusy soap and fresh-applied deodorant before, but today it filled my senses and made me want to scoot closer to him. I guess it had something to do with what April said about his liking me.

I fumbled around in my backpack for my notebook and dropped my pen three times before I got it to rest neatly at the top of my desk.

"Feeling a little weak in the knees?" Pete asked.

"What?" My chem book took a dive off the desk.

"Test jitters?" Pete retrieved my book. "Everybody's freaking. You should've seen it, Brett Johnson only snarfed down half a supreme pizza for lunch. I thought that was bad, but *you* look like you've just seen the Markham Street Monster."

I winced. That joke had never been funny to me. I snatched the book out of his hands. "I'm not nervous at all." I drew in another deep breath and forced out a long, calm sigh.

Pete flashed me one of his "triple threat" smiles, and my book hit the floor again. I chuckled as he picked it up, and I felt too warm in my sweater when he handed it back.

Why am I such a dumb girl? I mean, seriously, get it together.

There was only one other boy who could make me feel stupid like that, but since I wasn't going to give *him* a second thought, I turned my focus to Mrs. Howell as she passed out her thick stack of tests.

"Hey, Brett and I are going bowling at Pullman's after practice." Pete leaned in with his lingering scent. "You should come."

"Me?" I glanced up at Mrs. Howell as she put an upside-down test in front of me.

"Yeah. You and Jude. It'll be fun." Pete nudged me and grinned. "You can buy me that box of donuts you owe me."

"Jude and I are supposed to help Dad with his deliveries to the shelter."

Pete actually looked disappointed for a split second, but then he perked up. "Well, how about I come over to help you after practice. It'll take, what, a couple of hours? Then we can bowl."

"Really? That would be great."

"Eyes up front," Mrs. Howell said. "Your test begins"—she tapped her watch—"now."

Pete grinned and flipped his test over. I turned mine over and wrote my name at the top. That warm, bubbly sensation you get when you know something fresh and exciting is beginning swept through my body.

CHAPTER FOUR

D-vine Intervention

IN THE MAIN HALL, AT THE END OF SCHOOL

"Why didn't you tell me in English class, you dork?" April sidestepped around a sign-up booth for the spirit club's holiday fund-raiser. "I told you he was going to ask you out!"

"It's not a date," I said with a smile.

"Who asked you out?" Jude asked, coming out of the main office right in front of April and me. His question sounded more like an accusation, and his expression looked as cloudy as the winter sky beyond the hall's windows.

"No one," I said.

"Pete Bradshaw!" April practically squealed. "He asked her on a date for tonight."

"It's not a date." I rolled my eyes at April. "He offered to help out over at the parish after practice this afternoon, and then he wants to go bowling. You're invited, too," I said to Jude.

Jude jangled the parish's truck keys in his hand. I wasn't sure how he'd feel about my being interested in one of his friends—especially considering the last friend of his I'd liked. But Jude's expression brightened as he smiled. "It's about time Pete asked you out."

"See!" April pinched my arm. "I told you he likes you."

Jude playfully punched April in the arm. "So are *you* coming this time?"

April's cheeks flared red. "Uh . . . no. I can't." Little splotches of crimson spread from her face to her ears. "I, uh, I, have to . . ."

"Work?" I offered.

I knew from experience that no amount of coaxing was going to get her to come. April was absolutely mortified that Jude would think she was just a tagalong. Even getting her to occasionally eat lunch at the café with Jude and me was as difficult as taking a dog to the vet.

"Work . . . Yeah, um, that." April hitched her pink JanSport backpack up on her shoulder. "I've gotta get going. See you later," she said, and scurried off to the main doors.

"She's . . . interesting," Jude said as he watched her leave.

"Yep, that she definitely is."

"So . . ." Jude looped his arm around my shoulder,

leading me through a throng of sophomores toward the exit. "Tell me more about this date."

"It's *not* a date."

AN HOUR AND A HALF LATER

"Pastor D-vine is truly an angel of the Lord," Don Mooney said in awe as he scanned the jam-packed social hall of the parish. There were boxes upon boxes of food and clothing—and Jude and I were in charge of sorting through all of them. "I hope you still need these." Don adjusted the large box of tuna cans in his arms. "I got them from the market, and I even remembered to pay for them this time. You can call Mr. Day if you want. But if you don't need them . . ."

"Thank you, Don," Jude said. "Every donation helps, and we especially need high-protein foods like tuna. Right, Grace?"

I nodded and tried to pack one last coat into the bulging box marked MEN'S. I gave up and dropped it into a half-empty women's box.

"And it was good of you to remember to pay Mr. Day," Jude said to Don.

A huge grin spread across Don's face. He was as big as a grizzly, and his smile resembled a snarl. "You kids are truly D-vine. Just like your father."

"We do no more than anyone else," Jude said in that diplomatic voice he picked up from Dad that let him be humble but contradict someone at the same time. He grunted as he tried to lift the box out of Don's burly arms. "Wow, you brought *a lot* of tuna."

"Anything to help the D-vines. God's angels, you are."

Don wasn't the only one who treated our family like a group of celestial beings. Dad always said the pastor over at New Hope taught from the same good book as he did, but most everyone wanted to hear the gospel from Pastor Divine.

What would they think if they knew our last name used to be Divinovich? My great-great-grandfather had changed his surname to Divine when he immigrated to America, and my great-grandpa found it came in handy when he joined the clergy.

I often found it a hard name to live up to.

"Well, how about I let you carry that box out back." Jude clapped Don on the arm. "You can help us load the truck for the shelter."

Don paraded his hefty box through the social hall with his trademark snarl/grin on his face. Jude picked up my box of men's coats and followed him out the back door.

My shoulders relaxed once Don was gone. He was always lurking around the parish "wanting to help," but I usually tried to avoid him. I wouldn't tell my dad or brother this, but I still felt uneasy around Don. I couldn't help it. He reminded me of Lenny from *Of Mice and Men*—the way he was kind of slow and well meaning but could snap your neck with one movement of his baseball-mitt-sized hands.

I still couldn't shake the memory of the violence that lived in those hands.

Five years ago, Jude and I (and that person whose name starts with a *D* and ends in an *aniel*) were helping Dad clean up the sanctuary when Don Mooney stumbled through the chapel doors for the first time. Dad greeted him nicely despite his dirty clothes and sour stench, but Don grabbed my father and pulled a tarnished knife to his throat, demanding money.

I was so scared I almost broke my cardinal "Grace does not cry" rule. But Dad never faltered—even when blood started to roll down his neck. He pointed up at the big stained-glass balcony windows that depicted Christ knocking on a wooden door. "Ask and ye shall receive," he said, and promised to help Don get what he really needed: a job and a place to live.

It wasn't long before Don became Dad's most devoted parishioner. Everyone else seemed to have forgotten the way we met him. But I couldn't.

Did that make me the only Divinovich in a family full of Divines?

EVENING

"I don't know what to tell you, Grace." Pete lowered the hood of my father's decade-and-a-half-old, teal-green

Toyota Corolla. "I think we're stranded."

I wasn't at all surprised when the car didn't start up again. Charity and I regularly lobbied for my parents to get rid of the Corolla and buy a new Highlander, but Dad always shook his head and said, "How would it look if we got a new car when this one runs fine?" Of course, Dad meant "runs" in a relative sort of way. As in, if you said a heartfelt prayer and promised the Lord to use the car to help the needy, it usually started on the third or fourth turn of the ignition. But this time I wasn't sure if even divine intervention could get the car moving.

"I think I saw a gas station a couple of blocks back," Pete said. "Maybe I should walk there and get some help."

"That gas station is closed." I breathed on my frozen hands. "It's been abandoned for a while."

Pete looked back and forth down the street. Nothing much was visible outside the veil of orange light cast from the streetlamp. The night's sky was completely blotted out by clouds, and a frigid wind tousled Pete's rusty hair. "Of all the nights to forget to charge my cell phone."

"At least you have one," I said. "My parents are seriously stuck in the twentieth century."

Pete only half smiled. "Well, I guess I'll go find a pay phone," he grumbled.

Suddenly, I felt like all of this was my fault. Only a few minutes before, Pete and I had been joking about

Brett Johnson's hiccupping fit during the chem test. Pete looked at me when we laughed at the same time, and our eyes met in that cosmic sort of way. Then the car made this horrible clunking noise and lurched to a stop in an alley on our way to the shelter.

"I'll come with you." I flinched at the sound of shattering glass in the not-so-far distance. "It'll be an adventure."

"No. Someone needs to stay with this stuff."

The Corolla was packed full of the boxes that didn't fit in the truck. But I wasn't sure I was the one who should stay behind to protect it. "I'll go. You've done enough already."

"No way, Grace. Pastor or not, your dad would kill me if I let you walk by yourself in this part of town." Pete opened the car door and pushed me inside. "You'll be safer—and warmer—in here."

"But . . ."

"No." Pete pointed to the squatty building across the street. I could hear a couple of guys shouting at each other from one of the broken windows. "I'll just go knock on the door of one of those apartments."

"Yeah, right," I said. "Your best bet is the shelter. It's a mile or so that way." I pointed down the dark street. We were parked under the only working lamp on the block. "There are mostly apartments along the way, and a couple of bars. But stay away from those unless you want to get your teeth kicked in."

Pete smirked. "You spend a lot of time on the mean streets?"

"Something like that." I frowned. "Hurry . . . and be careful, okay?"

Pete leaned in through the doorway with one of his triple-threat grins. "This is some date, huh?" he said, and kissed me on the cheek.

My face prickled with heat. "So this *is* a date?"

Pete chuckled and rocked back on his heels. "Lock the car." He shut the door and shoved his hands into the pockets of his letterman's jacket.

I clicked the door lock and watched him kick an empty beer can as he walked away. I couldn't see him once he left the light of the streetlamp. I scrunched down in my coat for warmth and sighed. It might be going badly, but at least I was on a date with Pete Bradshaw, sort of.

Sc-rape.

I shot straight up. Was that the shuffle of gravel on the pavement? Was Pete back already? I looked around. Nothing. I checked the passenger's-side door. It was locked. I sat back and rested my hand on Pete's hockey stick, which lay in between the front seats.

I had almost died when Don Mooney asked if he could ride along with Pete and me in the Corolla. I couldn't tell if he was clueless or if he thought we needed a chaperone. Luckily, Jude had saved me by plunking down a box of women's coats on the backseat of the car. "No room here," he said, and convinced Don to squeeze into the truck with Dad and him. They pulled out first and Pete and I followed, but I had to drop off a bag from the pharmacy to Maryanne Duke on the way. Even though she looked tired, she invited us in for some rhubarb pie—she makes the best ever. But I knew she'd give Pete the third degree worse than my real grandmother, so I promised to stay longer the next time I came. Then, to make up time, when we got into the city, I took the shortcut down Markham Street, a decision I totally regretted at the moment.

Things had been quieter for the past few years, but this area of the city had once been infamous for strange happenings and disappearances. And then, on a monthly basis, dead bodies had started turning up like daisies. The police and the newspapers speculated about a serial killer—but others talked about a hairy beast that stalked the city by night. They called it the Markham Street Monster.

Nonsense, right?

Like I said, it had been years since something truly weird had happened around here, but I still found myself wondering if I'd be better off now if Don had come with us. Would I feel more or less uneasy if Don were alone in this alley with me?

More!

That thought was followed by an instant surge of guilt. I closed my eyes and let my mind wander, trying to stay calm. For some reason, I thought about the time I'd asked my father why he'd helped someone who'd hurt him.

"You know the meaning of your name, don't you, Grace?"

"Yes. It means heavenly help, guidance, or mercy," I'd said, repeating what my father had always told me.

"No one can make it in this life without grace. We all need help," he'd said. "There's a difference between people who do hurtful things because they're evil and people who do bad things because of their circumstances. Some people are desperate because they don't know how to ask for His grace."

"But how do you know if someone is bad or if they just need help?"

"God is the ultimate judge of what is truly in our souls. But *we* are required to forgive everyone."

My father left the conversation at that. To be honest, I was more confused than ever. What if the person who hurt you didn't deserve to be forgiven? What if what they'd done was so terrible—?

Sc-rape. Sc-rape.

It was the shifting of gravel again. On both sides of the car now? I gripped the hockey stick. "Pete?" No response.

Rattle. Rattle.

The door handle?! Electricity shot up my spine and surged through my arms. My heart hammered in my chest, and my lungs ached with heavy breaths. I peered out the window. Why couldn't I see anything?

Rattle, rattle, rattle.

The car shook. I screamed. A high, piercing noise echoed outside the car. The windows moaned and shrieked like they were about to shatter. I smashed my hands over my ears and screamed louder. The noise died. Something clanked on the asphalt outside my door. My pulse pounded in my ears—it sounded like running footsteps.

Silence.

Every nerve seared under my skin. I shifted and heard the rattling again. It was just my shaking knee against the dangling keys in the ignition. I let out a short laugh and closed my eyes. I waited, listening to the silence, for as long as I could hold my breath. I let it out in a long sigh and eased my grip on the hockey stick.

Tap, tap, tap.

My eyes popped open. My arm flew up. I whacked my head with the hockey stick.

A shadowed face stared at me through the fogged window.

"Pop the hood," a muffled voice said. It wasn't Pete.

"Get lost!" I shouted, trying to make my voice sound huskier.

"Do it," he said. "It'll be okay, Gracie. I promise."

I put my hand to my mouth. I knew that voice. I knew

that face. Before I could stop myself, I said, "Okay," and pulled the hood release.

His footsteps scraped against the frozen pavement as he walked around to the front of the car. I opened the door and saw a crowbar lying at my feet. My spine tingled as I stepped over it and followed Daniel. His head and shoulders disappeared under the hood, but I could see he wore the same ratty jeans and T-shirt from yesterday. Did he even own another set of clothes?

"What are you doing?" I asked.

"What does it look like I'm doing?" Daniel twisted off the cap to something in the engine and pulled up an oily metal stick. "You dating that Bradshaw guy?" He screwed the cap back on.

He was being so matter-of-fact I wondered if I'd dreamed all that commotion. Could I have fallen asleep while waiting for Pete? But that crowbar wasn't there before. "What just happened?" I asked. "Were you watching me?"

"You didn't answer my question."

"You aren't answering mine." I took a step toward him. "Did you see what happened?" *Did you stop what almost happened?*

"Maybe."

I ducked under the hood so I could see him better. "Tell me."

Daniel wiped his greasy hands on his pants. "Just some kids playing around."

"With a crowbar?"

"Yeah, they're all the rage these days."

"And you expect me to just believe that?"

Daniel shrugged. "You can believe whatever want, but that's all I saw." Daniel fiddled with something else in the engine. "Your turn," he said. "You going out with Bradshaw?"

"Maybe."

"You picked a real prince," he said sarcastically.

"Pete's a nice guy."

Daniel snorted. "I'd watch out for that prick if I were you."

"Shut up!" I grabbed one of his bare arms. His skin was like ice. "How dare you say things like that about my friends. How dare you come back here and try to weasel your way into my life! Stop following me around." I yanked him away from my father's car. "Get lost and leave me alone."

Daniel chuckled. "Same old Gracie," he said. "You're just as bossy as ever. Always ordering people around. 'Tell me.' 'Get lost.' 'Give it back.' 'Shut up.' Does your daddy know you talk like that?" He wrenched his arm out of my grasp and turned back to the engine. "Just let me get you moving, and then you'll never have to see my filthy face again."

I stood back and watched his movements. Daniel had that way about him that could shut me down in an instant. I rubbed my hands together and jumped up and down to generate some heat. Most Minnesotans have thick blood, but how could Daniel even stand to be outside in only short sleeves? I kicked the gravel a couple of times and worked up my courage again. "Tell me . . . I mean . . . why did you come back? Why now, after all this time?"

Daniel looked up at me. His dark eyes searched my face. There was something different about those too-familiar eyes. Maybe it was the way the orange light from the streetlamp illuminated his pupils. Maybe it was the way he stared without blinking. His eyes made him look . . . hungry.

He dropped his gaze. "You wouldn't understand."

I folded my arms. "Wouldn't I?"

Daniel turned to the engine, hesitated, and then looked back at me. "You ever been to the MoMA?" he asked.

"The Museum of Modern Art? No. I've never been to New York."

"I ended up there a while back. You know they have cell phones, and iPods, and even vacuums in the MoMA? I mean, they're everyday things, but at the same time they're art." His voice seemed softer and less raspy. "The way the lines curve and the pieces fit together. It's functional art that you can hold in your hand, and it changes the way you live your life."

"So?"

"So?" He came up real close to me. "Somebody

designed those things. Somebody does that for a living."

He stepped even closer, his face only inches from mine. My breath caught.

"That's what I want to do," he said.

The passion in his voice made my heart beat faster. But his hungry stare made me step farther away.

Daniel slumped back to the engine and yanked something loose. "Only that's never going to happen now." He leaned forward, and his black stone pendant dangled from his neck over the open engine block.

"Why?"

"You know the Trenton Art Institute?"

I nodded. Almost every senior in my AP art class was shooting for admission into Trenton. Usually only one student made it per year.

"They have the best industrial design department in the country. I took some of my paintings and designs there. This woman, Ms. French, looked them over. She said I have *promise*"—his voice skirted around the word like it was bitter to the taste—"but I need more training. She said if I get my diploma and graduate from a respectable art program, she'd give me another chance for admission."

"That's great, isn't it?" I shuffled closer. How did he always do that—make me completely forget I was mad at him so easily?

"The problem is, Holy Trinity has one of the few art

departments that Trenton even deems worthy as a pre-requisite. That's why I came back." He glanced at me. It seemed like there was something else he wanted to say, something more to the story. He brushed the pendant that rested against his chest. It was a smooth black stone shaped like a flattened oval. "Only that Barlow guy kicked me out the first day."

"What?" I knew Barlow was mad at Daniel, but I didn't think he'd actually kick him out. "That's so not fair."

Daniel grinned in that mocking way of his. "That's one of the things I always loved about you, Grace. You've got this overriding sense that everything in life should be fair."

"I do not. That's so not . . ." I cringed. "Justified."

Daniel laughed and scratched behind his ear. "You remember that time we went to the MacArthurs' farm to see their puppies, and one of the pups only had three legs and Rick MacArthur said they were going to put it down because nobody wanted it? And you said, 'That's so not fair!' and took that puppy home without even asking."

"Daisy," I said. "I loved that dog."

"I know. And she loved you so much she barked her head off whenever you left the house."

"Yeah. One of the neighbors called the sheriff so many times my parents said I'd have to give her away if it happened again. I knew no one else would want her, so I kept her in my bedroom whenever we were gone." I sniffed my running nose. "Then she got out of the house one day . . . and something killed her. Ripped her throat right out." My own throat ached with the memory of it. "I had nightmares every night for a month."

"It was my dad," Daniel said quietly.

"What?"

"The one who called the police all those times." Daniel wiped his nose with his shoulder. "He'd wake up in the middle of the day in one of his moods and . . ." He reached under the hood and jiggled something into place. "Start the car."

I backed away and got in the driver's seat. I said a small prayer and turned the key in the ignition. The engine chugged a couple of times and then made this sound like an asthmatic cough. I tried the key one more time and it started. I clapped my hands together and thanked the Lord.

Daniel dropped the hood. "You should get out of here." He rubbed his hands on his arms, leaving black, greasy tracks on his skin. "Have a good life." He kicked one of the tires and walked away.

As he slipped out of the light of the streetlamp, I jumped out of the car. "That's it?" I shouted. "You're just going to take off again?"

"Isn't that what you wanted?"

"I don't, I mean, aren't you coming back to school?"

He shrugged, his back to me. "What's the point? Without that art class . . ." He took another step into the darkness.

"Daniel!" My frustration fired like a pottery kiln. I knew I should thank him for fixing the car—for coming along when he did. I knew I should at least say good-bye, but I couldn't make the words come.

He turned and looked at me, his body almost lost in the shadows.

"Can I give you a ride somewhere? I could drop you at the shelter so you can get some clothes and something to eat, maybe."

"I'm not the shelter type," Daniel said. "Besides, I'm staying with some guys over there." He thumbed in the direction of the squatty building across the street.

"Oh." I looked at my hands. I'd actually thought he'd been following me, but he was probably just walk-ing down the street when he saw me with Pete. "Wait there." I went to the car and tore open one of the boxes in the backseat. I dug around and pulled out a red-and-black coat. I took it to Daniel and handed it to him.

He held it for a moment, fingering the embroidered North Face logo on the front. "I can't take this," he said, and tried to hand it back.

I waved it away. "It's not charity. I mean, you used to be my brother."

He flinched. "It's too nice."

"I'd give you another one, but the others in this car

are women's. Jude has the rest, so unless you want to come to the shelter?"

"No."

Shouts echoed in the background. A pair of headlights appeared around a corner.

"This will do." He nodded and took off into the darkness.

I stood and watched until he disappeared. I didn't even notice the headlights stop in front of my car until I heard someone call my name.

"Grace?" Pete ran up to me. "Are you okay? Why didn't you stay in the car?"

I looked over his shoulder to the white truck idling in the dark. Its cabin light barely revealed Jude's face as he sat in the driver's seat. His expression was blank and stiff as if carved out of stone.

"I got the car running," I lied.

"Good, but you're freezing." Pete wrapped his arms around me and held me to his chest. He smelled spicy and clean like always, but this time it didn't make me want to be closer to him.

"Can we skip bowling tonight?" I said as I pulled away. "It's getting late, and I don't feel up to it. We can go some other time."

"Sure. But you'll owe me." He draped his arm around my shoulder and walked me to the truck. "It's nice and warm in there, so you ride with Jude. I'll take the Corolla and then after we unload I'll drive you home. Maybe we can stop for coffee on the way back."

"Sounds good." But the thought of rich coffee made me ill. And that stony look on Jude's face as I climbed into the truck made me want to find a hole to bury my head in.

"He shouldn't have left you here," Jude said under his breath.

"I know." I held my fingers up to the heater. "But he thought he was keeping me safe."

"Who knows what could have come along?" Jude shifted the truck into drive. He didn't speak again all night.

CHAPTER FIVE

Charity Never Faileth

I wandered aimlessly around the house like a ghost all morning. Except I was the one who felt haunted.

All night long, I'd dreamed of rattling car doors and that strange, high-pitched noise. And then Daniel's eyes, glinting and hungry, staring back at me through the glass. I woke up more than once, cold and sticky with sweat.

In the afternoon, I sat in my room and tried to write a report on the War of 1812, but my gaze—and mind— kept drifting out the window to the walnut tree in the front yard. After I'd started the first sentence of my report over for the tenth time, I kicked myself mentally and went downstairs to the kitchen to make some chamomile tea.

I rummaged in the pantry and found a bottle of honey shaped like a bear. It was the same kind I'd loved when I was young enough to live off of peanut-butter-and-honey sandwiches with the crusts cut off. But now it seemed grainy and goopy as I squeezed it out in tiny globs on the surface of the brown tea and then watched them sink to the depths of my steaming mug.

"Got any more of that tea?" Dad asked.

I jumped at the sound of his voice.

He pulled off his leather gloves and unbuttoned his wool overcoat. His nose and cheeks were bright red. "I could use a pick-me-up."

"Um, yeah." I mopped up the puddle I'd spilled on the counter. "It's chamomile, though."

Dad crinkled his Rudolph nose.

"I think I saw some peppermint in the cupboard. I'll get it for you."

"Thanks, Gracie." He pulled a stool up to the counter.

I took the kettle off the stove and poured him a cup. "Bad day?" He'd been so busy with the charity drive and the endless studying in his office for the last month; it had been weeks since we'd really talked.

Dad wrapped his hands around his mug. "Maryanne Duke has pneumonia again. At least I think that's what it is."

"Oh, no. I just saw her last night. She looked tired but I didn't think . . . Is she okay?" I asked. Maryanne was my dad's oldest parishioner. I'd known her forever, and Jude and I had been helping out around her house ever since the last of her daughters moved to Wisconsin when I was twelve. She was practically our surrogate grandma.

"She refuses to go to the doctor. All she wants is for me to pray for her." Dad sighed. He looked worn, crumpled—as if the parish itself rested on his shoulders. "Some people expect miracles."

I handed him a peppermint tea bag. "Isn't that why God invented doctors?"

Dad chuckled. "Now, would you go tell that to Maryanne? Your brother can't even talk any sense into her, and you know how much she loves him. He told her that if she'd gone to the doctor last time, she'd probably be well enough to sing her solo tomorrow." Dad hung his head low; his nose just missed the brim of his mug. "I don't know where I'll find a replacement this late. And tomorrow is the kickoff for next semester's scholarship drive."

Dad believed that everyone deserved a quality Christian education, so he sponsored a biannual scholarship fund-raiser at the parish for Holy Trinity Academy. Eighty-something-year-old Maryanne Duke would always sing her infamous solo of "Holy Father, in Thy Mercy," and Dad and the principal and other members of the Board of Regents would give talks on charity and "doing unto others." Mom thought that Dad gave so much to the community that Jude and I should qualify for the scholarship fund.

"Maybe I should have opted for a children's choir this

year," Dad said before taking a sip. "Remember how much fun you and Jude had singing with your friends? That was the best children's choir in the state."

"Yeah, it was great," I said softly. I picked up a spoon and stirred my tea. It had grown cold unusually fast—or maybe that was just me. I was surprised that Dad would bring up the children's choir. Jude, Daniel, and I started the singing group while Daniel was living with us. But it had lasted only a few months before we lost our lead tenor. Daniel had had the voice of an angel—surprising depth and clarity for such a mischievous boy—before it turned raspy and bitter, like what I'd heard last night. When Daniel's mother took him back, it was a blow not only to our choir and our family, but to Daniel most of all.

"You could do it," Dad said.

I spilled my tea again. "What?"

"You could sing Maryanne's solo." Dad grinned, his eyes lighting up. "You have a beautiful voice."

"I'm out of practice. I'd sound like a frog."

"You would really be saving the day." He put his hand on mine. "Besides, you seem like you could use a spiritual lift."

I looked down at my mug. I hated it when Dad could see into my soul. It was like his own, special pastor superpower.

"I'll help," Charity said from behind us. She'd come in from outside with an armload of library books. "I can sing with you, Grace. It could be a duet." Charity gave me an eager smile. She loved to sing when she thought no one was around, but I knew her timid voice couldn't carry a whole solo in a crowded church.

"Thanks. I'd like that," I said to her.

Dad clapped his hands. "Charity never faileth," he said, and hugged the two of us together.

SUNDAY MORNING

I ended up sitting next to Don Mooney on the temporary choir benches behind the altar. Charity sat on the other side of me, wringing a bulletin in her hands. Don bellowed out "A Mighty Fortress Is Our God" about two octaves lower than the rest of the choir. He sang with such exuberance and clumsiness that I found myself almost warming to him for the first time.

"It's a shame about them windows," Don whispered to me while Principal Conway delivered his biannual address. Don looked up at the clear glass windows above the crowded balcony, where the beautiful depiction of Christ knocking on a door used to be.

When a fire, a little over three years ago, gutted most of the balcony but left the stained-glass windows intact, they were celebrated as a miracle. However, we all mourned their loss when Dad reported that a misplaced ladder during reconstruction had shattered the windows. And since they had been crafted over a hundred and fifty years ago, there was no way to replace the stained glass on our budget.

"I dreamed I had a time machine and went back and stopped the fire," Don whispered. "That way they'd still be there."

Principal Conway glanced back at us. Don's whispers were more like a low shout. I held my finger to my lips. Don blushed and slumped on the bench.

"As I was saying," the principal said, "Holy Trinity Academy can offer hope and guidance to all teens from every walk of life. However, it is up to us to help less fortunate students to succeed. So I ask each and every one of you to ponder this question: what can you do, how much can you give, to bring grace and salvation unto even one soul?" Principal Conway patted his handkerchief to his lips and took his seat next to my father.

The organ keyed up, and I sat there wondering if someone's salvation could really be linked to getting an education from HTA.

Charity pulled on my sleeve. "It's our turn," she croaked.

We stood at the podium, and even though we'd rehearsed for over three hours yesterday, my hands started to sweat. I looked out to the audience. Mom, Jude, and James sat in the front row, smiling at us. Pete Bradshaw had come in late but was now sitting with his mother a few rows back. He gave me a big thumbs-up.

My vision darted to the windows above the balcony and stayed there while Charity and I sang.

I imagined the stained-glass windows there, with Christ standing outside an old hardwood door. "Ask and ye shall receive, knock and it shall be opened unto you," my father had once told Don Mooney, and it had driven the giant man to tears. I remembered finding Daniel alone in the chapel shortly after Don's first arrival at the parish. He'd looked up at the stained-glass windows and asked the same question I had only days before—why my father had forgiven Don even though he had hurt him.

"Shouldn't he have told somebody or called the cops?" Daniel asked.

I tried to repeat what my father had told me, but I was still so confused I'm sure it came out all wrong. "Dad says we have to forgive everybody. No matter how bad someone is or how much they hurt you. He says people do bad things because they're desperate."

Daniel screwed up his eyes and wiped his nose on his sleeve. I thought he was about to cry, but then he punched me in the arm. "You Divines never make any sense." He shoved his hands into his pockets and limped up the aisle. At least his injured leg was getting better. It seemed like he could barely walk only a few hours ago when we picked him up for church. Daniel said he'd fallen out of the walnut tree the previous morning. But I knew he was lying. I'd been out front all day planting petunias with my mother, and I knew he hadn't come out of his house.

I wished he'd ask for help.

My voice faltered as we sang the line, "Bless them, guide them, save them."

A thought hit me like a slash of paint on canvas. What if Daniel, in his own sideways manner, had been asking for help the other night? Asking for *my* help?

When the song was over, I sat down in my seat with renewed resolve. It was too late to scrape the idea away.

I knew what I had to do.

MONDAY, BEFORE SCHOOL

"I'm sorry, Grace, but there's nothing I can do." Mr. Barlow stroked his mustache.

I couldn't believe how unreasonable he was being. My entire plan hinged on this factor. If I was going to help Daniel get his life back, I would have to get him back in school first. Then I'd find a way to make things right between him and my brother. "The decision is yours, Mr. Barlow. Daniel needs this class."

"What that boy needs is respect." Barlow shuffled a stack of papers on his desk. "Kids like that think they can waltz in here and screw around. This is AP art, not an easy-A course."

"I know, sir. Nobody takes this class lightly. In fact, I think it's an honor just to be in here—"

"Exactly. That's why your friend will not be joining this class. This is a place for serious artists. Speaking of which"—Barlow opened his desk drawer and pulled out a long slip of drawing paper—"I want to discuss your last project." He laid the paper on the desk. It was my shoddy teddy bear drawing.

I sank down in my chair. So much for fighting for Daniel's spot in the class; it was my own standing that was on the line now.

"I must say, I was quite disappointed when I saw this." Barlow waved his hand over the drawing. "But then I realized what you were up to. Quite a brilliant idea."

I sat up taller. "What?"

"Tell me if I'm wrong, because I would hate to make an improper interpretation. I asked the class to draw something that reminded them of their childhood, but I love your take on the assignment. This is plainly an example of your talent and skill level as a child. I'm impressed with your artistic vision."

I nodded, then wondered if I was doomed to hell for doing so.

"You should have turned in both of your assignments together. I almost gave you a failing grade before I saw this one." Barlow pulled a second drawing out of his drawer and laid it on the table. It was the charcoal sketch of the walnut tree.

I almost choked. At the bottom of the drawing was my name scrawled in April's unmistakable curly handwriting. "I didn't . . ." But I couldn't bring myself to admit the truth when I saw the admiration in Barlow's face as he looked over the lines of the tree.

"This is an excellent example of your growth and breadth of skill over the years," Barlow said. "To be honest, I didn't expect to see this level of skill from you before graduation." He pulled out a red pen and marked a bold A+ at the top of the paper. "It is an honor to have you in my class," Barlow said, and handed me both of the drawings. "Now get out of here so I can get some work done."

I stood up and started to walk away. Then I stopped and turned back. My resolve from yesterday returned. "Mr. Barlow?"

He looked up. "Yes?"

"You love to teach students who have a lot of promise, like what you saw in this drawing? You even said it was an honor."

"Yes, I did." Mr. Barlow stroked his mustache and squinted. "What are you getting at?"

I walked back to his desk. I took a deep breath and then blurted out, "I didn't do this." I handed him the tree drawing. "Daniel did."

Mr. Barlow sputtered. "You turned in his work!"

"No. This drawing is mine." I held up the teddy bear sketch. "This is the one I turned in. Someone else must have put that one"—I pointed at the drawing in his hands—"in the pile by accident. I'm sorry. I should have told you right away."

Barlow picked up his watercolor pens and shoved them, one by one, back into his handcrafted mug. He dropped the mug on top of a stack of files and then leaned back in his chair. "You say Daniel did this drawing?"

"Yes. He's trying to get into Trenton."

Barlow nodded.

"He really needs this class."

"Well, I'll tell you what. If you and your *friend* meet me here at seven twenty-five sharp, tomorrow morning, I'll have a talk with him and see what I can do."

I sprang up on my toes. "Thank you, Mr. Barlow."

"If Daniel misses another day of school, he'll lose his tuition scholarship." He shook his head and muttered, "How he got a scholarship in the first place is beyond me."

I cocked my head and smiled. "You're pretty cool, Mr. Barlow."

A couple of students filed into the class as the first bell rang.

Mr. Barlow glanced at them. "Don't tell too many people," he said. "And I expect to see a quality resubmission of your assignment by Monday."

CHAPTER SIX
Miracle Worker

AFTER SCHOOL

It wasn't until I was eating lunch with April in the art room that I realized the major fallacy of my brilliant plan: somehow I had to actually *find* Daniel to tell him that Barlow was willing to give him a second chance. All I knew was what apartment building he was "staying in." I didn't have an apartment number or even a way to get downtown. My parents absolutely forbade me from going into the city on my own—let alone to Markham Street. And I'm not exactly a fan of public transportation—April and I both got pickpocketed when we took a bus to the mall in Apple Valley last summer. So somehow I had to finagle one of my parents' cars and a decent alibi.

I wasn't a liar by nature. My chest and neck would turn bright red even when I told the slightest fib. Good thing no one bothered to ask how I'd gotten the car running again, or I would have turned into a shiny, blubbering radish. But I figured I might be able to get away with a half-truth when begging a car off my mom.

"I have to meet April at the library." I scratched at the thick wool scarf I'd wrapped around my neck to hide the blotching. "We're working on our research project for English." April and I *were* scheduled to meet at the library—but not until later.

Mom sighed. "I guess I can go to the grocery store tomorrow. We've got plenty of leftovers."

"Thanks. I probably won't make it home for dinner. I've . . . we've got a lot to do."

I zipped my coat up to my chin and took the car keys off the table. I was ready to bolt, but Mom reached out and clasped her hand on my forehead.

"Are you feeling okay, honey? You seem flushed."

"I just haven't slept well lately." I hadn't had a full night's sleep since I first saw Daniel on Wednesday. "I gotta run."

"You'll have to take the minivan."

Ugh. It was one thing to come rolling into the city in an old sedan, but it was another to show up in that part of town in my mother's Blue Bubble—that's what April called our royal-blue minivan, which resembled a bubble-gum ball on wheels and screamed "middle-aged mom out to get the groceries." I could just picture the snide look on Daniel's face.

I almost turned the car around three times. *I must be crazy*, I thought as I navigated through the alleys near Daniel's apartment. I pulled over under the same lamp from Friday night and studied the squatty building across the street—it didn't look *quite* as ominous in the waning afternoon light. It was constructed of yellowed bricks that looked like rows of rotting teeth with a wide gap in the middle where the front doors must have once stood. Cigarette butts and mucky trash littered the crumbling stoop.

I wasn't too anxious to learn what the *inside* of that apartment building looked like.

What was I supposed to do anyway, go knocking door-to-door, asking if anyone knew a tall, thin guy with the complexion of a ghost who answered to the name of Daniel—and hope that no one felt like taking advantage of a very innocent-looking girl?

I sat and watched the comings and goings of the street and hoped that Daniel might just happen by. I counted five homeless people hurrying along in the direction of the shelter, and at least seven different stray cats bounded down the street as if they were just as anxious to find refuge before nightfall. A black Mercedes with tinted windows pulled slowly to the curb and picked up what appeared to be a very tall man in a miniskirt who'd been fidgeting and pacing on the corner of Markham and Vine for the past thirty minutes.

The street got emptier as the sun sank deeper behind the city smog. Two guys walking in opposite directions paused briefly in front of Daniel's building. They didn't acknowledge each other, but something definitely passed between their hands before they walked on. One of them glanced right at the minivan. I ducked and stayed down for a few seconds and then peeked out the window. Markham was now just as deserted as it had been the other night. I checked the clock on the dash. It was past four thirty p.m.—I hate how early the sun sets in November—and I was going to be late meeting April if I didn't leave right away.

I was shifting the car into drive when I saw him. He wore a gray mechanics jumpsuit and tapped his fingers on his leg like he was playing along to a secret song in his head. He was just about to go inside the apartment building, so I turned off the ignition and lugged my backpack out of the car before I could lose my nerve.

"Daniel," I shouted as I crossed the street.

He turned back, looked at me, and went inside.

I stumbled up the stoop. "Daniel? It's me, Grace."

Daniel started up a dimly lit staircase. "Didn't expect to see you again." He made a slight "follow me" motion with his hand.

I crept up the steps behind him. The stairwell reeked

like stale coffee made in a dirty bathroom, and the walls had been spray painted over and over again with so many jumbled obscenities it looked like they had been wallpapered by a very disgruntled Jackson Pollock.

Daniel stopped on the third landing and pulled a key out of his pocket. "You just can't resist my good looks, can you?"

"Get over yourself. I just came to tell you something."

Daniel pushed open the door. "Ladies first," he said tersely.

"Whatever," I said, and brushed past him. I realized about one second later that maybe that wasn't such a good idea. Mom didn't let me have boys over when she wasn't home, and going into a guy's apartment alone was definitely not something she would have approved of. I wanted to stay close to the door, but Daniel walked inside and kept going. I followed him into a dingy room populated only by a TV set on a cardboard box and a short brown couch. Faint, thumping music wafted in from a room down the hall, and a lanky guy with a shaved head was draped over the couch. He stared up at the peeling ceiling with rapt, unblinking attention.

"Zed this is Grace, Grace this is Zed." Daniel motioned to the guy. Zed didn't move. Daniel kept walking.

I tilted my head toward the ceiling to see what was so fascinating.

"Grace," Daniel barked.

I jumped and went to him. Before I knew it, I was in what I presumed was his bedroom. It was about the size of my parents' closet, with a mattress, covered by a crumpled gray blanket, pushed into the corner next to a small dresser piled with stacks of Masonite boards. Daniel kicked the door shut behind us. Little tingling pricks ran up my spine.

It looked like someone had been keeping a large dog in this closet/room. The door was marred by several claw-like gashes—like the way Daisy would leave scratches on my bedroom door when I left her home alone, only these scratches were much larger and deeper. The door frame was splintered and cracked. Whatever animal had been kept in here had apparently gotten out.

I was about to ask about it when Daniel flopped down on the mattress. He pulled off his shoes and went for the zipper of his jumpsuit. A flash of panic went through my body. I turned my head and lowered my gaze.

"Don't worry, precious," Daniel said. "I'm not going to violate your virgin eyes."

His wadded-up uniform landed in a heap at my feet. I glanced, ever so slightly, and saw that he was fully clothed in torn jeans and a whitish T-shirt.

"So what could Her Graciousness possibly need to talk to me about"—he stretched out across the mattress and cradled his hands behind his head—"that would bring her all the way down here on a school night?"

"Forget it." I wanted to throw my bulging backpack

at his head. Instead, I unzipped it and dumped the contents on the floor—protein bars, soup cans, beef jerky, trail mix, a half dozen shirts, and three pairs of pants that I'd weeded out from the donations that had come into the parish over the weekend. "Eat something. You look like a starved dog."

Daniel reached down and sifted through the pile, and I started to leave.

"Chicken and stars," he said, holding one of the cans. "That was always my favorite. Your mom used to fix it."

"I know. I remembered."

Daniel ripped open one of the protein bars and wolfed the thing down in two bites. He moved on to a piece of beef jerky. He looked so eager I decided to tell him my good news after all.

"I talked to Mr. Barlow today. He says if you meet him tomorrow morning, he might give you a second chance. But you have to be there before seven twenty a.m.," I said, padding the time a bit. "And you should wear something respectable." I pointed at the pile. "There's a pair of khakis and a button-up shirt. Try not to be jerk, and he'll probably let you back in his class." I hitched my empty backpack onto my shoulder and waited for his response.

"Huh." Daniel grabbed another protein bar and leaned against the wall. "Maybe I'll show."

I don't know what else I expected—maybe he'd

jump up and hug me and call me a miracle worker? Or actually say thank you. But I could see the gratitude in his dark, familiar eyes—even if it would kill him to actually say so.

I wrapped my fingers around the straps of my backpack. "Um . . . I guess I should go."

"Don't want to be late to your Divine family dinner." Daniel chucked a wrapper onto the floor. "Meat loaf tonight?"

"Leftovers. But I've got other plans."

"Library," he said, like he was summing me up with one word.

I huffed out of his room and back into the living area. Zed still lay on the couch, but two other guys slouched in the room, smoking something that didn't smell like cigarettes. They stopped talking when they saw me. I suddenly felt like a marshmallow in my white puffer coat. One of the guys looked at me and then at Daniel, who came out of the bedroom behind me. "Well, 'ello there," he said, and took a drag. "Didn't know you liked 'em wholesome."

The other guy said something vile that I *will not* repeat, and then he made an even more disgusting gesture.

Daniel told him to go do something to himself and then took my arm and led me to the door. "Get out of here," he said. "Maybe I'll see you tomorrow."

I didn't peg Daniel as the type who would walk a girl to the car, but he followed me down the stairwell and, as I glanced over my shoulder while I unlocked the van, I saw him watching from the shadows of the doorless entryway.

LATER THAT EVENING

April Thomas had the attention span of an ADHD five-year-old when it came to computers and English books—reality television, on the other hand, could keep her occupied all day. Her latest favorite show was on Monday night, so I wasn't too surprised that she wasn't at the library when I got there. Which was totally understandable, considering I was almost an hour and a half late. I got stuck in rush-hour traffic from the city, and it was pitch-dark when I pulled up to the library. I wasn't much in the mood for tackling Emily Dickinson on my own, so I decided to go back home for dinner.

I whipped into the driveway and slammed on the brakes when a dark shadow lunged out in front of the car. My heart pounded against my rib cage as I peered out the window. Jude shielded his eyes from the headlights. His hair was disheveled, and his mouth was fixed in a thin, tight line.

"Jude, are you okay?" I asked as I got out of the car. "I almost hit you."

Jude grabbed my arm. "Where have you been?"

"At the library with April. I told Mom—"

"Don't lie to me," he said through clenched teeth.

"April came here looking for you. Good thing I answered the door. Mom and Dad can't deal with this right now. Where were you?" His eyes were sharp, like he wanted to tear me to the bone—and his fingernails, digging into my elbow, felt like they could finish the job.

"Let go," I said, and tried to pull out of his grasp.

"Tell me!" he shouted, wrenching my arm even harder. I'd rarely ever heard him shout before, even when we were kids. "You were with *him*, weren't you?" He wrinkled his nose in disgust, like he could smell Daniel on me.

I shook my head.

"Don't lie!"

"Stop it!" I shouted back. "You're scaring me."

There was a catch in my voice, and when Jude heard it, his eyes softened and he let go of my elbow.

"What on earth is going on?" I asked.

Jude put his hands on my shoulders. "I'm sorry." His face twisted like he was trying to hold back a rush of emotion. "I'm so sorry. I've been looking for you everywhere. This is just so horrible. I . . . I needed to talk to you, and when I couldn't find you—"

"What?" Flashes of horrible things happening to Baby James or Charity shot through my mind. "What happened?"

"I found her," he said. "I found her and she was all blue and cold . . . and those gashes . . . I didn't know what to do. Dad came, the sheriff, the paramedics. But it was too late. They said she'd been gone for hours, more than a whole day."

"Who?!" Grandma, Aunt Carol, who?

"Maryanne Duke," he said. "I was delivering Thanksgiving packages for Dad to all the widows. Maryanne was my last delivery. And there she was, sprawled on her porch." Jude's face splotched with red. "One of the paramedics said she must have fainted with weakness while leaving her house.

"Dad called Maryanne's daughter in Milwaukee. She's mad. She said it was Dad's fault. Said that he should have taken better care of Maryanne, that he should have made her go to the doctor." Jude wiped at his nose. "People expect him to work miracles. But how can you work miracles in a world where an old woman lay on her porch for over twenty-four hours and nobody stopped?" Lines furrowed around his eyes. "She was frozen, Grace. Frozen."

"What?" Maryanne lived in Oak Park. It wasn't nearly as bad as where Daniel was staying, but it was definitely a less desirable area. My head felt like I'd been standing over an open bottle of oil solvent too long. How many people could have passed her by? "She has a lot of potted plants on her porch, and with the railing . . . that's probably why nobody found her." At least that's what I wanted to believe.

"But that's not the worst of it," Jude said. "Something *had* found her. Some animal or something . . . some scavenger. She had all these gashes on her legs. And her throat, it was open all the way to her esophagus. I thought that's what had killed her, but the paramedics said she'd been dead and cold for a long time before it happened. There was no blood."

"What?" I gasped. My dog, Daisy, jagged through my mind. Her little throat ripped open. I pushed the thought down with my rising stomach. I couldn't let myself picture Maryanne the same way.

"Angela Duke said it was Dad's fault, but it wasn't." Jude bowed his head. "It was mine."

"How could any of this possibly be your fault?"

"I told her that if she'd gone to the doctor, then she would be able to sing in the program. I made her feel guilty." Tears welled in his eyes. "When I found her, she was wearing her green Sunday dress and that hat with the peacock feather she always wears when she sings." Jude burrowed his forehead into my shoulder. "She was trying to make it to the church. She was trying to sing her solo." His body lurched against mine, and he began to sob.

The world spun even faster. I couldn't believe I'd been singing while an old woman I'd known all my life was dying in the cold—alone. My legs gave out. I sank to the ground. Jude came with me. I sat in the middle of the driveway and held my brother's head to my shoulder. He sobbed and sobbed. I rubbed my hand up and down his back and thought of the only other time we had held each other like that. Only I was the one who'd needed comforting then.

It was a hot May night. I'd opened my window before bed and was awakened by echoing voices around two in the morning. Even now, when I can't sleep, I still hear those voices—like phantom whispers on the night wind.

My bedroom was on the north end of the house—the side facing Daniel's home. His window must have been open, too. The shouting got louder. I heard a crash and the sounds of ripping canvas. I couldn't help it. I couldn't stay put. I couldn't stand to be in my own skin until I did something. So I went to the one person I knew I could rely on most.

"Jude, are you awake?" I peeked into his room.

"Yes." He sat on the edge of his bed.

Jude's room was the one next to mine at the time—before my parents turned it into a nursery for James. Those horrible voices wafted in through his open window. They weren't as loud as they had been in my room, but they were just as chilling. My parents' bedroom was on the far south side of the house. If their window wasn't open, they probably wouldn't hear a thing.

"We have to do something," I whispered. "I think Daniel's father hits him."

"He does worse," Jude said quietly. "Daniel told me."

I sat next to Jude on the bed. "Then we have to help him."

"Daniel made me blood-brother swear I wouldn't tell Mom and Dad."

"But that's a secret, and secrets are wrong. We have to tell."

"But *I* can't," Jude said. "I promised."

A vicious roar erupted in the background, followed by the loud cracking of splintering wood. I heard a muffled plea cut off by a horrible smacking sound—like the noise the mallet made when my mom pounded out meat on the kitchen counter.

Six hard smacks and a thundering crash, and then it fell silent. So silent I wanted to scream just to break it. Then there was this tiny sound—a whimpering, doglike cry.

I clutched at Jude's arm and leaned my head on his shoulder. He brushed his hand through my tangled hair.

"Then *I'll* tell," I said. "So you don't have to."

Jude held me until I had enough courage to wake my parents.

Daniel's father split before the police arrived. But *my* father persuaded the judge to let Daniel stay with us while his mother figured things out. Daniel was with us for weeks, then months, and then a little over a year. But even though his fractured skull healed miraculously fast, he never seemed the same to me. Sometimes he was happier than I'd ever seen him, and then other times I would catch this pointed look in his eyes when he was with Jude—like he knew my brother had broken his trust.

DINNER

I sat at the table and ate dinner by myself for the first time in ages. Jude said he wasn't hungry and went down to the basement, Charity was in her room, James had already gone to bed, and Mom and Dad were in the study with the double doors pulled closed. As I picked at my plate of reheated macaroni casserole and beef Stroganoff, I suddenly felt smug toward Daniel, like I was glad he was wrong about my perfect family dinners. Then I knew thinking that was wrong. I shouldn't want bad things to happen to my family, just to prove something to Daniel. Why should he make me feel guilty or stupid for having a family that wanted to eat together and talk about our lives?

But tonight, it was too quiet to eat. I scraped my leftovers down the disposal and went to bed. I lay there for a while until those phantom voices found their way into my head. But then I realized the loud tones came from my own home. My parents were shouting at each other down in the study. They weren't violent shouts, but angry and annoyed. Mom and Dad occasionally disagreed and argued, but I had never heard them *fight* before. Dad's voice was low enough that I could hear his despair, but I couldn't understand his words. Mom's voice got louder, angrier, sarcastic.

"Maybe you're right," she yelled. "Maybe it is your fault. Maybe you brought this on all of us. And while we're at it, why don't we add global warming to the list? Maybe that's your fault, too."

I got up and closed my door all the way, slipped back under the covers, and pulled a pillow over my head.

CHAPTER SEVEN
Obligations

Dad usually went jogging early in the morning, but I didn't hear him go out while I was getting ready for school. The light was on in his study as I passed the closed doors on my way to the kitchen. I almost knocked but decided against it.

"You're up early," Mom said as she shoveled a stack of chocolate chip pancakes onto my plate. She'd already made two dozen of them even though none of us—except Dad—usually made our way down to breakfast for another thirty minutes. "I hope you slept well."

Yeah, with a pillow over my head.

"I have a meeting with Mr. Barlow this morning."

"Mm-hmm," Mom said. She was busy wiping down the already glistening counter. Her loafers reflected in the sheen on the linoleum floor. Mom had a tendency to get a little OCD when she was stressed. The harder things were for the family, the more she tried to make things sparkle. Like everything was perfectly perfect.

I poked my finger into one of the melting chocolate chips that formed a symmetrical smiling face in my pancake. Mom normally only made her "celebration pancakes" for special occasions. I wondered if she was trying to soften the blow for a discussion about Maryanne—prep us for one of Dad's sermons about how death is a natural part of life and all. That is, until I saw the look of guilt in her eyes when she placed a glass of orange juice in front of me. The pancakes were a peace offering for her fight with Dad last night.

"Fresh squeezed." Mom wrung her apron in her hands. "Or would you rather have cranberry? Or maybe white grape?"

"This is fine," I mumbled, and took a sip.

She frowned.

"It's great," I said. "I love fresh squeezed."

I knew right then that Dad wasn't coming out of his study this morning. We weren't going to talk about what happened to Maryanne. And Mom certainly wasn't going to talk about their fight, either.

Last night Daniel had made me feel guilty for having a family that sat around the dinner table and discussed our lives. But now I realized that we never actually talked about anything that was a problem in our home. It's why the rest of my family never mentioned Daniel's name or discussed what happened the night he disappeared—no matter how many times I'd asked. Talking would be admitting that there was something wrong.

Mom smiled. It looked as syrupy and fake as the imitation maple drizzled on my breakfast. She flitted back to the stove and turned over a couple of pancakes. Her face fell into a frown again, and she dumped the barely over-browned batch into the trash. She still wore the same blouse and slacks from yesterday under her apron. Her fingers were red and chapped from hours of cleaning. This was perfection overdrive, big-time.

I wanted to ask Mom why she would hide her fight with Dad by making ten pounds of pancakes, but Charity came stumbling into the room.

"What smells so good?" she yawned.

"Pancakes!" Mom shooed Charity into a seat with her spatula and presented her with a heaping plate. "There's maple syrup, boysenberry, whipped cream, and raspberry jam."

"Awesome." Charity dug into a container of whipped cream with her fork. "You're the best, Mom." Charity gulped down her pancakes and went for seconds. She didn't seem to notice Mom practically scrubbing a hole into the skillet.

Charity grabbed the raspberry jam and then froze.

Her eyes suddenly seemed glossy, like she was about to cry. The jar slipped out of her fingers and rolled across the table. I caught it just as it went over the edge.

I looked at the label: FROM THE KITCHEN OF MARYANNE DUKE.

"It's okay," I said, and put my hand on Charity's shoulder.

"I forgot . . . ," Charity said softly. "I forgot that it wasn't a dream." She pushed her plate away and got up from the table.

"I was just about to start some fried eggs," Mom said as Charity left the room.

I looked down at my plate. My smiling breakfast stared up at me and I didn't know if I could stomach any more. I took another sip of my orange juice. It tasted sour. I knew I could convince Jude to give me an early ride to school, but I didn't want to stick around and watch my mother's display of perfection start all over again when he came down for breakfast. I wrapped a couple of pancakes in a napkin and got up from the table. "I've got to go," I said. "I'll eat on the way."

Mom looked up from scrubbing. I could tell my not eating hadn't helped alleviate her guilt.

For some reason I didn't care.

I walked the few blocks to school in the cold and donated my breakfast to a stray cat I met along the way.

The clock in the art room ticked its way to 7:25 a.m. and I cursed myself for giving Daniel only a five-minute window for lateness. I closed my eyes and prayed silently that Daniel would come, just so I could prove Barlow wrong about him. But with every tick of the clock I started to think I was the one who was going to be disappointed.

"Worried I wasn't going to show?" Daniel flopped into the chair next to mine just in time. He wore the light blue woven shirt and khakis I'd left for him, but his clothes were crumpled like he'd had them wadded up in his pack until only a few minutes before.

"I don't really care what you do." I felt tiny pricks of red-heat forming on my neck. "It's your future, not mine."

Daniel snorted.

Mr. Barlow came out of his office and sat at his desk. "I see Mr. Kalbi decided to join us after all."

"It's just Daniel. No *Kalbi*." Daniel pronounced his last name like a cuss word.

Barlow raised an eyebrow. "Well, Mr. Kalbi, when you become a famous musician or the Pope you can drop your last name. But in my class you will go by the name your parents gave you." Barlow looked Daniel over like a critic appraising a new work in a gallery.

Daniel leaned back in his chair and crossed his arms.

Mr. Barlow clasped his fingers together on top of his desk. "You are well aware that your scholarship is contingent on your behavior. You will act and dress appropriately for a Christian school. Today was a nice try, but you might want to invest in an iron. And I highly doubt that is your natural hair color. I will give you until Monday to do something about it.

"As for my class," Barlow went on, "you will be here every day, on time, and in your seat when the bell rings. Every AP student is required to compile a portfolio of twenty-three works on a specific theme and ten more projects to show their breadth. You are coming into this class late, but I expect you to do the same." Mr. Barlow leaned forward and stared into Daniel's eyes like he was challenging him to a game of chicken—daring him to glance away first.

Daniel didn't blink. "No problem."

"Daniel is quite proficient," I said.

Barlow stroked his mustache, and I knew he was about to deliver the catch. "Your portfolio will consist only of work done *in* this class. I will monitor each of your assignments at the beginning, middle, and end of their progression. You will not turn in anything you have done previous to now."

"That's impossible," I said. "It's almost December and I'm not even a third of the way through my portfolio."

"That is why Mr. Kalbi will be joining us every lunch

period and will report directly to my classroom for one hour after school, each and every day."

Daniel almost lost the staring contest but regained his composure. "Nice try, but I have a job in the city after school."

"I've been informed that the school has given you a stipend for your living expenses. You are obviously in one board member's good graces, but don't expect any special treatment from me. You will be in this class every day after school, or you will not be here at all."

Daniel grabbed the edge of the desk and leaned forward. "You can't do this. I need the money." He finally looked away. "I have other obligations."

I sensed a twinge of desperation in his voice. The word *obligations* made my mouth go dry.

"Those are my stipulations," Barlow said. "It is your choice." He gathered up some papers and went into his office.

Daniel threw his chair aside and tore out of the room with the fury of a threatened bear. I followed him into the hall.

Daniel swore and smashed his fist into a locker door. The metal crunched behind his knuckles. "He can't do this." He punched the locker again and didn't even flinch with pain. "I have obligations."

There was that word again. I couldn't help wondering what it meant.

"He wants me to be his trained little circus pup. I

even wore this stupid shirt." Daniel clawed at the buttons and tore it off, uncovering his whitish tee and long sinewy muscles in his arms that I hadn't noticed before. He slammed his dress shirt against the locker. "This is total bullsh—"

"Hey!" I grabbed his hand as he pulled it back for another swing. "Yeah, those lockers really tick me off, too, sometimes," I said, and stared down a couple of gawking freshmen until they hurried along. "Damn it, Daniel!" I reeled on him. "Don't swear at school. You'll get kicked out."

Daniel licked his lips and *almost* smiled. He unclenched the fist I still held, dropping his blue shirt. I tried to inspect his hand, expecting his knuckles to be purple, considering the deep dent in the locker door. He pulled out of my grasp and shoved his hand in his pocket.

"This completely sucks," Daniel said, and leaned against the abused locker. "That Barlow guy doesn't get it."

"Well, maybe you can reason with him. Or maybe if you tell me about your *obligations*, I can explain it to him for you. . . ."

Yeah, could I be any more obvious?

Daniel looked at me for a long moment. His eyes seemed to reflect the fluorescent lights in the dimly lit hall. "You want to get out of here?" he finally asked. "You and me." He held out his uninjured hand. "Let's blow these jerks off and do something fun."

I was an honors student, daughter of a pastor, citizen-of-the-month winner, and a member of the One for Jesus Club, but for the briefest nanosecond I forgot all of those things. I ached to take his hand. But that aching scared me—made me hate him.

"No," I said before I could change my mind. "I can't miss class, and neither can you. You skip one more day, and you'll lose your scholarship. You still want to get into Trenton, don't you?"

Daniel balled his hand into a fist. He took a deep breath, and his face shifted into a cool, unruffled façade. He pulled a crumpled slip of paper from his pocket. "So, precious, how do I get to geometry?"

I studied the list, relieved that AP art was the only class we would have together. "Room 103 is down the hall and to the left. Past the cafeteria. You can't miss it. And don't be late. Mrs. Croswell loves to give detention."

"Welcome back," Daniel mumbled. "I forgot how much I hate this sh—crap." He smirked at me and laughed to himself.

"Yeah, welcome home," I said. And this time I was the one who walked away.

LATER

I didn't know how many people would remember Daniel Kalbi. He'd had only a handful of friends growing up, and he'd moved away from Holy Trinity before his sophomore year. Regardless, I expected the appearance of someone like Daniel to at least spark some controversy and gossip. However, there was another scandal sweeping through the halls of school that upstaged Daniel's return tenfold: the sudden death and mutilation of Maryanne Duke, devoted Sunday-school teacher, childhood babysitter of many, and—despite her old age and meager means—volunteer at almost every school activity.

I was the recipient of many sidelong glances and backhanded whispers as I made my way from class to class. I was used to people talking about me. Watching me. It was just part of being a Divine. Mom always said I had to be careful about the clothes I wore, how late I stayed out, or what movies I was seen going into, because people would set their own behavior by what the pastor's kids were allowed to do—like I was some kind of walking morality barometer. Really, I think she was more concerned about people having a reason to talk bad about the pastor's daughter.

Kind of like the talk that was going on today. Except, it was Jude's and Dad's names that came up in conversations that halted as I approached. A lot of people had the decency to stick up for my dad against Angela Duke's accusations of mistreatment, but stories spread fast in a small town. It was only inevitable that wild speculations about my family's "involvement" in Maryanne's death would be everywhere. Crap like, "I heard that Mike said that the pastor refused to take Maryanne to her doctor's appointment and then he said he was going to kick her out of the parish if she didn't . . ." Or this gem I heard outside the gym: "They said that Jude's on some type of meds that made him go all nutso on Maryanne about being sick . . . ," which I'm ashamed to say made me break the rule I'd set for Daniel about not swearing at school.

But as sad and distraught—and prone to bad language and dirty looks—as I was, I could only imagine how Jude must have felt. April was the only person considerate—or clueless—enough to actually speak to me in person about all the things that had happened in the last twenty-four hours.

"Okay," April said the second I sat next to her in art. "Number one: where the heck were you last night? Number two: what the heck is *he* doing here?" She pointed to Daniel, who sat with his feet up on a table in the back of the room. "Number three: what the heck happened to your brother, and is he okay? And number four: numbers one, two, and three had better the heck not have anything to do with one another." She scrunched her lips and crossed her arms in front of her chest. "I want answers, sister!"

"Whoa," I said. "First of all, I'm sorry I missed you last night. I got stuck in traffic."

"Traffic? Around here?" She pointed her finger at Daniel. "You were in the city," she whispered. "You were with him."

"No, I wasn't—"

"I know he lives downtown because I saw him by the city bus stop this morning."

"That could mean anything. . . ." But really, what was the point in lying? "Okay, I was. But it's not what you think."

"It isn't?" April did this sassy little head shake that made her curly hair bounce like spaniel ears.

"No, it isn't. I was just delivering a message for Barlow. It's your fault, anyway." I mimicked her feisty stance. "You're the one who turned in his picture and made Barlow want him back in class."

"Oh, no. Did I get you in trouble? I didn't mean to. How did he know it was Daniel's?"

"I told him."

"What, are you crazy?" April's eyes widened. She leaned in close and whispered, "You're in love with him, aren't you?"

"With Barlow?"

"You know who I'm talking about." She looked back at Daniel, who was playing the drums on his leg. "You're still in love with him."

"I am not. And I never was to begin with. It was just a stupid crush." I knew she was wrong, but I felt heat rushing up my neck. I grasped for the first thing I could think of to change the subject. "Don't you want to hear about Jude and Maryanne Duke?"

April's demeanor changed immediately. Her eyes

softened, and she brushed her fingers through her hair. "Oh, my gosh. He looked so sad last night when I came looking for you at your house. And then this morning I heard Lynn Bishop—her brother is an Oak Park paramedic—talking about Maryanne Duke in the hall. I heard her say that Jude and your father had something to do with it. But I couldn't tell what she was saying. And these guys in bio were going on about the Markham Street Monster."

I shook my head. "You know the monster's just a story, right? Besides, Maryanne doesn't—didn't—live on Markham." I knew it was just a story—one I hadn't heard since I was a kid—but it gave me chills to hear people talk about the monster again. And I also knew not living on Markham didn't make one immune from strange happenings, either. I hadn't been able to get the memory of my mutilated little dog out of my head since I'd heard about Maryanne.

"Yeah, but what happened to Maryanne wasn't a story," April said. "And why is everyone saying that Jude was involved?"

I glanced up at the window of Barlow's office. Barlow was on the phone, and he looked like he was going to be a while. April seemed genuinely concerned, and I really wanted to talk to someone about what had happened. I lowered my voice so no one else (especially Lynn) could hear, and I told April about how Jude had found the body and how the Dukes blamed my father. I told her about the aftermath, too. How Jude had freaked out and how my parents had fought.

April gave me a hug. "It's going to be okay."

But how could she know that? She hadn't felt how strange it was to eat dinner at the table by myself, or heard the way my parents shouted at each other. But I guess April *would* know how those things felt. She moved here when her parents split when she was fourteen, and her mom's work hours had been getting longer and longer lately. I'd invited her to our Thanksgiving dinner so she wouldn't have to spend the day alone.

None of that seemed "okay" to me.

Barlow came out of his office. He dumped a box of empty Pepsi cans on his desk and went to work without any instruction to the class.

"Do you want to go to the café for lunch today?" I asked April. "Jude totally wouldn't mind if we just showed up. In fact, I think he could use the change."

April bit her lip. "Okay," she said. "He could probably use some consoling." She half frowned, but trembled in that excited way of hers.

LUNCH

It usually took *a lot* of coaxing to get April to come with me to the Rose Crest Café. And the few times she had come, she'd hung back from the group with Miya, Claire, Lane, and a few of the other juniors who watched the seniors with nervous reverence. April was so like my old dog Daisy that way. She had a lot of yap and spunk when it was just the two of us, but she totally cowered in most social situations.

Except today she seemed like a totally different breed.

We had been there only long enough to order our food before she was the center of attention, talking animatedly about her trip to Hollywood with her dad last summer. Brett Johnson and Greg Divers were practically drooling at her feet, but when Jude came through the door, she ditched them and went to his side. Within a matter of minutes, they were sitting together in a corner booth. April patted his hand sympathetically as he spoke to her in low, confidential tones.

"Wow," Pete said as he pulled up a chair next to me. "I can't believe April's cracked his stoic shell." He tipped his soda can toward Jude. "I haven't gotten a word out of him all day. In fact, he's been acting strange for almost a week now."

"I know what you mean," I said, and picked at the uneaten sandwich on my tray.

"You doing okay?" Pete asked.

"Yeah. Just tired of being sad." What's weird is that the only time I hadn't felt sad or hurt all day was the few minutes I'd spent with Daniel. But maybe that's just because he's so darn aggravating.

Pete tapped his soda can. "Well, I had fun the other

night," he said with a slight upturn in his voice like it was a question.

"Me, too," I said, even though "fun" wasn't how I'd describe Friday evening.

"I plan on calling in that rain check for bowling, you know." Pete grinned. "It'll give me a chance to prove I've got better skills than my ability to fix a car."

"Good." I glanced down at my tray. "But give me some time."

Pete's grin wavered. "Oh, okay." He started to scoot away.

"Things are really crazy right now," I said quickly. "You know, with Maryanne and Thanksgiving and everything. I just won't have time for a . . . uh . . . date for a while." I half smiled. "I am looking forward to it, though."

"I'll take your word for it," he said.

"See you in chem." I jumped out of my seat. "I'll let you be my shoulder to cry on when we get our tests back," I said, and went to collect my best friend from my brother.

FIFTH PERIOD

"Jude asked me out for coffee this afternoon!" April squealed as we crossed the street to the school.

"That's nice." I kept walking, my feet keeping pace with the chirping of the crosswalk meter.

"That's it?" April padded up behind me. "You're supposed to freak out and jump and down for joy with me." She grabbed my sleeve. "Are you mad?"

"No." *Yes.* "I am excited for you." *Not.* "It's just that . . ." *You're supposed to be* my *best friend.* "Jude's acting really weird lately. Now doesn't seem like the best time for you to try to be his girlfriend."

"Or maybe now is when he needs a girlfriend the most," she said with a trill of excitement. "Come on, Grace. Be happy for me. You went out with Pete, and he's one of Jude's best friends." She smiled all sheepish and innocent. "And it's just coffee anyway."

I smiled. "*Just* coffee, huh?"

"Okay, so the best freaking cup of coffee I'll ever have!" April popped on her toes. "Come on, be excited for me."

I laughed. "Okay, I'm excited."

We got to class a few minutes before the bell. Daniel leaned back in his seat, tearing scratch paper into strips and rolling them into tiny wads. I had to pass him to get to my supply bucket. My back was to him when I felt something plink against my head. A paper ball landed at my feet.

"Hey, Grace," Daniel stage-whispered.

I ignored him and rummaged in my bucket. Another paper ball hit my head and stuck in my hair. I nonchalantly dislodged it.

"Graa-ciee," he intoned like a hyena calling its prey.

I collected my supplies and made my way back to my seat. He flicked another paper wad, and it bounced off my cheek. I kept my eyes averted. I wanted to be finished with him. I wanted to tell myself that I'd fulfilled my duty. I'd done what I said I was going to do. But really, I knew I hadn't. Getting him back into this class was just the first phase of my plan. I still had to find out what had happened between Daniel and Jude so I could fix it. And since Jude wasn't going to tell me, I knew I had to get that information from Daniel. But I couldn't face him yet. I still hated the way he'd made me want to forget—even for a moment—who I was.

How could I help Daniel find his way, without losing mine?

AFTER SCHOOL

"So what are you going to do?" April asked as we hiked through the parking lot separating the school from the parish.

I unrolled my chem test and stared at the red *D* marked on the page, followed by a scribbled note from Mrs. Howell: *Please have parent sign your test. Return after the holiday.* "I don't know," I said. "Dad usually handles this sort of thing the best, but I don't want to bug him right now. And Mom's all hopped up in Martha Stewart mode, so if I show her this, she'll probably make me drop art next semester."

"No way," April said. "Maybe you should sign it yourself."

"Yeah, right. You know I can't do that." I rolled the test up again and stuck it into my back pocket.

"He's here!" April yelped.

Jude pulled up to the curb in front of the parish in the Corolla. He was picking April up here for their "coffee date." I waved to him, but he didn't wave back.

"Lipstick check." April smiled so I could inspect her teeth.

"You're good," I said, not really looking. I watched Jude idling in front of the parish. He had that stony look on his face.

"Good luck with the test," April said, positively shaking.

"Hey." I reached out and took her hand. "Have a good time. And . . . watch out for Jude for me, okay? Let me know if he needs anything."

"Will do." April squeezed my hand and then bounded across the rest of the parking lot to the Corolla. I was surprised Jude didn't get out to open the door for her—not very Jude-like at all. But at least his expression softened slightly when she hopped into the car.

As much as I wasn't too keen on the idea of my best friend dating my brother, I hoped Pete was right about April—that she could crack Jude's stoic shell when nobody else could.

After Jude and April drove away, I pulled my rolled-up test out of my pocket and went down the alley between the parish and the school. I stopped at my father's outer office door and tentatively listened for signs of life. I figured Dad was still the best bet for signing off on my grade, plus I wanted to check on how he was doing, but I had no idea if he had even ventured out of his study at the house yet. My question was answered before I could even knock on the door.

"I can't do this anymore," I heard someone say. The strained voice sounded somewhat like my father's. "I can't do it again."

"I didn't mean to," someone else said. It was a masculine but childish voice. "I didn't mean to scare nobody."

"But you did," the first voice said, and this time I was certain it belonged to my father. "This is the third time this year. I can't help you again."

"You promised. You promised you'd help me. You fix things. That's what you do."

"I'm done!" my father shouted.

I knew I shouldn't, but I pushed open the door and saw Don Mooney throw his hands over his head. He wailed like a gigantic baby.

"Dad!" I yelled over Don's cries. "What on earth is going on?"

Dad looked at me, startled that I was suddenly there. Don noticed me, too. He fell quiet, trembling in his chair. Fluid streamed from his nose and his great, swollen melon eyes.

Dad sighed. His shoulders slumped like the weight on them had increased tenfold. "Don decided to take his knife to work. Again." Dad pointed at the hauntingly familiar dagger that lay on his desk. It was the same knife Don had once held to my father's throat. "He scared off a bunch of customers, and Mr. Day fired him. Again."

"I didn't know he'd been fired before."

Don cringed.

"That's because I always smooth things over. Don screws up, and I fix it." Dad sounded so distant, not with the normal kindness and compassion so characteristic of his deep, melodic voice. His face sagged with lack of sleep, his eyes shadowed by dark circles. "I try and I try to fix everything for everyone, and look where it's gotten me. I can't help anymore. I only make things worse. Both of them are on their own."

"Both?" I asked.

Don wailed, cutting me off.

"Dad, this is Don we're talking about," I said, shocked at the sudden rush of feeling I had for the blubbering man—even with his knife so close by. "You weren't trying to scare anyone, were you?"

"No, Miss Grace." Don's huge lower lip quivered.

"Them people were already afraid. They was talking about the monster—the one that tried to eat Maryanne. So I showed them my knife. It's pure silver. My great-great-grandpa used it to kill monsters. My granddaddy told me so. All my ancestors took an oath to kill monsters. I was showing the people that I could stop the monster before it—"

"That's enough," Dad said. "There's no such thing as monsters."

Don cowered. "But my granddaddy—"

"Don." I gave him my best *don't push it* look. I turned to my dad. "Don needs you. You said you'd help him. You can't just quit because it's hard. I mean, what ever happened to seventy times seven and all that 'be your brother's keeper' stuff you're always talking about?"

Guilt washed through me. How could I say all that? I mean, I was the one who wanted to give up on Daniel just because helping him had turned out to be difficult in ways I hadn't expected. And I really couldn't believe I was the one expounding scripture—however crudely—to my father.

Dad rubbed his hand down the side of his face. "I'm sorry, Grace. You're right. These are my burdens to bear." He put his hand on Don's shoulder. "I guess I can talk to Mr. Day one more time."

Don lunged and wrapped his arms around my father's middle. "Thank you, Pastor D-vine!"

"Don't thank me yet." Dad sounded breathless from

Don's death-grip hug. "I'll have to take your knife away for a little while."

"No," Don said. "It was my granddaddy's. The only thing I've got of his. I need it . . . for the monsters. . . ."

"That's the deal," Dad said. He looked at me. "Grace, put that thing in a safe place." He led Don from the room, the latter gazing longingly at his knife as they went. "We'll discuss its return in a few weeks."

I put my test in my backpack—today was obviously not the right time to get it signed—and picked up the dagger. I held it out in my hands. It was heavier than I'd expected. The blade was stained with tarnish and other strange, dark-colored marks. It seemed ancient, valuable even. I knew where Dad wanted me to hide it. I tipped back the potted poinsettia on the bookcase and slid out the key it concealed. I unlocked the top drawer of my father's desk, where he kept important things like the cash safe for the Sunday offerings and his first-aid kit. I placed the knife under a flashlight and locked the drawer.

I replaced the key and felt a pang of remorse. I knew what Don was capable of doing with that blade of cold silver, but I couldn't help feeling sorry for his loss. I couldn't fathom having only a single item to remember a loved one by.

"Hey." Charity slipped into the office. "That was really nice, what you did for Don."

"I did it more for Dad," I said. "I don't want him to

wake up tomorrow regretting the things he did today."

"I don't think Dad will be back to normal tomorrow."

I looked up at her. She seemed to be blinking back tears. "Why?" I asked, though I really didn't want to know the answer. I'd been holding on to the fantasy that I would wake up tomorrow and everything would be the way it was supposed to be: oatmeal for breakfast, uneventful day at school, and a genial chicken-and-rice supper with the whole family.

"Maryanne's daughters want her funeral to be tomorrow, before Thanksgiving, because they don't want to cancel some big trip they've been planning."

I sighed. "I guess I should have thought of that. Death is usually followed by a funeral." Helping Mom prepare loads of rice pilaf and all varieties of casseroles for bereaving families was just another part of the pastor's-kid gig, but I hadn't been to a funeral for someone I was actually close to since my grandpa died when I was eight.

"That isn't the bad part," Charity said. "Maryanne's family asked the pastor from New Hope to come over for the funeral. They don't want Dad to do it. They still blame him."

"What? That's not fair. Dad knew Maryanne all his life, and he's been her pastor for as long as you've been alive."

"I know. But they won't listen."

I sank down in the desk chair. "No wonder he's talking like he wants to give up."

"You know the worst part? Pastor Clark heard about our duet from Sunday, and he wants us to sing it at the funeral because it was Maryanne's favorite song."

I opened my mouth to protest.

"Mom says we have to." Charity sighed. "She says it's our obligation or something like that."

Obligation. I was beginning to hate that word.

CHAPTER EIGHT

Temptation

A somber shadow cast over the parish, touching the hearts of all those who shuffled into the sanctuary for Maryanne Duke's funeral. School had even let out early for the afternoon service. Everyone was affected by the gloom of it all—everyone except my mother. I could tell she was still in perfection overdrive when she started banging around the kitchen at four a.m. to make a feast big enough for a thousand mourners. Her enthusiastic tone startled more than a few sullen people as she greeted them before the service with Pastor Clark, and she invited anyone who looked the slightest bit lonely to tomorrow's Thanksgiving extravaganza at our house.

"Invite whomever you'd like," she said to Charity and me as we loaded trays of food into the Blue Bubble. "I want this to be the warmest Thanksgiving your father can remember. He could really use the company."

But I wasn't sure she was right about that. Dad shrank away from his greeter duties before the funeral and ended up sitting in the only deserted corner of the chapel by himself, rather than taking his seat on the pulpit as the presiding pastor of the parish. I had the overwhelming urge to go to him, but I was stuck on the choir benches with Charity, watching the back of Pastor Clark's robes sway as he talked in melancholy tones about Maryanne's warm heart and giving nature, even though he barely knew her. I scanned the sanctuary and wished I could send a telepathic message to either my mother or brother to go put their arms around Dad, but Mom was busy setting up for the dinner in the social hall, and Jude was nuzzled close to April in the third row.

My eyes shot back to the hem of Pastor Clark's robes and stayed there until it was my turn to sing. The organ belted out the notes of the song, and I tried to choke out the words. My face began to quiver. I knew I was on the verge of crying, but I pushed that urge way down like always and pursed my lips together. I couldn't sing another note or I'd lose it. And Charity's voice was so high and shaky that I couldn't even tell what part of the song she was singing. I looked out the windows at the dreary, smog-filled sky—even the clouds looked like they were about to burst with emotion—and that's when I saw him.

Daniel sat in the back of the crowded balcony with his arms folded and his head bowed. He must have felt the heat of my stare because he lifted his chin. Even from that distance, I could see that his eyes were rimmed with red. He looked down into me for a moment, like he could see every painful feeling I was holding back, and then he lowered his head again.

Curiosity replaced grief as I sat down in my seat. Charity wrapped her arm around my shoulders, no doubt mistaking my shocked expression for extreme emotional distress. The Duke daughters' droning eulogy went on for ages. Angela Duke even worked in a few well-placed jabs at Dad. When the service finally ended, and the procession of those mourners headed for the grave site had filed out, I watched Daniel move toward the balcony staircase that led to an outside exit. I jumped out of my seat, waving off someone who tried to thank me for my singing—or lack thereof—and pulled on my charcoal-gray dress coat and leather gloves.

"Mom wants our help," Charity said.

"In a minute."

I made my way through the aisle, sidling around the church ladies who murmured about the lack of heart in Pastor Clark's portion of the service. Someone pulled at my sleeve as I passed and said my name. It may or may not have been Pete Bradshaw, but I didn't stop to find out. It was like an invisible thread was hooked into my belly and drew me out the doors of the parish and into the parking lot. My pace quickened without any direction from my brain when I saw Daniel hop onto a motorcycle in the far reaches of the lot.

"Daniel!" I called as the engine roared to life.

He shifted forward on the seat of the bike. "You coming?"

"What? No. I can't."

"Then why are you here?" Daniel looked at me then, his mud-pie eyes—still splotched with red—searching my face.

I couldn't stop it—that invisible thread pulled me right up next to him. "You got a helmet?"

"This is Zed's bike. You wouldn't want to wear his helmet if he had one." Daniel booted the kickstand. "I knew you'd come."

"Shut up," I said, and climbed on the back of the motorcycle.

ONE HEARTBEAT LATER

The hem of my simple black dress hiked up my legs and my matching Sunday heels suddenly seemed sexy as I placed them on the footrests of the bike. The engine roared again, and the bike went flying forward. I threw my arms around Daniel's waist.

Cold air clawed at my face, ripping tears from my eyes. I buried my face deep into Daniel's back and breathed in a mixture of familiar scents—almonds, oil paint, earth, and a hint of varnish. I didn't even question why I was on that bike. I just knew I was supposed to be there.

We rode in a straight, steady shot for downtown. Daniel's shoulders tensed and trembled like he craved more speed but was taking it slower for my sake. The sun was drowning in a crimson sunset behind the city skyline when we finally pulled over in a deserted alley in an unfamiliar part of town.

Daniel cut the ignition. The following silence made my ears throb.

"I want to show you something," he said, and got off the bike with ease. He hopped up onto the curb and kept walking.

Shocking pain surged up my frozen legs when I hit the ground. I wobbled and swayed as I followed, like it had been years since I stood on solid ground. Daniel disappeared around a corner.

"Wait," I called, trying to pull my more-than-wind-blown hair back into the French twist it had been in before we left the parish.

"It's not far," his voice wafted back.

I rounded the corner and went down a dark, narrow alleyway. Daniel stood at the end of the passage in front of two brick pillars and a wrought-iron gate that blocked his path.

"This is my sanctuary." He grasped one of the iron bars of the gate. A brass plaque on one of the pillars said: BORDEAUX FAMILY MEMORIAL.

"A graveyard?" I hesitantly approached the gate. "You hang out in a graveyard?"

"Most of my friends worship vampires." Daniel shrugged. "I've hung out in a lot of weird places."

I stared at him, openmouthed.

Daniel laughed. "This is a memorial, not a cemetery. There are no graves or dead people—unless you count the security guard. But this is the back entrance, so we shouldn't run into him."

"You mean we're sneaking in?"

"Of course."

A jangling noise echoed from the street behind us. Daniel grabbed my arm and pulled me into a shadowed alcove of the adjacent building.

"They lock the gates in the evening to keep vandals out."

His face was so close to mine that his breath grazed my cheek. The deep chill in my bones disappeared and warmth tingled through my body.

"We'll have to hop the gate and stay out of spot-lights." Daniel leaned his head to the side to check if the way was clear.

"No." I shrank back in the alcove, feeling colder than ever. "I don't do stuff like this. I don't sneak into places, or break laws—even little ones." At least I tried not to. I really did. "I'm not going to do it."

Daniel leaned toward me until his warm breath lingered on my face again. "You know, some religious scholars believe that when faced with overwhelming temptation"—he reached out and brushed a tangled strand of hair off my neck—"you should commit a small sin, just to relieve the pressure a bit."

In the shadows, his eyes seemed darker than usual, and his stare didn't just make him look hungry—he was starving. His lips were almost close enough to taste.

"That's stupid. And . . . and . . . I don't need any pressure relieved." I shoved him away and stepped out of the alcove. "I'm going home."

"Suit yourself," Daniel said. "But I'm going in there, and unless you know how to drive a motorcycle, you'll have a long wait until you can get home."

"Then I'll walk!"

"You drive me crazy!" Daniel shouted at my back. He paused for a moment. "I just wanted to show you," he said, his tone much softer. "You're one of the only people I know who could truly appreciate this place."

I stopped. "What's in there anyway?" I half turned toward him.

"You just have to see for yourself." He cradled his hands together. "I can give you a boost, if you want."

"No, thanks." I took off my heels and flung them over the gate. I shoved my gloves into my coat pockets and mounted the brick pillar, finding a foothold with my barely thawed toes. I climbed up a few feet, grabbed one of the pointed iron fleur-de-lis spikes, and pulled myself up to the top of the pillar.

"I thought you didn't do this sort of thing," Daniel said.

"You know I could always climb higher and faster than you boys." I stood up on top of the pillar and tried not to show that I was just as shocked by my performance as he was. I put my hands on my hips. "You coming?"

Daniel laughed. His feet scraped against the brick as he climbed up behind me.

I felt a bit dizzy as I inspected the at least ten-foot drop down to the other side. *Crap, that's high.* I was wondering how I was ever going to get *down* when I lost my balance and stumbled off the pillar. Before I could shriek, something hard and tight wrapped around my arm, wrenching me to a stop a couple of feet from the ground.

I dangled for a moment, my feet swinging above the frozen earth. I tried to catch my breath before looking up. But I found it even harder to breathe when I saw Daniel kneeling on the top of the pillar, holding me with only one hand. His face was completely smooth and calm, not puckered or creased by the strain of my weight.

His eyes seemed too bright to be real as he stared down at me. "Nice to know you don't do everything perfect," he said, and rather than just letting me drop the last two feet, he tightened his grip around my arm and pulled me effortlessly up to meet him on top of the pillar.

"How . . . ?" But I was unable to speak when I looked into his bright eyes.

Daniel wrapped his arms around my trembling body and jumped. He stuck a perfect landing on the gravel inside the memorial, and set me on my feet.

"How . . . how did you do that?" My legs felt as soft as a couple of well-kneaded putty erasers. My heart beat too fast. "I didn't know you were so close behind me."

Or that he was so strong.

Daniel shrugged. "I've had a lot of practice climbing since we used to race up the walnut tree."

Yeah, from sneaking into a lot of places, no doubt.

"But how did you catch me like that?"

Daniel shook his head like my question didn't matter. He shoved his hands into his coat pockets and started down a narrow walkway that stretched in between two tall hedges.

I bent over and slipped my heels on. My head swam a bit when I straightened up. "So what's so special about this place?"

"Come," Daniel said.

We walked down the path until it opened into a wide gardenlike expanse. Trees, vines, and bushes, which were probably dotted with blossoms in the springtime, filled the open area. A misty fog swirled around us as we followed the meandering path deeper into the garden.

"Look there," Daniel said.

I followed his gesture and found myself standing eye to eye with a white-faced man. I gasped and jumped back. The man didn't move. The fog parted, and I realized he was a statue. I stepped to the edge of the path and stud-ied him closer. He was an angel, not of the cute cherub variety, but a tall, slender, majestic figure, like an elfin prince from *The Lord of the Rings*. He was dressed in robes, and his face was carved with great detail. His nose was narrow and his jaw was strong, but his eyes looked as though he had seen the wonders of the heavens.

"He's beautiful." I ran my hand along one of the statue's outstretched arms, tracing my finger along the folds of his robe.

"There's more." Daniel gestured to the rest of the garden.

Through the fog, I made out more white figures, standing as majestically as the first. Little spotlights shone on their heads from above, making them look particularly divine in the dimming evening light.

I drew in a breath. "The Garden of Angels. I heard someone talking about this place once, but I never knew where it was." I moved down the path to the next regal statue. This one was a woman with long, beautiful wings that tumbled down her back like Rapunzel's locks.

Daniel followed behind me as I floated from angel to angel. Some were old and ancient looking. Others were young children with eager faces, but they were still slender and noble like the rest. I stretched up on my toes at the edge of the path to brush another angel's wings.

Daniel laughed. "You never stray from the path, do you?" He passed close behind me, his arm brushing across the small of my back.

I looked at my toes perched on the border of the

gravel trail, and rocked back on my heels. If only he knew how imperfect I felt most days. "Isn't that supposed to make life easier?"

"Doesn't that make life boring?" Daniel flashed me a wicked grin as he slipped between two of the statues and disappeared into the mist. A few moments later, he reemerged onto the path near an angel statue that was taller than the rest.

"This place was built as a memorial for Carolyn Bordeaux," Daniel said, his voice drifting back to me. "She was rich and greedy and hid away her wealth, until one day, in her seventies, she took in a stray dog for no apparent reason. She told people that the dog was an angel in disguise, who revealed to her that she was supposed to help people. After that, she devoted the rest of her life and fortune to helping the needy."

"Really?" I walked closer to him.

Daniel nodded. "Her family thought she'd gone crazy. They even tried to have her committed. But at the moment she died, an otherworldly chorus of beautiful voices filled her bedroom. Her family thought the angels must have returned to claim Carolyn's soul, but then they realized the house was surrounded by singing children from the orphanage where Carolyn volunteered. The Bordeaux family was so touched they built this memorial for her. They say there is an angel for each of the people she helped. There are hundreds of them throughout the garden."

"Wow. How do you know all that?"

"It says it on that plaque over there." Daniel grinned, as devious as ever.

I laughed. "You had me going there. I was starting to think you were some kind of intellectual, what with all this knowledge of obscure local history and quoting religious scholars."

Daniel bowed his head. "I had a lot of time to read where I was."

The air felt thick between us. Did Daniel *want* me to ask him where he'd been for the last three years? I'd wanted to—since the moment I first saw him. That question was just as important as finding out what happened between him and Jude. No doubt those two answers were connected. I told myself to seize the opportunity—to finally find the answers I needed so I could fix things for good.

I clenched my hands, digging my fingernails into my palms, and asked before I could change my mind, "Where did you go? Where have you been all this time?"

Daniel sighed and looked up at the tall statue next to him. This angel was a young man—early twenties, maybe—who was accompanied by a stone dog that sat at attention at his side. The dog was tall and slender like the angel, its triangular ears stretched to the man's elbow. It had a long snout, and its bushy coat and tail seemed to get lost in the intricately carved folds of the angel's robes.

"I went back east. Down south. Out west. Pretty much every other directional cliché you can think of." Daniel crouched down and studied the dog. "I met him when I was back East. He gave me this." He brushed his black stone necklace with his fingertips. "He said it would keep me safe."

"The dog or the angel?" I goaded. I should have known better than to think Daniel would give a straight answer to my question regarding his whereabouts.

Daniel swept his shaggy hair out of his eyes. "I met the *man* this statue was carved for. Gabriel. I learned a lot from him. He talked about Mrs. Bordeaux and the things she did for other people. He was the one who made me want to come back here. To be close to this place again . . . and other things." Daniel stood and sucked in a deep drag of foggy air. "Coming here always gave me such a high."

"You mean you used to come here to get high," I said, hazarding a guess.

"Well, yeah." Daniel laughed and sat on a stone bench.

I instinctively took a step farther away from him.

"But I don't do that anymore." He tapped his fingers on his legs. "I've been clean for a long time."

"That's good." I dropped my hands to my sides and tried to look casual and unshaken by his admission. I knew that he was no saint. I knew that his life had gone to a dark place long before he'd disappeared. I'd seen him only three times in the six months after he moved away to Oak Park with his mother—the six months that led up to his vanishing altogether. The last of those three times was when the Oak Park public high school called Dad because Daniel had been expelled for fighting. They couldn't reach his mother, so Dad and I had to escort him home. But in some ways it was like thinking of my own brother doing drugs or something worse.

I glanced at the tall statue of Gabriel the Angel looking down on us. His carved eyes seemed to rest on the crown of Daniel's head. That thread of curiosity pulled me to the seat next to him on the bench. "Do you believe in angels? Real ones?"

He shrugged. "I don't think they have feathery wings or anything like that. I think they're people who do good things even if they get nothing out of it. People like your father . . . and you."

I looked up into his glinting eyes. Daniel reached out his hand like he wanted to brush my cheek—little tingles sparked under my skin—but he pulled his hand back and coughed.

"You're all crazy, if you ask me," he said.

"Crazy?" My cheeks flamed even hotter.

"I don't know how you all do it," he said. "Like Maryanne Duke. She had nothing and she still tried to help people like me. I think she was an angel."

"Is that why you came to the funeral? For Maryanne?" *And not for me?*

"I used to stay with Maryanne when things got messy between my parents. If I wasn't at your house, I was with her. She was always there for me when others weren't." Daniel wiped at his nose with the back of his hand. His fingernails were blackened with what looked like marker ink. "I just felt like I should pay my last respects. . . ."

"I guess I forgot. Maryanne took care of a lot of people."

"Yeah, I know. I'm not special or anything."

"No. That's not what I meant. . . . I'm just sorry I didn't remember." I put my hand on his shoulder. He shrank away, and I could barely feel the firmness of his body under the fabric of his coat. "Things were really hard for you. I'm sure Maryanne made you feel—"

"Loved?"

"I guess. Loved, or at least normal."

Daniel shook his head. "I felt close to loved sometimes. Like when Maryanne read me stories at night, or when I'd sit around the table with your family. There's nothing like a Divine family dinner to make you feel like someone might care about you. But I never felt normal. Somehow, I always knew I didn't . . ."

"Belong?" For some reason I could understand.

"I never did belong, did I?" Daniel reached up and wrapped his long fingers around my wrist. He moved like he was going to cast my hand away, but then he hesitated and turned my hand over, cradling it in both of his. "But I can't tell you how many times over the last few years I wished I could be eating at that table with your family. Like I could take back everything I did, change things so I could be a part of it again. But that's impossible, isn't it?" He traced his warm fingers up the heart line in my open palm, and slipped his fingers in between mine.

It may have been the glimmering from the spotlights or the swirling of the fog, but for a moment he looked like the old Daniel, the one with white-blond hair and mischievous but innocent eyes—like the years had melted away and the darkness had drained out of him. And in that moment, something—an energy—passed between us. Like the thread that had drawn me to him was now a live wire, a lifeline, that bound us together, and I needed to pull him to safety.

"We're having a big Thanksgiving dinner tomorrow," I blurted out. "You should come. I want you to."

Daniel blinked. "You're freezing," he said. "We should go inside somewhere."

Daniel stood up, still holding my hand, and led me down the gravel lane. I didn't know when he was going to let go of my hand—and I didn't want him to. And I held on because I knew he needed me.

He finally let go as he stepped off the path and into a patch of decaying plants. "The fence isn't as high if we go this way," he said.

I hesitated for a moment on the edge of the path,

watching him slip away into the mist. I stepped off the gravel walkway and followed him through the depths of the garden. When we made it to the iron fence, I let him help me over, his hands skimming my waist and legs as I climbed. We walked side by side as we found our way back to the motorcycle. Our fingers brushed once, and I longed for him to take my hand in his again. I climbed on the back of the motorcycle and took in a deep breath of Daniel's earthy scent as the bike shot into the city night.

A FEW MINUTES LATER

The motorcycle lurched to a stop in front of Daniel's building. I slammed into his back and almost flew right off into the gutter.

Daniel gripped my thigh and steadied me. "Sorry about that," he mumbled, and let his hand linger for a moment.

Daniel got off the bike, and I followed. He rested his arm on my shoulder and steered me up the sidewalk and through the doorless entry of the apartment building. My heart thumped so hard as we went up the stairs I feared that Daniel might hear it. The thumping grew louder and heavier as we climbed, and I realized there was music coming from behind a door on the third landing. Daniel put his key in his pocket and tentatively pushed open his door. Sound engulfed us. Gyrating dancers packed the front room, and Zed—looking much more lively than he had before—sang (i.e., screamed) into a microphone while a few other guys banged on musical instruments with reckless abandon.

Daniel led me into the throng. I choked on the sickly sweet smoke wafting in the air. I was coughing and sputtering when this person, who looked more woman than teenage girl, emerged from the crowd. She came toward us, moving and convulsing to the indiscernible beat of Zed's song. Her short hair feathered out like she was some type of exotic bird, and her bleached white bangs made three perfect triangles on her forehead—the tips of them were dyed a garish shade of pink.

"Danny Boy, you made it," she said in an Eastern European–sounding accent. She turned her thick kohl-lined eyes on me and plumped her blood-red lips.

Daniel released my shoulder.

"Oh, look"—she took me in from head to toe—"you brought treats. I hope there's enough to share."

"Grace, this is Mishka. We knew each other a long time ago," Daniel said about the female clad in a black leather mini and what I think is called a bustier.

"Not *so* long, Danny Boy." She leaned her breasts up against him. "But you were more fun then." She traced a long, red, talonlike fingernail down his cheek. "You must come with me now." She pulled Daniel away from my side. "You have kept me waiting, and Mishka is not a patient woman."

"Come on, Grace." Daniel held his hand out to me.

I was about to slip my fingers into his when Mishka scowled.

"No!" she said. "I do not perform for an audience. This one stays here."

"I won't leave her behind."

Mishka leaned in even closer to Daniel, her gleaming teeth brushed his ear as she spoke. "You and I are the only real players here. Your *girl* will be fine without you for a few minutes. Mishka will not wait for you any longer, Danny Boy."

She pulled on his arm, but he didn't budge.

"Do you need a reminder of how I get when you disappoint me?" She narrowed her eyes and licked her lips.

"No . . . but Grace . . . ," he protested halfheartedly.

Mishka turned her glare on me. The irises of her eyes looked jet-black in the apartment's murky light. She brushed my arm with her talons, and her teeth seemed awfully sharp as she smiled. "You do not mind if I borrow my Danny Boy for a few moments," she said, but I could have sworn that her lips never moved—like I'd heard her voice inside my head.

"Um . . . no," I said, suddenly not minding much of anything. Maybe it was just the sick sweet smoke engulfing the room, but as Mishka stared into my eyes, I couldn't think, let alone care, about anything.

"That's a good girl," Mishka said. She looped her

arm through Daniel's and led him away from me.

Daniel glanced back and said, "Stay put. And don't talk to anyone."

At least that's what I think he said. My brain felt too fuzzy and my tongue felt too heavy to say anything back. I stood there in bewilderment until I was almost knocked flat by someone. I blinked at her through my fog. All I could make out was a girl with green hair and more piercings than face. She stopped "dancing" and leaned in close, squinting her seemingly too-large eyes. She said something I didn't understand, and I tried to ask her if we knew each other from somewhere. But what came out of my mouth didn't even sound like words. She stumbled away, laughing hysterically to herself.

I retreated to the dark hallway that led to the bedrooms and took in a few breaths of slightly fresher air. I was about to knock on Daniel's door when I heard Mishka laughing from behind it. My stomach churned, and as Zed's noxious song drifted into another melody (this one eerie and pulsing, with Zed breathing heavily into the microphone), my hazy thoughts cleared and I realized that I had been abandoned. Any moment, or connection, or energy that Daniel and I had shared was gone.

"Well, 'ello there, darling," a guy said as he approached me from the crowd. "Didn't expect to see you 'ere again." He smirked, and I realized he was one of the foulmouthed guys I'd met here before.

"Neither did I." I pulled my wool coat closer around my chest. Any sexiness I had felt in my Sunday clothes suddenly felt overly naïve.

"You look like you could use some fun." His voice was as slippery as a serpent's. He offered me a plastic cup filled with dark amber-colored booze—something fizzled ominously at the bottom. "I can show you a good time if you're feeling neglected."

I waved the cup away. "No, thanks, I was just leaving."

"That's what you think." He slammed his arm out in front of me, blocking my escape. "This party's just starting." He tried to brush his cup-filled hand where it didn't belong.

I dove under his arm and through the crowd to the door. The green-haired girl teetered in the open doorway. She slurred a nasty name at me as I pushed past her. I went down the stairs and out of the building. I listened carefully at the exit, and when I heard footsteps on the metal stairs, I bolted down Markham Street.

My luck must have turned because as I came to the end of the block, a bus headed in the direction of home pulled up to the curb. I bounded up the steps when the doors swung open and prayed I had enough money for the fare. The driver grumbled as I counted out my change, but I had enough, with thirty-five cents left to spare.

The bus was almost empty, except for a couple of grizzly men shouting at each other in a language that reminded me of Mishka's accent, and a forty-something-year-old guy with bottle-thick glasses who cradled a baby doll in his arms and crooned to it in deep, fatherly tones. I took a seat in the back and hugged my knees to my chest. The bus lurched and jolted and smelled faintly of urine, but I felt safer there than I had in that apartment's hallway.

I couldn't believe that Daniel had abandoned me to those people. Couldn't believe that I went with him into his apartment in the first place. What might have happened if it hadn't been for that party? But mostly, I was ashamed that part of me had *wanted* something to happen.

Temptation bites.

HOME AGAIN

I rode the bus until it pulled into the stop by the school. I used the last of my spare change to call April from a pay phone, but she didn't answer. It wasn't too hard to guess who might have been distracting her at the time.

I pulled my coat tight around my body and walked home as quickly as I could in my heels—feeling the whole time like that nasty guy from the party was following me. I slipped into the house and hoped to sneak up to my room without being noticed. Like I could pretend I'd been in bed all along. But Mom must have heard the soft click of the door closing because she called me into the kitchen before I had a chance to disappear up the stairs.

"Where have you been?" she asked, sounding more than a little annoyed. I watched her rip thick slices of bread into chunks to dry overnight for Thanksgiving stuffing. "You were supposed to help serve dinner after the funeral." Apparently, it wasn't late enough in the evening for her to be worried about my safety—but plenty late enough for her to be ticked off about my absence.

"I know," I mumbled. "I'm sorry."

"First you disappear, and then Jude." She grabbed another slice of bread and tore into it with her fingers. "Do you know how it looked to have half of our family missing from the dinner? And your father nearly threw out his back putting away chairs while you two were out gallivanting with your friends."

"I'm sorry. I'll make it up to you." I turned to leave the kitchen.

"You're darn right you will. We've got at least twenty people coming for Thanksgiving tomorrow. You're doing the pies, and then you'll scrub the floors. Your brother will get his own list of chores."

For a moment I contemplated bringing up the chem test I needed signed since I was already in trouble—but decided not to push it. Mom can get pretty elaborate with chore assignments when she's aggravated. "Okay," I said. "That's fair."

"Set your alarm for five forty-five!" Mom called as I headed toward the stairs.

Seriously, like I *needed* another reason to curse my impulsive decisions at that moment.

CHAPTER NINE
Thanks Giving

"I could never paint like that," I said as I looked over the project Daniel had set out to dry on the kitchen counter.

It was a painting of my father's hands slicing a green apple for Daniel's birthday cobbler. The hands looked lifelike—gentle, kind, and steady. The self-portrait I'd been working on seemed so flat in comparison.

"Yeah, you can," Daniel said. "I'll teach you."

I crinkled my nose at him. "Like you could teach me anything."

But I knew he could. This was my first reattempt at oils in almost two years, and I was about ready to give it up all over again.

"Only because you're so darn stubborn," Daniel said. "Do you want to learn how to paint better or not?"

"I guess so."

Daniel pulled a Masonite board from his supply bucket under the kitchen table. The board looked like a mess, smeared with a dozen different colors of oil paint. "Try this," he said. "The colors come through as you paint. It gives more depth to your work."

He coached me as I started my self-portrait over again. I couldn't believe the difference. I loved the way my eyes looked with flecks of green and orange coming through behind the violet irises. They looked more real than anything I had ever painted before.

"Thank you," I said.

Daniel smiled. "When I get some more, I'll show you this really great trick with linseed oil and varnish. It gives the most amazing quality to skin tones, and you won't believe what it does for your brushstrokes."

"Really?"

Daniel nodded and went back to work on his own portrait. Only, instead of painting himself like Mrs. Miller had assigned, he was painting a tan-and-gray dog, with eyes shaped like a person's. They were a deep, earthy brown like his.

"Daniel." Mom stood in the kitchen entryway. Her face was pale. "Someone is here to see you."

Daniel cocked his head in surprise. I followed him into the foyer, and there *she* was. Daniel's mother stood in the doorway. Her hair had gotten a lot longer and blonder in the year and two months since she'd sold their house and left Daniel with us.

"Hi, baby," she said to him.

"What are you doing here?" His voice crackled like ice. His mother hadn't called in months—not even for his birthday.

"I'm taking you home," she said. "I got us a little place in Oak Park. It's not like the house, but it's nice and clean, and you can start high school there in the fall."

"I'm not going with you," Daniel said, his voice climbing in anger, "and I'm not going to a new school."

"Daniel, I am your mother. You belong home with me. You need me."

"No, he doesn't," I practically shouted at her. "Daniel doesn't need you. He needs *us*."

"No, I don't," Daniel said. "I don't need you." He pushed past me, almost knocking me over. "I don't need anybody!" He ran past his mother and out into the yard.

Mrs. Kalbi shrugged. "I think Daniel just needs some time to get adjusted. I hope you will understand if he doesn't see your family for a while." Her eyes flicked in my direction. "I'll send for his things later." She closed the door behind her.

THANKSGIVING MORNING

I woke up early to the sound of wind battering my window. I shivered and shook in my bed. Daniel was right. He didn't need anybody. I'd been fooling myself in that garden. Daniel didn't need my lifeline. He didn't need *me* at all.

I pulled my comforter over my shoulders and hunched into a ball, but no matter what I did, I couldn't find warmth in my bed.

The clinking of flatware in the distance was evidence that my mother was already setting the table in anticipation of today's Thanksgiving dinner to end all dinners.

I decided to get an early start on making amends for yesterday's absence and lurched out of bed. The sleepiness in my brain vanished the second my feet hit the frigid hardwood floor. I scurried over to the closet and pulled on my slippers and robe and then made my way downstairs.

Mom had two of the tables from the parish's social hall pushed together so they stuck out into the foyer from the dining room. They were draped with pressed linen tablecloths the shade of maple leaves, and she was setting places for at least twenty-five with her best china and crystal goblets. Festive floral arrangements and candles adorned the table instead of the usual papier-mâché pilgrims I'd helped her make when I was nine.

"Looks nice," I said from the last step.

Mom almost dropped a plate. She steadied herself and placed it on the table. "Hmm," she said. "I don't need you up until a quarter to six to get the pies started."

Obviously, all had not been forgiven yet.

I sighed. "I was awake anyway." I rubbed my hands together. "You could stand to turn up the heat, though."

"It will get plenty warm in here when the ovens get going and this place starts filling up with people. We've got a crowd this year. I'm doing two turkeys." She placed silverware around the table as she spoke. "But that means the pies need to be done by eight at the latest. I bought fixings for two of your caramel apple pies and a couple of spiced pumpkin. Your dad is making his famous crescent rolls, so we need to time those just right."

"Thank goodness for two ovens."

"Like I said, it will get plenty warm in here."

"But can't we turn up the heat for a few minutes?" I peeked through the window curtains and was actually surprised that the lawn was still bare and dead and not blanketed with snow. "Aren't you afraid Baby James will freeze to death or something?"

Mom almost laughed. "It's not *that* cold." She came up and swatted me on the butt. "Go get an early start on those pies. Or if you're so cold you can go work up a sweat helping Jude clean out the storage room."

"The storage room?"

"Somebody might want a tour of the house."

I raised my eyebrows. "You don't have to show them the storage room."

Mom shrugged. "Jude was up looking to get his penance over with an hour ago, and we both know that your father is the only male in this family who can cook."

"Oh." I didn't bother to point out that she could have had Jude set the table because she was repositioning the floral centerpieces to be exactly the same distance apart. "Is April still coming?"

"Yes. Didn't she tell you?" Mom gave me an inquisitive glance.

"Seems like she talks more to Jude these days than she does me." I knew it was petty to be bothered by April and Jude hanging out—but I couldn't help it.

Mom wrinkled her nose. "I guess that explains why he seems so anxious lately." She clucked her tongue.

"I guess so." I fingered the tie of my robe. "April is a good person."

"I'm sure she is." Mom adjusted the fold on one of the linen napkins. "I'm sure she is."

"Um, I guess I'll get dressed and then start in the kitchen."

"That would be nice," she mumbled, and started straightening all the goblets.

PIES

Mom was right. Things got pretty heated around the house later that morning. It all started when Dad revealed that he had no idea Mom wanted him to make his famous crescent rolls for the festivities.

"You never asked me," Dad said after she made a snippy remark about how he should have gotten started on the dough a half hour before.

"You make them every year." She banged a tray of dried bread chunks onto the counter. "I shouldn't have to ask."

"Yes, you should. I'm not in the mood for baking right now. And I'm not in the mood for this big dinner, either."

"What do you mean?" Mom swatted the bread crumbs into her mixing bowl and jabbed at them with her wooden spoon. "I put this big dinner together for *you.*"

"You should have asked me, Meredith," he said from the other side of the counter. "I don't want all these people coming over. I don't want a big fancy dinner. I don't even know if I feel like giving thanks today."

"Don't say things like that!" Mom brandished her wooden spoon. A brownish glob landed at my feet. Neither of my parents seemed to notice that I was still in the kitchen making filling for my caramel apple pies.

"If it's such a problem for you," Mom said, "then I'll do the rolls, and the turkeys, and the stuffing, and the cranberries, and the mashed potatoes, and the green bean casseroles, and the spinach salads. All you'll have to do is say the blessing and put on a happy face for the crowd." Mom stabbed the spoon back in her bowl.

"You are these people's pastor. They don't want to hear you talking like that."

Dad slammed his fist onto the counter. "Like what, Meredith? Like what?" He stormed out of the room and into his study before Mom could respond.

"Insufferable man," she mumbled, "thinks he isn't worth anything if he can't save the whole world." She marched over to the fridge and flung open the door. She riffled through the shelves and swore under her breath.

I cleared my throat and made loud noises as I scraped apples into my piecrusts.

Mom stiffened, no doubt realizing I had been there through that whole exchange. "Finish those pies," she snapped. "And then run over to Apple Valley and get some cranberries. The berries. Not that canned garbage."

Mom slammed the fridge door. Her shoulders dropped. "I'm sorry. I forgot," she said. "They were out at Day's Market yesterday and I forgot to check elsewhere. I think Super Target opens at seven for a few hours." She opened the fridge again. "Would you mind running to get a couple of things?"

"Not at all." Normally, I would have grumbled and whined on principle at being asked to run errands on such a frigid morning, but that was one heated kitchen I was anxious to get out of.

I drifted without direction up and down the grocery aisles, unable to remember what I'd come to the store to get in the first place. I'd left the house as soon as I stuck my pies in the ovens—and, in my haste, left the dozen-item shopping list Mom had dictated to me on the counter.

That was the second time in a week that I'd heard my parents shout at each other. Had things been strained at my house for longer than I realized? I thought of Dad holed up in his study for the last month. And Mom flipping into perfection overdrive wasn't a new thing. The first time I'd noticed it was a few days after Charity and I had come home from our unplanned trip to Grandma Kramer's three years ago. I'd found Mom frantically trying to brush, measure, and cut all the fringe on the area rugs to be the exact same length. Dad hid the scissors for weeks after that. I guess I'd been too young to fully clue in to the weirdness between them then. And, of course, no one ever talked about it.

Was this how it started for April's family? Was this anything like it had been for Daniel in his broken home?

But I knew it had been worse for him. My parents' shouting was nothing like what Daniel had lived through.

I dropped a bag of cranberries into my basket and pushed all thoughts of Daniel aside. I foraged through the picked-over shelves for whatever else I could remember from the list, paid for my stuff, and headed back home.

When I opened the door into the mudroom, I was slammed by a wall of stench. Something was burning. I dropped my grocery bags and ran to the kitchen. All but one of my pies was cooling on the counter. I yanked open the oven door. Black smoke billowed out, making me cough and gag. I pushed open the window above the sink and tried to direct the smoke outside. But it was too late. The smoke detector started screaming from the hallway.

I covered my ears and ran for Dad's study. The detector was right in front of the closed doors. I flung the doors open and was surprised that Dad wasn't in there—and even more surprised that no one else in the family had responded to the screeching alarm.

I struggled to open the study window, almost snagging my hand on a protruding nail in the sill. Stupid old house. I finally pried the window open and grabbed a book from the stacks on my father's desk. I used it to fan the smoke away from the detector until the blaring stopped.

My ears were still ringing as I took the book back to the tower of babble that used to be Dad's desk—books and notes were scattered everywhere in heaps. The book I held was cased in crackling leather and looked older than anything I had ever checked out of the local Rose Crest library branch. A delicate hooded flower was etched in silver on the cover. The title was also engraved in worn silver: *Loup-Garou.*

I'd never heard such a word. I flipped the book open. It was all in what I assumed was French. I checked the next book in the stack where I'd gotten the first. This one didn't look quite as old, but it was just as battered. *Lycanthropy: Blessing or Curse?* I was about to open it when I saw a long, slender velvet box sitting in the stacks of papers. It looked like one of those necklace boxes from a high-end jewelry store. I put down the book and popped open the lid of the box. It held Don's silver knife. The one I'd locked in Dad's office over at the parish. Why would Dad bring it here? And why would he leave it out like this with a toddler in the house?

The front door rattled open.

"What on earth?" Mom's voice echoed down the hall.

I stuck the knife box on the highest shelf of the bookcase and went out to meet her.

Mom had James on her hip and a Day's Market bag in her hand. "Great. I forgot one of the pies, didn't I?"

I nodded. Though I felt like it was my fault for taking so long at the store.

"Just great!" she said. "I remembered a few more

groceries just after you left, so I ran over to Day's. . . . And now the house stinks. Just what I need."

I contemplated reopening my petition for a cell phone but thought better of it as James started to fuss when Mom tried to put him down. He wrapped his legs around her knee and clung to her shirt. I offered to take him from her.

Mom peeled him from her legs and handed him over.

"It'll air out," I said, and tried to bounce James on my hip.

Why did it seem like *I* was the one holding everyone together lately?

James dropped his blanket in a desperate attempt to jump from my arms to Mom's. "Banket!" he shrieked, and burst into tears, kicking his Curious George slippers against my legs.

I picked it up and wadded it into a puppet. "Mwah, mwah," I said, and pretended to kiss his face. His whines turned to laughter, and he hugged his blanket in his skinny little arms.

"I'll open a few more windows," I said to Mom, "and then find Charity so she can entertain Baby James while I help you cook."

"Thanks." Mom rubbed her temples. "Charity should be back soon. She went over to the Johnsons' to feed their birds. Tell her to make James some lunch in a couple of hours. Dinner is at three, so I want him to go down for a nap by two. Oh, but we'll have to put him down in his Portacrib in the study. Aunt Carol will be staying in his room."

Great. Just who my dad needed today—Aunt Carol.

DINNER

My mother's family is half Roman Catholic, half Jewish—kind of ironic for the wife of a protestant pastor. And even though she was raised Catholic, her family still celebrated Passover and Hanukkah. I think that is where they got this interesting tradition of always setting an extra place at the table for special occasions. According to Aunt Carol, it was supposed to be an expression of hope and faith in the Messiah who would someday come. While I thought it was kind of cool, it usually bugged Dad because, of course, he believed that the Messiah had already come, in the form of Jesus Christ, and that such a tradition was an affront to his devotion for Him.

Mom, trying to appease both him and her sister, would tell him to think of it as an extra place for an unexpected visitor. However, today Dad seemed to find my mother's family's tradition especially irksome as he scanned the ragtag group of lonely hearts, young families, widows, widowers, and single moms who congregated around our holiday table, and noticed that there was not only one empty seat but two. One was at his end of the table.

The other, across the table from me, was set with a special golden goblet and golden utensils.

Dad glared at the goblet and mumbled something under his breath. Then an almost-genial smile spread across his face. "Shall we get started?" he asked the crowd.

Eager faces nodded, and April actually licked her lips—but she was staring at Jude when she did it, so it may have had nothing to do with the food.

"Who's missing?" Pete Bradshaw gestured to the two empty seats. He and his mother sat to one side of me. I'd felt bad when Pete told me his dad had cancelled their annual Thanksgiving cruise because he had an emergency meeting in Toledo, but I was glad Pete was there to close the distance between my mom and dad—who threw each other pointed looks when Pete asked this question.

"Don Mooney had to close up at Day's Market," Dad said. "Meredith does not feel like waiting for him."

Mom coughed. "Don did not RSVP, so there is no point in waiting if we don't know if he's coming."

"I'm sure he will be along soon." Dad smiled at her.

I wondered if he was right or if Don was still brooding over his encounter with my father the other day. I actually got this heavy feeling when I imagined him sitting alone in his apartment behind the parish.

"The other seat," Mom started to explain, "is a family tradition of ours—"

Dad grunted. "Meredith has asked me to say a special blessing over the food."

Aunt Carol gave Dad the evil eye, most likely on my mother's behalf.

Dad extended his hands to Jude on his right side and Leroy Maddux on his left. We all joined hands around the table, my fingers slipping tentatively into Pete's. Dad began his blessing. His voice was even, and he sounded like he was speaking words he had rehearsed in his office at the parish or wherever he had disappeared to until dinner.

"We are gathered here, O Father, to celebrate thy bounty. Thou art giving and kind unto us, and we wish to share that with others. That is why we leave a space at our table for any unexpected visitors. To remind us to open our home to those in need. And also to remind us of those who should be here: our extended family, my father, and Maryanne Duke." He paused for a moment and then went on. "Let us give thanks for thy blessings—"

The doorbell rang. Mom fidgeted in her seat.

"Let us give thanks for thy blessings. Keep us and bless this food that it will nourish and strengthen us as Thou strengthens our souls. Amen."

"Amen," the rest of us intoned.

My seat was at the end of the table that stuck out into the foyer. I jumped up, went to the door, and flung it open, expecting to find Don. Instead, there was this amazingly attractive guy with shortish, light brown hair, dressed in khakis and a blue button-up shirt, standing on the porch.

"Sorry I'm late," he said.

"Grace, who is it?" Mom called from the dining room.

"Daniel?" I whispered.

CHAPTER TEN
Unexpected

"You came?"

"I was invited, wasn't I?" Daniel said.

"I didn't expect . . . and you look so . . . different."

"Compliments of Mishka," he said. "That's why she was there last night. I needed to change it for school. Couldn't strip all the dark out, though"—he brushed his hand through his shorter, brown hair—"so we settled for this."

The mention of Mishka made me want to slam the door in his face. Oh, but what a nice face he had now that it wasn't obscured by long, black hair.

I shook my head. "You should go."

"Grace, who is it?" Mom repeated as she came to the door. "Is this a friend from school . . ." She stopped mid-step beside me. "Grace, what is the meaning of this?" She pointed an accusatory finger at Daniel, who stood motionless on the porch. "What is *he* doing here?"

"I invited him."

"You invited him?" she said too loudly. I was sure we had an audience by then. "How could you? How dare you!"

"You told her she could invite whomever she wanted," Dad said as he came up behind us. "You must be prepared to deal with the consequences if she interprets your suggestion literally."

"You're right, Grace. I should go." Daniel glanced at Dad. "I'm sorry, Pastor, this was a mistake. I'll leave."

Dad dropped his gaze. "No," he said. "You were invited; therefore, you are welcome."

Mom gasped. I looked back at my father in shock and a bit of awe.

"If we say we're going to do something, then we do it. Right, Grace?" Dad looked at Daniel. "I'm sorry I forgot that."

Daniel nodded.

"He can't stay," Mom said. "There's no room. He was not expected."

"Don't be silly. You set a place for him yourself." Dad turned to Daniel. "Come in then, before the food gets cold."

"Thank you, Pastor."

Dad took my mother by the shoulders and steered her back to the table. I think she was too shocked to protest. I gestured Daniel inside and closed the door behind him. He followed me to the table, and I pointed to the empty seat across from mine.

Everyone sat there staring at him, probably trying to figure out what the big deal was.

"Is that that Kalbi guy?" Pete whispered to me.

I nodded and he turned and whispered something to his mother.

Daniel tentatively prodded the golden fork next to his plate. He looked up at me and winked.

Jude rose from his chair. "This is ridiculous. He can't stay. He doesn't belong here."

"He stays." Dad put a heaping scoop of mashed potatoes on his plate. "Pass this to Daniel," he said, and handed the bowl to Leroy.

"Then I'm leaving," Jude said. "Come on, April, let's get out of here." He held his hand out to her.

"Sit!" Dad said. "Sit, eat, and be grateful. Your mother made this fabulous meal, and now we—all of us—are going to eat it."

April shrank into her chair like a scolded pup. Jude looked for a moment like he was going to do the same. He clenched his fists and then relaxed into his sullen shell. "I'm sorry, Mother," he said in an even tone. "I just remembered that I volunteered to serve dinner at the shelter. I should get going so I won't be late." He sidled his way past the dining room chairs.

"What about *our* dinner?" Mom called after him.

But Jude kept going. He took a set of keys off the hook and headed for the garage.

"Let him go," Dad said.

Mom smiled to her guests. "You know Jude. Always thinking about others first." She grabbed the bowl of cranberry sauce from Aunt Carol. "Eat up," she said to everyone. But as she shoveled cranberries onto her turkey, she shot me a look that made my heart shrivel with guilt.

I stared at the lump of green bean casserole on my plate. It didn't look right to me. Too soggy—I'd over-cooked it for sure.

Pete brushed my arm. Warmth crept up my face.

I felt someone's foot nudge my leg. I looked up at Daniel, and he raised his eyebrows and smiled like he was completely innocent. My face got even warmer when I noted how much I liked the way his sandy hair flopped above his dark eyes as he raised his golden goblet to me. I scowled and turned back to my food, feeling like a silly little kid.

The meal went on in awkward silence for another ten minutes or so. I literally jumped when there was a loud bang on the front door. The banging got louder, and the doorbell rang several times. Everyone looked at me like I was also responsible for this mysterious interruption.

"Who did you invite now, the Ringling Brothers Circus?" Mom asked as I got up from the table.

Aunt Carol chuckled. She always got a kick out of our Divine little family.

"Pastor? Pastor?" a loud voice shouted from behind the door. The second I pulled it open, Don Mooney came barreling into the house. He almost knocked me flat. "Pastor D-vine!" he shouted.

Dad shot up from the table. "What is it, Don?"

"Pastor D-vine, come here quick. You have to see."

"What's going on?"

"There's blood. Blood all over the porch."

"What?" Dad flew out the door, and I followed. There was blood—a small pool of it on the porch step and several drops around it.

"I thought maybe one of you was hurt," Don said. "Maybe the monster—"

"We're all fine," Dad said.

I followed Dad as he followed the trail of blood. Our porch wrapped around the side of the house, and so did the trail—little red gems of blood instead of bread crumbs. It led to the outside of the study's open window. There was a spattering of blood there, like someone had shaken a wounded hand. Or paw. Dad crouched to inspect the mess. I looked inside the study. James's Portacrib was on its side next to my father's disheveled desk.

"Mom!" I whirled around, almost smacking into Daniel, who was suddenly behind me. "Mom, where's Baby James?" I couldn't remember him being at dinner.

"He's still asleep," Mom said. She'd appeared on the porch with most of the dinner crew. "I'm surprised he didn't wake up with all that racket. . . ." She looked at the blood at her feet. Her face went white. She bolted into the house.

Dad, Carol, and Charity followed. I didn't have to. Mom's screams were enough to confirm my fears.

Daniel inspected the window frame. "Was the screen missing before?"

"Yes. Jude broke it out a couple of months ago. We locked ourselves out of the house. No one knew how to fix it."

Mom's voice grew shriller from the other side of the window. Dad tried to calm her.

"Perhaps James wandered off," old Leroy said. "Everyone, let's go search the yard." Leroy hobbled off the porch. "James?" he shouted as he went around to the back.

Pete and April followed.

Dr. Connors, Mom's friend from the clinic, handed his tiny baby daughter to his wife. "Stay here. I'll go down the lane." He and most of our other guests fanned out into the yard. They all shouted for James.

"Do you think it was the monster, Miss Grace?" Don asked. "If only I had my knife . . . I could kill it . . . hunt it down like my great-great-granddad."

"There's no such thing as monsters," I said.

Daniel winced. He'd found the nail I'd almost snagged

myself on earlier. His finger was stained with blood—but not his. He brought it to his nose and sniffed. He closed his eyes, as if to think, and smelled the blood again.

Don made a blubbering noise. He sounded just like my mom.

"Is there anywhere James loves to go?" Daniel asked me.

"I don't know. He really likes the horses at the MacArthurs' stables."

"Don," Daniel said. "Go get as many people as you can and search the route toward the MacArthurs' farm."

I knew I should go, too, but I waited for Daniel.

He wiped the blood on his sleeve. "Pastor," he called into the open window.

Dad held Mom to his chest. "He'll be okay," he said, and cradled the back of her head with his hand.

Mom was usually so on top of things. Seeing her act so helpless made me shake with anxiety.

"Pastor," Daniel said.

Dad glanced at us. "One of you go call the police. They'll organize a search party."

I started to move.

Daniel grabbed my arm. "No." He looked at my dad. "The police can't help us."

Mom whimpered.

Daniel let go of my arm. "I'll find him for you."

Dad nodded. "Go."

Chapter Eleven
Revelations

INTO THE WOODS

Daniel launched himself over the porch railing and flew around to the backyard. I stumbled down the steps and went after him. Pete and Leroy inspected the wood fence Dad had had installed after Daisy was killed. It shielded our yard from the encroaching woods. Daniel stopped where the fence ended in a narrow gap. It was the same section that blew down whenever there was a windstorm like the one this morning. He scanned the ground as if searching for tracks. I didn't see any.

Daniel squeezed through the gap. "Go help Don search the way to the MacArthurs'," he said through the fence. It sounded like a blanket order to all three of us.

I started after Daniel.

"Grace?" Pete asked.

"Go call the shelter," I said. "Tell them to send Jude

home as soon as he gets there. Then take Leroy and help Don."

Pete nodded.

I slipped through the fence.

Daniel was up ahead. He scratched at the dirt near the hiking path we used to explore as children. I rubbed my arms for warmth, wishing I'd grabbed my coat. My thin sweater and cotton slacks would have to do.

"You really think he's in the woods?" I asked.

Daniel dusted off his hands and grunted. "Yes."

"Then why did you send everyone down to the farm? Don't we need them here?"

"I don't want them mucking up the trail."

"What?"

Daniel grabbed my hand. "Doesn't this path lead to the creek?"

I swallowed hard. "Yes."

Daniel wrapped his fingers around mine. "Hopefully, it's dry by now."

We jogged down the trail for what felt like half a mile. The farther we went into the forest, the muddier the path became. And the more my feet sank into the earth, the more I doubted that James could have toddled this way.

Daniel stopped. He turned in a small circle like he'd lost his bearings.

"We should turn back." I pulled off one of my flats, and thanked my lucky stars I *hadn't* worn the stupid kitten heels Mom had wanted me to wear to dinner.

"This way." Daniel stepped off the narrow path into the brush. He drew in a breath and closed his eyes, as if savoring the taste. "James is this way."

"That's not possible." I flexed my foot. "He's not even two yet. There's no way he could have come this far."

Daniel stared into the dark of the woods. "On his own, no." He rocked up on the balls of his feet. "Stay," he whispered, and bolted into the thicket of trees. He was there and then gone.

"Wha . . .Wait!"

But he kept moving.

And I'm apparently not very good at doing what I'm told.

"He's my brother!" I yelled, and crammed my foot into my shoe.

I could barely see Daniel as I followed. Only flashes of his back in the distance as he wove through the trees. He was like an animal, running on instinct without even looking where his feet landed. I, on the other hand, lumbered and crashed into trees that seemed to leap right in front of me. Branches cracked under my shoes, and I stumbled over rocks and roots as I tried to catch up to him.

It seemed like he'd picked up on a scent or something. Was that even possible? All I could smell with each stabbing breath were decaying leaves and pine needles. Those smells reminded me of only one thing—it was nearly winter. And if Daniel was right, Baby James was out here somewhere.

The temperature fell as the sun sank below the tall pines. Looming shadows made it even harder to pick my way through the woods. I caught my heel in the root of a large pine and toppled forward. Pain slammed up my arms as I hit the ground. I pushed myself up and brushed my hands off on my slacks, leaving a bloody smear on the fabric.

I looked around. Daniel was nowhere. And another few steps would have taken me down a deep ravine. If I hadn't stumbled, I would have fallen a sharp thirty feet. Was that what had happened to Daniel, or did he veer left or right? I grabbed a branch of a nearby tree and leaned out over the steep slope. I could only see more rocks and dirt and thick ferns at the bottom.

"Daniel!" I shouted. All I got in return was my echo. Wouldn't I have heard something if Daniel had fallen? Wouldn't I be able to make out his path if he'd climbed down?

A half-moon would rise soon to replace the sun. I didn't have a flashlight, and I'd never ventured this deep into the woods before. How would I find James, or Daniel, or even my way back now? Maybe I deserved to be lost. It was my pie that had burned, and I was the one who had opened that window. It was so stuffy in the house from the two ovens going all day; Charity wouldn't have noticed that it was still open when she put the baby down for his nap.

How can I go home without James?

A howl filled the void below, echoing off the walls of the ravine. Only an animal could have made that noise. But it was like a shout of frustration. Like a wolf anxious to capture its prey. I had to find a way down. I had to find my brother before that animal did.

Parts of the ravine wall were much steeper than others—a sheer drop-off in some places, but where I was seemed like a somewhat doable incline for climbing down. I grabbed at the roots protruding in the eroded hill and climbed, with my back to the open air, over the side of the steep slope. The toe of my shoe slipped in the mud, and my chest hit the earthen wall, knocking a scream right out of me. I slid several feet before I was able to claw my hands into a tangle of roots above my head. I held on with desperate force, the roots searing like lightning in my injured hand. I tried to determine with my dangling feet how far I was from the bottom. *Please be only a couple of yards*. I couldn't hold on much longer.

"You're safe," Daniel shouted from somewhere below me. "Push off and let go, and I'll catch you."

"I can't," I said. His voice sounded too far away—too far to fall. I couldn't look.

"It's just like jumping from the gate in the Garden of Angels."

I panted into my shaking arms. "I almost killed myself then, too."

"And I caught you then, too." Daniel's voice seemed closer now. "Trust me."

"Okay."

I pushed off and fell. Daniel whipped his arms around my chest, stopping me before I hit the boulder-strewn ground. He pulled me tight against him.

I couldn't breathe.

"So what part of 'stay' did you not understand?" he whispered. His warm breath brushed down my neck like caressing fingers. Heat encircled my whole body.

"Well, since I'm not a golden retriever . . ."

Daniel set me down gently. I turned toward him. My legs wobbled as I moved. His blue shirt and slacks were still spotless. Only his forearms, where he caught me, were smeared with mud.

"How did you . . . ?"

But then I noticed what was in his hand. Small, brown, fuzzy, and all too familiar. One of James's Curious George slippers.

"Where did you find this?" I asked, snatching it out of his hand. Strangely, the slipper was almost completely clean, not caked with mud like my shoes from wandering in the forest.

"There," Daniel said. Pointing to a heap of decaying ferns between two boulders about twenty feet from where we stood. "I thought for sure . . ." Daniel backed away, looking around at the ground as if searching for some kind of trail.

"James!" I shouted, my voice echoing through the ravine like hundreds of desperate cries. "James, are you here?"

Daniel kept searching the ground. His face became rigid with frustration. I followed him as he crossed to the other side of the ravine, opposite from where I'd slid down. He crouched, spreading a few ferns with his hands, and inhaled deeply. "I thought for sure I was on the right trail."

"Like you followed his scent?" I asked.

Daniel tilted his head slightly as if listening. He shot straight up and spun around, staring back up at the ravine wall, about a hundred feet from where we stood now. Then I heard something, too. A faraway cry from somewhere back up on the ridge. The monkey slipper fell from my fingers. And my heart stopped beating as I watched something that looked like a little white ghost in the twilight toddle out from behind a boulder, and right toward the edge of the cliff.

"James!"

"Gwa-cie!" he wailed with his arms outstretched to me.

"Stop!" I screamed. "James, stop!"

But his little legs kept moving. "Gwa-cie, Gwa-cie!"

Then Daniel was moving. Running across the ravine floor toward James—faster than I thought possible.

James took another step, slipped in the mud, and toppled over the edge.

"James!" I shrieked as he fell like a limp doll.

Daniel dropped to all fours and leaped like a mountain lion off a boulder. He sailed into the air toward James—twenty feet high, at least. I watched in paralyzed amazement as he caught James in midair and wrapped him in his arms, simultaneously twisting until his back slammed with bone-breaking force into the jagged rocks of the ravine wall. In that split second I saw a look of pain rip through Daniel's face, but he clutched Baby James closer as they ricocheted off the wall and started to fall, twisting out of control, the last twenty feet.

"No!" I clamped my eyes shut and said the fastest prayer ever. I waited for the gruesome sounds of a skull-cracking impact. But instead, all I heard was the shifting of rocks and the crunch of a branch, like someone had jumped a mere few feet on top of it.

I opened my eyes and saw Daniel *standing* on the ground with Baby James clinging to his chest like a little wolverine. My mouth dropped open.

"Holy sh . . ."

THE WAY HOME

"Nice word to teach your little brother," Daniel said as I pulled James out of his arms.

Baby James clapped his hands and repeated my expletive with his happy baby lisp. He patted my face with his icy hands. His jumper and his one Curious George slipper were caked with mud. His lips were a ghastly shade of blue, and he shivered in my arms. But thankfully, he seemed uninjured.

"What else did you expect me to say?" I hugged James close, hoping to share some of the panicked heat that had flashed through my body when I watched them fall. "How on earth? What on earth? That was a freaking miracle."

"Fweaking," James said.

"How did you do that?"

"Miracle," Daniel said with a shrug. He winced. That's when I noticed the bloody tear in his shirt across the back of his right shoulder. I remembered the look of pain on his face when he hit the ravine wall.

"You're hurt." I touched his arm. "Let me look at it."

"It's nothing," Daniel said, and turned away.

"No, it's not. And what you did wasn't *nothing*." I'd heard of people doing extraordinary things when pumped full of adrenaline—but I couldn't believe what I'd just seen, no matter what the circumstances. "Tell me how you caught him like that."

"Later. We need to go."

"No," I said. "I'm sick of everyone dodging my questions. Tell me what's going on."

"Gracie, James is freezing. He's going to get hypothermic if we don't get him home." Daniel grabbed my uninjured hand and pulled me to a patch of mud. He pointed at some animal tracks. They obviously belonged to something large and powerful. "These are fresh," Daniel said.

I remembered that strange animal howl. I hugged James even tighter.

"We need to get out of here." Daniel unbuttoned his long-sleeved oxford shirt and pulled it off, uncovering his faded Wolfsbane T-shirt underneath. He tied the two long oxford sleeves together at the cuffs.

"What are you doing?"

"Making a sling."

"I thought your shoulder wasn't—"

"It's not for me, it's for James." He made a couple more knots in his shirt. "If I wear him up front, it'll be easier for us to make a run for it." Daniel pulled his homemade sling over his shoulder and took James out of my arms. The baby squealed as Daniel situated him in the fabric folds, but sure enough, the shirt had made a perfect little seat for him to sit in against Daniel's chest. "I've been here before. This ravine curves around back toward your neighborhood." Daniel took my hand again.

He started running, pulling me with him.

"But how are we getting *out* of the ravine?" I asked. "My hand is trashed. I don't think I can climb."

"Leave that to me," Daniel said, and picked up his pace.

I had to sprint to keep up with him. I couldn't believe how fast he ran, especially while hefting James. Daniel never missed a step, even though it was getting quite dark—we'd probably been gone from the house for more than an hour. I had to concentrate hard on my footfalls just so I wouldn't slip in the mud or trip over boulders. Anytime my feet faltered, Daniel would pull me up before I could fall. His hand twitched as he held mine. I could tell his shoulders were tightening and relaxing like they had when we rode on the motorcycle. He craved more speed. But I was thankful he didn't pull me any faster. I was breathing so hard I couldn't even speak.

The ravine wrapped around toward the east, and it felt like we'd been running for at least a mile. My feet burned with blisters. My legs and lungs ached. I couldn't see anything now in the dark, so I closed my eyes. I listened to my heart pounding in my ears, and to Daniel's breathing. His sounded so even compared to mine. Just when I thought I couldn't go any farther, it happened: I felt a wave of energy pass from Daniel's hand into mine. That connection, that lifeline, from the Garden of Angels was binding us together again. Only this time the energy rushed through my body, and I felt a sudden liberating release, and I knew I could trust that Daniel would keep me safe while I ran blind. I let go of myself and let his graceful movements flow through me, let him be my guide in the darkness, as we ran with total abandon in the night.

I'd never felt so free.

I almost forgot where I was until Daniel leaned into me. "Almost there," he said. He let go of my hand and slid his fingers up my arm. In one fluid movement, he gripped me tight underneath my arms, and lifted me up off the ground and onto his back. "Hold on!"

I latched my arms around Daniel's neck and wrapped my legs around his almost-nonexistent boy-hips. James giggled and tugged on my hair. I'm sure I did look funny. Daniel picked up a sudden burst of speed. We shot forward, and I opened my eyes just in time to realize that he was running headlong into the ravine wall. He jumped onto a fallen tree and leaped.

Daniel grabbed at a root, but he barely touched it. He kicked off the wall and flew another six feet up the slope. His feet touched down on a rock outcropping. He jumped again. I slipped on his hips. My fingers dug into his throat. James clung to my arms. Daniel grabbed a tree branch that sagged over the top of the cliff—with only one hand. And then we were up and over the top. Safe.

Daniel jogged a few more paces into the trees and then leaned forward, panting. I slipped off his back, and the three of us went tumbling onto the dirt-packed ground. I lay next to Daniel for a moment, my body shaking with shock and a whole lot of awe. "That . . . was . . . was . . ."

I'd spent two weeks once watching parkour videos

online because my art camp roomie, Adlen, had been totally in love with a French free-style runner. But compared to those films, the things Daniel had done today—while carrying two people, no less—weren't *humanly* possible.

Daniel looked at me, his eyes twinkling in the moonlight.

James clapped and squealed, "More!"

Daniel drew in a deep breath. "But we're home, little guy." He pulled James out of the sling and pointed through the woods to where my neighborhood's lights called like a beacon in the distance.

James pouted with disappointment, and I felt the same way.

Daniel rolled over onto his stomach, still breathing hard. I fingered the tear in his T-shirt and realized that even though the rip was matted with blood, there wasn't a cut in his skin. Only a long, jagged scar where a bleeding wound should have been. I brushed my fingertip down the warm, pink mark. Daniel started to flinch away, but then he sighed, as if my touch was soothing to his skin.

"How . . . ? I mean . . . *What* are you?" I asked.

Daniel laughed—a real laugh. Not a snort or sarcastic snicker. He stood up and offered me his hand. "I think it's best if we walked from here," he said, and pulled me to my feet. He picked up James and motioned for us to keep going toward my house.

I frowned. Did he really expect me to just walk away?

"Tell me, please. That was so not normal. How did you do all that?"

"Let's get your brother home first. We'll talk when this is all over. I promise."

"Don't promises always get broken?"

Daniel reached out and brushed my cheek.

James coughed. His breath fogged out of his lips. I was so hot from running so fast, I'd completely forgotten that it was cold. I felt a chill creeping up my sweaty arms, and knew James must be even colder. But I also knew once we passed through the fence into my yard, the magic—the connection—I'd felt while running with Daniel would be gone. And my chance for getting answers might never come.

What if Daniel decided to disappear again?

But I knew James had to come first, so I swallowed my questions and followed Daniel through the woods until we came to the fence behind my house. I climbed through the gap.

BACK IN THE YARD

Blue and red lights flickered from the street, illuminating the patched roof of the house. Beeping and shouting and a lot of movement filled the shadows cast by the light. It seemed like half of Rose Crest, including the sheriff and deputy, had converged on the neighborhood.

"Looks like they organized a search party anyway," I said.

Daniel stiffened as he came through the fence. "I should go. Take James. Tell them you found him yourself."

"No way." I grabbed his hand. "You're the hero here. I'm not taking credit." I dragged Daniel toward the front yard. "Mom, Dad!" I shouted. "We're here. We've got James."

"James!" Mom pounded down the porch steps.

"How did you . . . ? Where did you . . . ? My baby." She tried to take James from Daniel.

James squealed and locked his little arms around Daniel's neck. Daniel went pink. But that might have just been the glow from the flashing police lights.

"Daniel saved him, Mom." I touched Daniel's elbow. "I think Baby James is a bit attached to his hero."

"Okay, little guy. Let me breathe." Daniel pulled James from his throat. "I bet you're hungry. You want some turkey and a piece of pie?"

James nodded.

Daniel passed James to my mom. She hugged him so tight he whined, and she kissed him all over his face.

"James?" Dad came up the driveway.

The sheriff followed.

Daniel moved slightly behind me.

The deputy tried to bar our neighbors from entering the yard, but he let Dad and the sheriff pass.

Dad grabbed James and swung him around. He looked at Daniel. "Well done," he said, and wrapped his arm around Daniel's shoulder. "Well done, my son."

"I don't mean to bust up this little reunion," the sheriff said, "but I'll need to get your statement." He looked at Daniel.

"There's not much to state." Daniel shrugged. "I found him wandering in the woods, and I brought him home. He must have knocked over his playpen and decided to go on a little adventure."

I stared at him. That's it? I guess I didn't expect him to tell the truth—he followed the baby's scent through the forest, caught James midair when he fell off a thirty-foot cliff, and then used his very own superhuman powers to get us out of the ravine—but he sounded so nonchalant. No drama at all.

"That's not all that happened!" I practically shouted. Daniel shot me a wide-eyed look, like he was afraid that I'd tell everyone his secrets—which I totally wouldn't. My mind latched on to the first plausible, but furthest from the real scenario, lie I could think of. "He stopped James from falling in the creek!"

Mom cried and pulled James out of Dad's arms.

I was glad it was too dark for anyone to see the "lie marks" spreading up my cheeks. "Daniel's a hero. He saved James's life." I wanted people to know that truth, even if Daniel didn't want them to hear the real story.

"And the baby was alone? Uninjured?" The sheriff

raised his eyebrows and motioned to the bloody tear in Daniel's makeshift shirt-sling.

Daniel and I nodded.

"So how do you explain the blood on the porch?"

Daniel's face went blank.

"That's not his job to explain," said Dad. "It could have been anything—probably one of the neighborhood cats. Don't you have a forensics lab to tell you for sure?"

The sheriff snorted. "The Rose Crest Sheriff's Department is a trailer behind the Gas 'n' Go. I'll have Deputy Marsh take a sample and send it to a lab in the city. It'll take a while before we hear anything." He looked at me. "And there's nothing more you'd like to add? Nothing else you can remember?"

"Daniel saved my brother's life," I said. "That's all there is to it."

A car whipped into the driveway, scattering a gaggle of spectators onto the lawn.

"Mom. Dad." Jude jumped out of the minivan and pushed through the crowd. Not even the deputy could stop him. "I've brought the cavalry! I've got half the volunteers from the shelter coming to help us—" He stopped. The look of triumph on his face shifted into stony nothingness. I followed his hardened glare from James in my mother's arms to the sight of Dad holding Daniel in a fatherly embrace.

"James is safe," Mom said.

"Thanks to Daniel." Dad squeezed Daniel's shoulder. "James would have been lost without him."

The sheriff extended his hand toward Daniel. Daniel flinched—then stared back in disbelief as the sheriff gave him a hearty handshake.

"Well done," the sheriff said. He shined his flashlight along the back fence. "You should get that fixed," he said to Dad. "You're lucky this case turned out for the best. If it hadn't been for your son here . . ." At first I thought he was talking about Jude, but then I realized he was smiling at Daniel.

Dad did not correct him.

"We'll wrap up a few things here and then get out of your hair." The sheriff clapped Daniel on the back. "My wife had a conniption when I left dinner early. Her parents are in town. . . . They wanted her to marry an accountant."

"We'll get to work on that fence right away," Dad said, and shook hands with the sheriff. "Daniel, you're handy, aren't you?"

Daniel nodded.

"I'm going to take James inside." Mom smiled slightly and squeezed Daniel's arm. I think it was her way of saying thank you.

I couldn't help smiling. It may have taken some twisting of the truth, but my plan to help Daniel get his life back was working—the lifeline I'd offered seemed to be reeling him in.

But then I heard a deep rumbling coming from the direction of my older brother. He was positively shaking.

"Ju—"

Jude lunged at Daniel. "You did this!" he shrieked, and smashed his fist into Daniel's face.

Daniel fell back, knocking me to the ground with him. Jude went in for another blow, practically stepping on me to get to Daniel. But then the sheriff was on top of him. He pulled Jude back. Mom shouted.

Jude flailed and screamed, "He did this! He did this! Don't you see?"

Daniel scrambled up from the grass. "Jude?" He reached for his former best friend. "I swear I didn't do this."

Jude wrenched out of the sheriff's grasp and tried to fly at Daniel again. Dad stepped between them. The sheriff grabbed Jude from behind.

"Calm down," Dad said.

"He did this. He stole James." Jude looked up at the sheriff. "Arrest him. Get *him* before he runs away!"

Daniel stepped back. I knew he could be a quarter of a mile away by now, but he made no attempt to escape. He let Deputy Marsh seize his arm.

"Stop it," I yelled at Jude, and tried to stand on my aching legs. "Stop lying. Daniel *saved* James. He saved him from drowning in the creek."

"You stop lying!" Jude's face looked twisted like

it had the night he found Maryanne's body and then couldn't find me. I was afraid he was going to punch me, too—even though I hadn't known he was capable of hitting anyone until just now. "The creek's dried up and you know it," he said.

Mom gasped. The noise was echoed by the bystanders who'd edged closer to us when the deputy left his post. The sheriff must have loosened his grasp because Jude pulled away.

"Arrest him," Jude said. "Arrest that *monster*." He lunged at Daniel.

"Stop!" Dad grabbed Jude's arm and swung him away.

Jude stumbled back on his heels and fell to the ground.

Dad stood over him, one foot planted on each side of Jude's prostrate body. I'd never seen Dad look so domineering. "Back down!" he commanded. "Stop these lies now."

Jude moaned and rolled onto his side. It was like hitting the ground had knocked some sense into him. His face and fists relaxed.

"What do you want us to do?" Deputy Marsh asked. He still had Daniel by the arm. "We can take this one down to the station if you want."

"On what charges?" Dad turned to the crowd, his voice raised. "The baby simply wandered away. Daniel brought him back to us. That's all there is to it." He inclined his head to the deputy, telling him to release Daniel. "Thank you, everyone, for helping us in our time of need," he said in his best pastor voice. "I'm sure you all have festivities waiting for you. And if you don't mind, my family has a few things to attend to."

Dad turned to my mom. "Meredith, take James inside. I'm going to see what I can do about the fence. Daniel, Jude, come with me."

Jude was standing now, but he cowered from Dad's touch. He shook his head and then jogged into the house. April appeared from the crowd and padded after him.

"Daniel?" Dad asked.

Something was very wrong with the look in my father's eyes.

Daniel gave a slight nod and went with him.

Dad must have sensed my longing to follow. "Gracie, go help your mother," he said. His voice was so strained it sounded like he was holding his breath as he spoke.

I stood in the grass and watched them go around behind the house. The deputy and sheriff grumbled and trudged over to their car. Our friends and neighbors trickled away—just like my hope for fixing Daniel and Jude.

Chapter Twelve
Questions Unanswered

My mother flipped into full Florence Nightingale mode. She refused to let the sheriff take James to the hospital in Oak Park, insisting that she and Dr. Connors were quite capable of looking him over. After a very thorough examination by the doctor, she finally let James out of her arms and ordered Charity to get started on a bath to warm him up. Then she put Superman Band-Aids on the scratches Don Mooney had somehow gotten up his arm, and sent the last of our lingering guests home with leftovers from our abandoned dinner. I was about to sneak out the back door to try to find Daniel when Mom called me over to the kitchen table.

"Let's take a look at your hand."

I winced as she picked a few rocks out of the cut.

She clucked her tongue. "You're lucky you don't need stitches."

I let her clean my hand and tried not to squirm. I figured the less I protested, the faster I could get to Daniel. He'd promised to explain things to me. But what if he decided to slip away? I'd seen the things he could do, and with Jude's false accusations, Daniel could be out of the state before I could even start looking for him.

Mom placed my hand in a bowl of hydrogen peroxide. "Just relax for a minute," she said, and unpacked the gauze and tape from her first-aid kit.

Little bubbles tingled up from all over my skin. My mind wandered, replaying the things Daniel had done in the woods—and how it felt to run with him in the dark. I barely noticed as Mom dried my hand and wrapped it with gauze.

"All done." She patted down the last piece of medical tape and held my hand for a moment. "Gracie," she said without looking up at me. "Please do not invite that boy into our home again." She laid my hand on the table between us and busied herself packing everything back into her kit.

I nodded even though she probably couldn't see.

"Mom," Charity called down the stairs. "James refuses to get out of the bath until he has his blanket."

"I'll get it," I said, glad for the momentary distraction.

Mom nodded. "I'll be up in a minute," she called back to Charity.

I checked James's room first, but Aunt Carol was

asleep in the guest bed in his room. She'd excused herself with a headache as soon as Dr. Connors announced
that James was in perfect health. I remembered that
James's blanket was probably still in the study.

The doors were slightly ajar when I slipped inside.
James's Portacrib was still on its side. I tipped it
upright and found the blankie. I picked it up and was
about to dash off to the upstairs bath when a sudden
thought stopped me. If James had really wandered off,
wouldn't he have taken this with him? That blue rag of
a crocheted blanket went everywhere my little brother
did. He never left it behind.

Daniel's words when I said that James couldn't have
gone so far into the woods echoed in my ears: *On his
own, no.*

Was it a mistake to send the sheriff away? It seemed
like they had just arrived when Daniel and I returned
with James. Had they taken pictures or looked for any
clues? Jude had accused Daniel, but that couldn't be.
My father insisted that it was just an accident. But
Daniel—he had been afraid of something.

I looked around the study, really noticing things
for the first time since I entered. Dad's books and
papers were strewn across the floor. His lamp was
tipped over, and the drawer of his desk was open. It
looked like a small earthquake had erupted inside of it.
Had an intruder been in here looking for something?
But wouldn't we have heard any of this commotion in the

dining room? Maybe Mom had started throwing things while she was so distraught? Several books were missing from the bookcase.

The bookcase!

I lunged over to it and stretched up on my toes. I fingered along the top shelf, back and forth. The black velvet case—the one that held Don's silver dagger—was gone.

UPSTAIRS

My first instinct was to tell Dad about his study. But then I realized that he'd been in there with Mom. Wouldn't he have seen all this mess already? And still, he was the one who sent the sheriff away. He was the one who insisted that nothing out of the ordinary had happened. Perhaps it *was* my mother who had made the mess, and he wanted to spare her any questioning by the police. It would not have bode well with her OCD tendencies to have Deputy Marsh poking through our things or tearing up the house. But why was that knife missing? Did Dad even know? I hadn't told him I'd moved it.

"Grace. We need that blanket," Charity yelled down the stairs.

I shut the study doors behind me and dashed up to the bathroom. "Here." I handed the blanket to Mom.

"Banket!" James stood up in the bath. Bubbles ran down his little body.

"Finally," Charity said, and pulled him out of the tub. She wrapped him in a towel and handed him to Mom.

He nuzzled his blanket to his face. Mom held him tight.

I decided not to mention anything about the study to her. I didn't know what mode she'd flip into if I said anything to worry her. I'd question Dad later.

But the person I really wanted to talk to was Daniel. What did he know about all this? Why had he seemed so afraid? Was it somehow related to the things he could do?

"Bathroom's all yours," Mom said to me. "Clean up before you do anything else." She shook her head at my mud-caked sweater and slacks.

"You smell like a dog that's been running in the cold." Charity made a gagging face.

"Howy shwit," James cooed.

Mom blinked at me. "What did he just say?"

"No idea," I said, and shooed them out of the bathroom.

I took a quick shower—at least as fast as I could without getting my bandaged hand wet.

What if I couldn't get to Daniel before he was done helping my dad?

I wrapped up in a towel and wiped the steam from the bathroom window. I peered out through the filmy glass. All I could see was the narrow gap in the white outline of the fence. I flipped off the bathroom light and made out what looked like my dad, kneeling in the grass near the decaying rosebushes. It looked like he was praying—perhaps giving thanks for James's safe return. But then he rocked forward and back on his knees, and his hands flew up to his face. His shoulders bounced up and down in a weird jerking way.

I grabbed my bathrobe. Dad needed me with him. But someone else stepped out of the shadows near the fence. He knelt next to my father, hesitated for a moment, and then wrapped his long, lean arms around Dad's quaking shoulders. I stepped back and blinked, and the window fogged over with steam.

I pulled tight the tie on my terry-cloth robe, bounded down the stairs, and ran smack into my mother.

"Where do you think you are going in that, young lady?" She scoffed at my robe and pointed to the dining room, where Don was telling Charity a story about his grandfather. "We still have guests in this house."

"But Da—" I saw the annoyed look on her face and remembered the way she'd sarcastically yelled at Dad for blaming himself for Maryanne's death. He didn't need that now. "I just have to do something real quick."

"Go put something decent on."

I grumbled under my breath and started up the stairs for a quick change of clothing.

"And did you take your muddy clothes down to the

laundry or dump them on the bathroom floor?"

"I'll do it later. I need to—"

"What you need to do is get dressed and then get your dirty clothes in the wash before they're ruined. Money doesn't appear like manna around here."

"But—"

"*Now.*" And I swear she gave me this look like she thought I was up to something she wouldn't approve of.

"Fine."

My legs ached and protested as I staggered up to my bedroom. All that running in the woods had taken its toll. I pulled on the first clothes I could find—a long-sleeved tee and a pair of paint-splattered overalls my mother particularly hated. I grabbed my dirty laundry from the bathroom and hobbled all the way down to the basement.

I was busy blaming Mom in my head for potentially ruining my chances to talk to Daniel and my father, when I heard low voices coming from Jude's bedroom. I could make out Jude's somber voice and April's cocker spaniel–like yips of reassurance. I clutched my bundle to my chest and inched toward Jude's door.

"It's not fair," I heard him say.

"Why?" April asked.

"You don't understand. They don't understand." Jude's voice went lower. "How can they not see what he's doing?"

April said something I couldn't make out.

"It's wrong. He's wrong. Everything about him is wrong," Jude said. "I'm the good one. I'm the one who does everything this family needs. I'm the one who is here every day for them, and now he's back for a few hours, and they believe him over me. Dad and Grace act like he's some kind of hero." His voice twanged. "How can Dad believe *him*, after what he did?"

"What?" April asked. "What did he do?"

Jude sighed.

Any pang of guilt I felt for eavesdropping was overpowered by my desire to hear the answer to that question—and by burning jealousy that he might tell April the thing he'd refused tell *me* for three years.

Jude whispered something, and I leaned in closer to hear.

"Grace!" Mom shouted down the stairs. "Make sure you use stain spray."

I jumped back from the door and dropped my bundle. Jude's voice cut off, followed by shifting noises behind his door. I gathered up my clothes and hurried off to the laundry room.

LATER THAT NIGHT

Daniel was gone by the time I made it outside. He wasn't in the back or the front yard. Neither was Dad. It had been only about fifteen minutes since I'd seen them through the bathroom window, so I decided to take a car and track Daniel down at his apartment—catch him with my questions before he could skip town—but no keys were on the hooks. Dad kept the truck at the parish, and Jude must have still had the van keys. But strangely, the Corolla was not in the garage.

I resigned myself to the fact that any more searching would be futile, and decided to help Mom and Don Mooney clean up the dining room.

I wasn't surprised Don had stuck around. He'd probably ask to move into Jude's room when my brother went off to college next year. However, Don's idea of "cleaning" involved eating the food off of people's forgotten plates.

I reached for the half-empty goblet in front of him.

Don stopped picking at the Band-Aids on his arm and gave me a huge turkey-in-his-teeth grin. "You look real pretty tonight, Miss Grace."

I fingered my wet curls and wondered if I'd gained a new admirer for sticking up for him with my father the other day. "Thanks, Don," I mumbled, and picked up the goblet.

"You were real brave, too," he said, "going into the woods to find your brother. I wish I'd been there. I'd have protected you from the monster. My granddaddy told me how. He was a real hero." Don rubbed his injured arm against his chest.

I smiled. But then I thought of the jumbled contents of my father's office. Mom had taken a load of dishes into the kitchen, but I lowered my voice just in case. "Don, while everyone was searching for James, did you go into the study?"

His eyes shifted sideways. "I . . . I . . . was just lookin' for something. I didn't mean to make such a mess. Everyone came back inside before I could clean up." He rocked in his chair like he was about to bolt.

Relief washed over me. "It's okay, Don." I smiled at him. "I won't tell anybody. But you really should put the knife back."

Don lowered his droopy eyelids. "Yes, Miss Grace."

Mom came back and noticed me fumbling her china plates with my bandaged hand and sent me off to bed. I went without protest, even though I didn't have much hope for sleeping—or much hope for anything else. Mom was upset with me for inviting Daniel over; Dad's roller coaster of despair had hit maximum velocity; my older brother was on the verge of a breakdown of his own; and Daniel was most likely gone. But at least I knew where that knife was. And it hadn't been stolen by some sinister intruder.

Strange—that was the first time I'd ever thought of Don as harmless.

I lay on top of my bed, my mind racing with all of the strange things that had happened during the day, until the house grew dark and silent. It felt like hours had passed since I heard Don make his loud good-byes. I was still in my clothes, so I decided to get up and change. I pulled off my overalls and shirt and found my most comfortable pair of pajamas. White flannel dotted with little yellow rubber duckies. I was standing in my flannel pants and pink bra when I heard a tapping noise behind me.

I turned and saw a dark silhouette outside my second-story window. I jumped and almost screamed. Images of the study's bloodstained windowsill ripped through my mind.

"Grace," came a muffled voice through the glass. The shadow moved closer to the window. It was Daniel.

Embarrassment replaced fear. I crossed my tingling arms in front of my chest—not that I had much to hide, but still. I turned my back to him and grabbed my terry-cloth robe. It was still damp from my shower, but I pulled it on anyway. I went to the window and pushed it open. "What are you doing here?"

Daniel balanced on the sloping roof outside my room. "I promised we'd talk." He stared at me through the thin mesh screen. "Can I come in?"

CHAPTER THIRTEEN
Hounds of Heaven

ROOFTOPS

Heat flushed up my arms and chest. I'm sure I went as pink as my bra. I pulled my robe tighter around me. "I . . . I can't let you in."

Mom hadn't made me *promise*, but I felt like I should respect her wishes not to invite Daniel in the house again. It was the least I could do for her now.

"Then you'll have to come out." With a flick of his hand, he pushed the screen out of my window. It landed at my feet, looking perfectly untouched. Not mangled and broken like the time Jude had shimmied the screen out of the study's window just below us. "Come on." He reached for me through the window frame.

Before I could even think, I put my hand in his. He pulled me up and out and into his arms. He held me to him, his fingers twisting with the sash of my robe against my back.

"I thought you were gone," I whispered.

"A promise is a promise." His breath warmed my damp hair. He grasped both of my hands and lowered me to sit next to him on the narrow eave of the roof. He wore jeans now and the red-and-black coat I'd given him. He hadn't had it with him when he showed up earlier for dinner.

My robe wasn't as warm as a coat, and my feet were bare, but I didn't mind. "I'm glad you came back."

Daniel grinned. It was an almost-grimacing smile—pained. That's when I noticed, in the dim light from my bedroom, the purplish-green bruise across his cheekbone.

"You're hurt." I touched his face.

He leaned his cheek into my hand.

"I'm sorry. You're hurt because of me. I'm the one who made up the story about the creek. I'm the one who made Jude—"

"Don't be sorry. None of this was ever your fault." Daniel clasped his hand over mine. "I'll be fine soon anyway."

He closed his eyes and pressed my bandaged hand against his cheekbone. His skin grew warmer under my touch. My palm started to sweat. His skin flared hot. Just as it felt like it was going to burn me, the heat tingled away. Daniel dropped his hand, and I pulled mine back.

His skin was bare. No bruises or marks of any kind.

"You really are a superhero," I whispered.

Daniel leaned against the house. His feet dangled over the side of the roof. "I'm nothing of the sort."

"How can you say that? I've seen the things you can do. You could totally help people. And you saved James." I scratched at my bandage. My hand and feet throbbed, and I ached all over. The power to heal myself would come quite in handy right about now. "I wish I could do some of those things."

He clasped his fingers around his smooth stone necklace. "You wouldn't like the side effects."

"Are you kidding? I'd do anything to be like you."

"No, you wouldn't." Daniel glanced at me. His eyes flashed with that hungry glint. "That's what makes you so special."

A frightened shiver rushed through my body. Part of me wanted to climb back into my room and lock the window. But most of me wanted him to take me in his arms and run away from everything and everyone.

"You are special, you know," Daniel said, and brushed my arm.

"Daniel, I . . ."

Daniel winced and pulled away. He clutched the black necklace tighter and mumbled something I couldn't understand between sharp breaths.

"Are you okay?" I stretched out my hand to him.

"Please, don't." He shrugged off my touch and backed up against the side of the house. He pulled his legs to his chest, as if creating a barrier between us. His body quaked. He closed his eyes, panting. His trembling stopped, but he still clenched his pendant in a rigid fist.

"Is that what gives you your . . . abilities? The necklace?"

Daniel kept his eyes closed. "No."

"Then how? What?"

He let air out between his teeth. "I should leave you."

"But I want to know everything."

"I'm sorry, Gracie. I really should go."

I folded my arms. "You're not getting off that easy. A promise is a promise, remember," I said in my bossy Grace voice.

Daniel stopped and his mouth edged into a grin. "You have no idea what you do to me."

I blushed, but I wasn't going to let him distract me. "Is this why you left town? Or did this happen to you while you were gone? How did you become what you are? Tell me, please."

"Nothing *happened* to me. Not exactly. I guess you could say I was born this way."

"I don't remember you being like . . . this." But then I remembered all those times as a child that he seemed to have bruises in the morning that were gone by the afternoon, or limps that mysteriously disappeared. I remembered how baffled Daniel's doctor had been when his skull fracture healed in a matter of weeks rather than months.

"It develops with age . . . and experiences."

"Superpowers are a little more intense than armpit hair and zits," I said.

Daniel laughed. "It's kind of a family thing." He lowered his voice. "You know what your father says in his sermons about how the devil works—among other things—through flattery, jealousy, and complacency?"

I nodded. That was one of Dad's favorite subjects.

"Well, the devil wasn't always so subtle. In the beginning, he used demons, vampires, and other evil spirits to do his bidding. Real things-that-go-bump-in-the-night monsters." Daniel looked at me for my reaction.

I didn't know what to say—or even think. Was he being serious? Did he really want me to believe that monsters existed? But then again, up until today, I thought people with superstrength and the ability to heal themselves were just characters from comic books.

When I didn't respond, Daniel went on. "With demons running loose on the earth, God decided he needed to 'fight fire with fire,' so to speak. My family—the Kalbi family—dates back before written language. Back before real civilization even existed. My family was part of a tribe of warriors. They were strong defenders of their land, but they were also stalwart in their belief in God and followed his teachings. He decided to reward them— bless them with special abilities. He infused them with the essence of the most powerful animal in their highland forests, giving them enhanced speed, agility, strength, cunning, and tracking." He rubbed his hand across his cheekbone. "I'm not sure where the healing ability came from—must have been part of the benefits package."

"So God made the ultimate soldier in His fight against evil?" My question sounded so logical, even though I still couldn't believe what I was hearing.

"Exactly. He even marked them with white-blond hair like the angels." He fingered his shaggy, sandy-brown hair. "Hounds of Heaven. That's what He called them. Or something like that—the actual word has been lost. The closest I know of is the Sumerian word *Urbat*. It was their job to track down demons. Keep mortals safe from the wrath of the devil."

"These . . . Urbat . . . what became of them? Why haven't I ever heard of them before?"

Daniel shrugged. "They overstayed their welcome in the mortal world. There are only a relative handful of them today. They prefer to live in groups—packs, actually. Many of them are artists like me. It must be that animal connection to nature. There's a group out west. They live in a sort of artists' colony. I went there for a while. That's where I met Gabriel."

"The angel from the garden? You said he gave you that necklace. What is it?"

Daniel touched the black stone. "A piece of the moon."

"What?" I don't know why that seemed more impossible to believe than his story.

Daniel smiled at my inquisitive look. He wrapped his arm around my back and let me hold the flat black stone as it hung from his neck. It was surprisingly warm and wasn't as smooth as it looked. It was slightly porous, like lava rock. I pressed my fingertip into the small crescent carved in the middle.

"It helps me control the things I do." He stroked his fingers over mine.

I leaned my head against his chest and was surprised I could hear his heart thumping through his coat. His breaths were deep and steady, but his heartbeat seemed erratic. Too fast, but too slow at the same time—almost as if two hearts pounded inside of him. Both telling me to believe his words.

Daniel pulled me closer in his embrace. He traced his hand along the collar of my robe, his fingers grazing my skin. One of his heartbeats quickened, fluttering as it pulsed.

I dropped the stone pendant. It bounced slightly against his chest. "Daniel? If people like you—these Urbat—still exist, does that mean monsters do, too?"

Daniel turned his head away. "I should go now." He pulled me up with him as he stood.

My feet felt uneven on the slope of the roof. Daniel steadied me. I didn't want him to leave. I would have kept him with me all night if I could. But I knew he wouldn't stay. He wouldn't answer any more questions tonight.

He helped me through the window and popped the screen back in place. "Good night, Grace."

"Will I see you again?" I placed my hand on the screen that separated us. "You're not going to disappear now that your secret identity is blown?"

He put his hand against mine, the thin metal mesh between our skin. "Tomorrow. I'll be here tomorrow. I told your dad I'd fix the fence." He made no guarantee beyond that.

"I'll see you then."

Daniel pulled his hand away.

"Wait," I said.

He stopped.

"Thank you. For what you did for my dad . . . out in the backyard."

Daniel bit his lip. "You saw that?"

I nodded.

His face colored slightly. "Don't worry about it, Gracie. Your dad was just feeling the aftereffects of what happened today—thinking he'd lost a son forever." Daniel stepped backward to the edge of the shingled eve. He sprang up onto his toes. "Lock your window," he said, and did a backflip dive off the roof.

CHAPTER FOURTEEN
Such Great Heights

IN BED

I curled up with my comforter and tried to make my brain stop whirling. But I couldn't stop thinking about Daniel: how it felt to be held in his arms, the exhilaration and freedom of running with him in the woods, what he told me about his ancestors . . . about himself. But most of all, I couldn't stop wondering why Daniel hadn't answered my question about the existence of monsters.

I have to admit I didn't know much about that sort of thing—monsters, demons, *vampires*. A lot of people in the parish thought it was a sin to read books or watch movies about such things. My parents limited the shows we were allowed to watch, and I had friends who were banned from reading the Harry Potter books because they supposedly celebrated witchcraft. I always thought that was silly—those things were just make-believe anyway.

At least that's what I'd believed.

But restrictions didn't stop people in Rose Crest from talking. I'd always tried to believe that the Markham Street Monster was just some kind of morality tale to scare us kids into behaving. The stories started out as just sightings of some kind of hairy beast on Markham Street. Then people in that part of the city went missing. Mostly shelter guests, prostitutes, and kids who were wasted, so no one seemed all that concerned. That is until their mangled bodies started turning up on Markham about once a month. At least those were the rumors I'd heard when I was a kid. Things closer to Rose Crest weren't as bad. Mostly dead animals—like my little dog, Daisy, ripped to pieces. Dad had said it was probably just a raccoon from the woods, but I'd always feared something worse. And what if I was right? What if it had been the Markham Street Monster? What if it had been as close as my front yard?

Those strange things had stopped years ago—before Daniel ever left town—but now they were happening again. Maryanne had died from the cold, but her body had been abused like the ones found on Markham Street. Then James went missing . . . and the blood on the porch. And I couldn't forget what had happened while I was stranded on Markham Street itself. What might have happened if Daniel hadn't come along?

Could it really be a coincidence that any of these things started happening again only after Daniel had come home? Could the monster have followed him here? Or maybe he was the one who was tracking it.

Daniel said he'd returned because of art school, but I'd felt there was something more to it. Was this it? Was the Markham Street Monster back? Was Daniel here to protect us from it?

MORNING

I must have fallen asleep eventually, because I was startled awake by a loud *thunk* outside my bedroom window. I rolled over and looked at the clock: 6:00 a.m. I heard the *thunk* again, so I stumbled out of bed and went to investigate. It was mostly dark out, but I could still see that the side yard was empty. The *thunk*ing continued. It seemed to be coming from the backyard. My legs were so stiff I practically had to slide down the stairs on my butt.

I was in the kitchen when I saw Daniel out in the backyard. He was driving a wood fence post into the frozen dirt—with his bare hands. I couldn't tell for sure because his back was to me, but it looked like he was holding the post in one hand and then swinging his arm, presumably whacking the top of the post with the butt of his hand. No mallet, or hammer, or any tool was even nearby from what I could tell. He'd probably gotten such an early start so he could do it *his* way.

I was about to go out and join him when I ran my

hand through my hair, and my fingers lodged in a nest of snarls. I watched Daniel take another swing, sinking the post a good three inches into the ground, and I suddenly felt compelled to be cleaned and dressed in something more flattering than my flannel yellow-ducky pj's.

By the time I'd done my makeup, flat-ironed my hair, and changed my sweater three times—why was everything I owned so boxy?—Charity was in the kitchen perusing one of her science books and eating sugared cereal from her private stash. Which meant that Mom wasn't up yet. The *thunk*ing noise had stopped, so hopefully Mom and James would sleep in for a while longer.

I peered out the window. "Did you see where Daniel went?"

"Nope," Charity grumbled. "I was about ready to go strangle him for making all that racket, but he was gone by the time I got down here."

"Sorry," I said, like anything Daniel did was my fault.

"Meh." She shrugged. "I was gonna get up early today anyway. I've got to write a whole first draft for my research paper this weekend."

"Oh." I stared farther out the window. "I wonder where he went."

"The Corolla's gone. Maybe Dad took him to the hardware store or something."

Or maybe whoever took the car last night never came home. I didn't hear the garage door last night, and I hadn't fallen asleep until at least three a.m. Dad's study was closed and locked, and the light was out. If Daniel wasn't with Dad, then where had he gone?

I sank into a kitchen chair. Perhaps Daniel's reason for fixing the fence so early was because he'd changed his mind about wanting to see me again.

"May I?" I reached for Charity's box of Lucky Charms.

She nodded. "Did you hear about Mr. Day's granddaughter?"

"Jessica or Kristy?"

"Jess. She's missing."

Little frosted three-leafed clovers tumbled into my bowl. I hadn't seen Jessica in years. She was in Daniel and Jude's grade growing up, but her family had moved to the city when she was a sophomore. "Doesn't she run away on a bimonthly basis?"

"Yeah, but never seriously. She's never missed a holiday before. When she didn't show up for Thanksgiving, her parents called the police. Her friends said they were with her at a party downtown the other night. They said she was there one minute and gone the next. It was in the paper." Charity scraped the bottom of her bowl. "The Markham Street Monster strikes again."

I dropped the cereal box. "Is that what they're saying?"

"Yep. There was even a little blurb at the end of the article about James wandering away. I don't know how they even heard about that. They say the monster might have tried to take him." There was a sudden edge to her voice. She looked at me over the cereal box. "You don't think—"

"They're just trying to freak people out to up their sales." I wished I could believe what I was saying, but I knew now the article might be right. "Where's the newspaper anyway?"

"Jude surfaced a few minutes ago. He took it back downstairs," Charity said. "The paper said the police are waiting for test results on that blood before they release a statement."

My heart did a little flip-flop in my chest. What *would* they find with those test results? I pushed away the bowl of too-sweet cereal.

Charity turned the page of her book. A large silver-gray wolf stared back at me from the page. I couldn't help shuddering as I thought of those animal tracks deep in the ravine.

AFTERNOON

I told myself I was not *waiting* for Daniel. I was simply working on my make-up assignment for Mr. Barlow, out on the porch, in November, where I might just happen to see Daniel if he decided to come back. I settled sideways into the porch swing, where I could see the walnut tree in the side yard, and the street—but like I said, I was not sitting around waiting for a *guy*.

It may have been the lack of focus, but no matter how hard I tried, my attempts to draw the walnut tree still didn't *feel* right at all. I was fighting the urge to chuck my charcoal pencil across the porch when I heard someone come up beside me.

"I'm glad to see you haven't given up on me," Daniel said.

"Took you long enough," I said, trying not to betray that I'd worried he wouldn't show. "Where'd you take off to anyway?"

"Maryanne Duke's."

I glanced up at him.

"Apparently, she left her house to the parish. Your dad is letting me stay in the basement apartment until I figure some things out. I moved my stuff over there this morning."

"I'm sure Maryanne's daughters are just crazy about that."

Daniel smirked and sat down next to me on the swing.

"Did you see the newspaper this morning?" I asked, trying to sound nonchalant.

Daniel's grin fell into a frown.

"Do you think they're right? That the Markham

Street Monster is responsible for what happened to Mr. Day's granddaughter? That it tried to take James?"

He shook his head.

"But you're the one who said James couldn't have gone that far on his own. And how did his slipper get down in that ravine?"

Daniel just stared at the palms of his hands, like he was hoping the answer would somehow be written there.

"Monsters *are* real," I said. "They still exist right here in Minnesota, and in Iowa, and in Utah. Don't they?"

Daniel scratched behind his ear. "Yes, Gracie. My people wouldn't still exist if monsters didn't."

I suddenly shivered, even though we were sitting in the sun. I'm not sure I *wanted* to be right. "That's just too weird to wrap my head around. To think that for nearly seventeen years I've been walking around completely oblivious to what the world is really like. I mean, I could have walked right past a *monster* without even knowing it."

"You've met one," Daniel said. "The other night."

"I did?" Then my mind drifted back to the party at Daniel's apartment. "Mishka," I said, thinking of her black, black eyes and how I'd felt so fuzzy in the head around her. "And you're friends with her?"

"It's complicated," Daniel said. "But she's only dangerous when she doesn't get what she wants. That's why I went with her. I didn't just abandon you for a haircut.

I knew if I chose you over her, she might decide to . . . target you."

My heart felt like it was twisting into a knot. "You don't think that's what happened, do you? Maybe she followed you here and decided to go after my little brother—"

"No. That's not what happened."

"Then what did?"

"I don't know," he mumbled. He was quiet for a moment, and then he looked at the drawing I held on my lap. "I can help you with that."

"You're doing it again," I grumbled.

"What?"

"Dodging my questions, like everybody else. I'm not stupid or fragile or weak, you know."

"I know, Grace. You're anything but." He blew his floppy bangs off his forehead. "I'm not dodging your questions. I just don't have any more answers to give you." He tapped my sketch pad with one of his long fingers. "Now, do you want help with your assignment, or not?"

"No, thanks. I'm in enough trouble over the last time you 'fixed' one of my drawings."

"That's not really what I meant," he said. "I'll be staying after school every day to work in the art room. I could use your company. Help keep that Barlow guy off my back. But we could start today. I could show you some new techniques I've picked up over the years."

"I bet you could." I sighed, realizing that our discussion about monsters was over—for now. "But this drawing is totally hopeless." I tore the page out of my sketch pad and was about to crumple it up.

"Don't." Daniel grabbed it from me. He studied it for a moment. "Why are you drawing this?" He pointed at my skeleton of a tree.

I shrugged. "Because Barlow wants us to draw something that reminds us of our childhood. This is all I could think of."

"But why?" Daniel asked. "What exactly about this tree are you trying to capture? What does it make you feel? What does it make you want?"

I gazed at the real tree in the yard. Memories trickled into my mind. *You,* I thought. *It makes me want you.* I looked down at my drawing pad and hoped mind reading wasn't one of Daniel's many hidden, demon-hunter talents.

"Remember when we used to race up that tree—see who could go the highest the fastest?" I asked. "And then we'd perch up there, and we could see the whole neighborhood? It felt like if we could just climb a little bit farther into the thin branches, we could stretch up and brush the clouds with our fingers." I rolled the charcoal pencil between my hands. "I guess that's what I want to feel again."

"Then why are we down here?" Daniel grabbed my pencil and tucked my pad under his arm. "Come on."

He pulled me up from the swing and down the porch to the base of the walnut tree. Before I could blink, he'd kicked off his shoes and was halfway up the tree. "You coming?" he goaded from his perch.

"You're crazy," I shouted up to him.

"You're losing!" He jumped from his branch to a higher one above.

"You're cheating!" I grabbed the lowest branch and tried to swing myself up. My stiff legs groaned. I grabbed a different branch and climbed up a few feet. This was a lot less scary than the ravine, but a lot harder than the stone pillar in the Garden of Angels. My injured hand didn't make it any easier.

"Pick up the pace, slowpoke!" Daniel shouted down at me like we were kids all over again. He was higher in the branches than I'd ever climbed.

"Zip it, or you're going to lose an appendage."

My feet scraped against the ashy-white bark as I pushed and pulled myself up through the tree. I was a few feet below Daniel when the branches felt too thin and wavering to support me. I stretched to reach him— to reach the sky, like I tried when I was a kid. I slipped a bit and hugged the closest branch. Daniel swung down to meet me. The tree shuddered when he landed. I hugged my branch tighter. Daniel didn't even blink. He sat in a crook of the tree, his legs swinging in the open air.

"So what do you see now?" he asked.

I willed myself to look down. I gazed out across the

neighborhood—a bird's-eye view of the world. Through the branches, I could see the tops of houses, smoke coming out of the Headrickses' chimney. Kids playing street hockey in the cul-de-sac where Jude, Daniel, and I used to run with our light sabers. Where Daniel, after much bossing on my part, taught me how to skateboard. I looked up. Tree branches swayed above me, dancing in the blue, cloud-spotted sky.

"I see everything," I said. "I see—"

"Don't tell me. Show me." He pulled my sketch pad out of his shirt. "Draw what you see." He tried to hand me my things.

"From up here?" I was still hugging my tree branch. How did he expect me to be able to draw without falling? "I can't."

"Stop worrying." He leaned against the trunk. "Come here."

I slowly edged over to him. He helped me sit in front of him and then handed me my things. I leaned my back against his chest, and he wrapped his arms around my waist.

"Draw," he said. "I'll hold you until you're done."

I put the charcoal pencil to the paper. I hesitated for a moment. What was it I wanted to draw? I looked out across the yard in the other direction. From here, most of my Craftsman-style house was obscured by branches, but it looked like it had when I sat up here as a kid. Not patched and old, but solid, inviting, and safe. My hand started moving, drawing what I saw. Glimpses of my childhood home from my perch in the walnut tree.

"Good," Daniel said as he watched my progress. He stayed mostly silent except to point out something here and there. "See how the sun glints off the wind vane? Draw the dark, not the light itself."

I drew, letting charcoal lines flow right out of me, until my hand felt cramped and tired. I stopped to stretch, and Daniel pulled the sketch pad off my lap. "It's good. Real good." He nuzzled his nose against the top of my head. "You should do this in oils."

"Yeesh." I leaned forward.

Daniel trailed his fingers down my spine. "Still not a fan?"

"I haven't tried oils in years." Not since the day his mother took him away.

"You'll never get into a place like Trenton if you don't get the hang of it."

"I know. Barlow's been after me all year about that."

"It wouldn't be the same there without you."

I scooted away from him and dangled my legs along the sides of the branch. Daniel thought about us together at college? It felt weird to think about the future—our future—when so many weird things were happening. What were we doing up here anyway? We'd held hands, brushed skin, talked into the late hours of the night. But what did any of this mean? What could it mean?

"You never did show me that technique with linseed oil and varnish," I said. It was the "trick" he'd promised to teach me just before he'd left with his mom.

Daniel cleared his throat and pulled himself to his feet. "You remember that?"

"I tried to forget," I admitted. "I tried to forget everything about you."

"You hated me that much?"

"No." I grabbed a branch and pulled myself up, my back still to him. "I missed you that much."

Daniel slid his fingers through my hair, sending little chills down my back. "God only knows the things I did to try to numb you out of my brain."

"Me?"

"Grace, I . . . You have . . ." Daniel rested his hand on my shoulder. He sighed, and I knew he was about to change the subject.

I stepped away from his grasp, annoyed that I wouldn't know what he wanted to say.

Daniel laughed uneasily. "I can still see right into your bedroom from here."

"What?!"

Sure enough, I could see right into my bedroom window. It was afternoon, so the window reflected the sunlight, but if it had been night and the light was on, I'd be able to see just about everything. "You perv!"

"I'm just teasing," he said. "I mean, I used to sit up here and watch your family, but I didn't—"

Just then, something—someone—moved behind my window. I leaned forward, balancing myself with a thin branch, to see who was in my room.

"Careful," Daniel said.

My foot slipped. The branch I held snapped. I shrieked.

Daniel caught me along the waist. He whirled me around so I was now on the thicker portion of the branch, and he stood where I had been. He pulled me tight against his body.

Am I the one shaking so much, or is that him?

Daniel rested his chin on my head and we stood together, precariously perched at such great heights. The only thing holding me, keeping me from falling, was Daniel. But he didn't try to balance himself in any way—he didn't need to.

"You've got to stop doing that," he said about my near fall. "I don't remember you being such a klutz."

Neither did I—at least not before he came back. "You're the one who is always making me climb on things." I smacked his chest. "Who knew hanging out with you could be so dangerous?"

"You have no idea," he mumbled into my hair.

I looked down at my hand on his hard chest. "You're worth it."

"Gracie," Daniel whispered. He lifted my chin so I was looking up at him. He cupped my face with both hands. His eyes glinted with the sun. He touched his nose to my brow. He tilted his head.

All my fears and worries about monsters, all my concerns about my older brother, all my questions about Daniel melted away as I stretched up on my toes to meet him.

"Grace, Daniel," someone shouted.

Daniel dropped his hands from my face and stepped away.

Disappointment washed over me with the flood of my returning doubts. I sighed and looked out at the house. For the briefest of seconds, I thought I saw Jude watching us from my window. But that wasn't who called our names. It was my dad.

He stood at the base of the tree, wearing the same clothes from yesterday. It looked like he had a wooden box tucked under his arm. The Corolla was parked in the driveway.

Daniel moved as far away from me on the branch as he could.

"Oh hey, Dad." I gave a slight wave.

Dad crouched and picked up my sketch pad from the grass. It must have fallen when Daniel caught me. He looked at the drawing and then up at us.

"We were just working on an assignment for class," I said.

Dad shielded his eyes from the sun. "Come down

now," he said, sounding more tired than I'd ever heard him.

"Are you okay?" I asked.

He looked at Daniel. "We need to talk."

Daniel nodded. He turned to me and said softly, "Meet me on the porch after dinner. We'll go to the store and get some linseed oil and varnish."

"Can we go for a run afterward?"

He brushed my cheek. "Anything you want."

CHAPTER FIFTEEN
The Lost Sheep

"Grace!" Charity bellowed from the front room.

I came in from the kitchen. She was sprawled across the couch, watching TV.

"What?"

"Phone." She waggled the cordless over her head.

I grabbed it from her. I was about to put it to my ear when I noticed two wolves on the TV screen. They were gnawing on bloody, fleshy bones.

I covered the receiver. "Gross. What are you watching?"

"It's for school." She lowered the volume a bit. "I'm doing my paper on wolves. Did you know there haven't been any in our county for over fifty years?"

"Really?"

One of the wolves howled. It sounded just like what I'd heard in the ravine.

I watched as a third, smaller wolf approached the eating pair. It tried to snatch a bite from the bloody carcass. The two other wolves growled. One of them lunged at the third, snapping and snarling. The small wolf retreated a few feet and watched longingly as the two larger wolves devoured their food.

"Why won't they let that one eat?" I asked. "There's plenty to share."

"That one's the omega." Charity pointed at the smaller wolf. "He's the lowest member of the pack. They treat him like a whipping boy."

"That's so not fair."

"At least the alpha of this pack isn't totally brutal. He'll let the omega eat eventually."

The large wolf bared its teeth as the small one tried to approach again. It lunged at the omega's throat.

I turned away. I'd hate to see an alpha more brutal than that.

"Don't forget about your boyfriend." Charity pointed at the phone.

"Oh." I knew that she was teasing, but I wondered if I'd ever be able to call Daniel that. I walked into the kitchen. "Hello?" I said into the phone.

"Grace?" It wasn't Daniel.

"Oh hey, Pete."

"Hey, so my mom wants to know how James is doing."

"He's fine."

"Good." Pete paused. "I hope you don't hate me for not saying good-bye yesterday. My mom wasn't feeling too great after everything that happened."

"No worries," I said. To be honest, I hadn't even thought of Pete since I went into the woods with Daniel. "So what's up?"

"I'm calling in my rain check."

"Rain check?"

"For bowling. You still owe me a date."

I could tell from the sound of his voice he was using his "triple threat" smile.

"For tonight?"

"Yeah. We're doubling with Jude and April," he said, like the date was already set in stone. "Dinner, bowling, and then a party at Justin Wright's."

"Oh."

I wondered if I should go. Not for Pete's sake, but for Jude's. I hadn't talked to him since he'd freaked out the night before. The fact that he even wanted to go out and have fun with his friends was a good, but surprising, sign. How would he feel if he knew I was passing on spending time with him and April so I could hang out with the person he hated most? But as much as I felt I should go, nothing could make me blow off a chance to run with Daniel.

"I'm sorry, but I already have plans for tonight."

"Then change them," Pete said.

"I can't." I tried to sound apologetic. "I've got to go. I'll see you at church, okay?"

"Yeah, okay." His voice sounded hard. No smile at all.

DINNER THAT NIGHT

Every year, the day after Thanksgiving, my mother makes her famous turkey à la king. It's this creamy sauce with chunks of leftover turkey and fresh veggies she serves in little flaky pastry cups. And since we have it only once a year, no one in my family ever misses this meal.

Except that Charity, Don, and James were the only ones sitting with me at the table when Mom brought the steaming pot from the stove. Don and Charity banged their forks and knives on the table in happy anticipation.

"Save some for the others," Mom said as Don ladled a second scoop of creamy sauce into his already overflowing pastry cups.

"No way!" Charity grabbed the ladle from Don.

"Their loss," I said, and passed the salad to my mom.

"Where'd Jude take off to anyway?" Mom asked with a hint of annoyance. "It's not like him to miss this meal."

"He has a date with April."

Mom frowned.

"Where's Pastor D-vine?" Don asked.

"He's not back yet," Mom said. "He'll be here soon . . . I hope."

James smacked his hand into his à la king, sending a spray of peas and cream sauce across the table. He laughed and shouted his new favorite four-letter word.

"James!" Mom went a little red in the face. "Where would he possibly learn that?"

Charity chuckled.

"Haven't a clue," I said, trying to keep a straight face. Daniel would have laughed his head off had he been here. Really, it was a shame that he wasn't. This was one of his favorite meals, too. I checked the contents of the pot, and then ladled up a smaller portion for myself than normal.

After everyone was finished and gone, I dished up a Tupperware of leftovers for Daniel. He deserved it—especially if the others weren't going to show up to enjoy it. He'd put on weight since I'd first seen him last week—like a stray dog thriving under the care of a new owner. He was still thin, but his face was less hollow. My food donations must have done him good, but Meredith Divine's turkey à la king would truly be appreciated.

I stuck the container behind the milk, deciding to save it as a surprise for after our run, and then I went to meet Daniel.

I could see the walnut tree creaking and swaying in the wind, so I decided to wait for Daniel in the front room. I settled into the sofa with my history book—Daniel was *always* late, after all—and used the opportunity to do some homework. But once I'd finished the assigned reading for the whole next week, I couldn't shake the creeping feeling that Daniel wasn't going to show—like something was wrong.

The house was quiet. Mom and James had gone to bed hours ago, Dad had finally come home and gone straight to his study, and Charity had left for a sleepover with her friend, Mimi Dutton, next door. But I couldn't concentrate anymore, not with the noise in my head telling me that even Daniel would know that ten p.m. was way too late to be considered "after dinner." I would have just called it a night and gone to bed if it hadn't been for the eerie feeling that accompanied that thought.

I was standing in front of the window when I noticed something moving in the grass near the walnut tree. The movement happened again, and I wondered if the Duttons' cat had gotten out. I hated the idea of something happening to Mimi's cat—like what had happened to Daisy—so I decided to take action. I draped an afghan around my shoulders and went outside.

I slinked toward the side yard, so as not to scare the cat away. But as I approached, I realized that the huddled mass under the tree was much too large to be anything but human.

"Daniel?"

He was wearing the same outfit from earlier—dark indigo jeans and a red long-sleeved shirt I'd given him. He sat with his knees pulled up to his chest and his arms wrapped around his legs. He stared, unblinking, at the front of his old home.

"Daniel, what are you doing? I've been waiting for you."

"I'm just looking," he said. "I like this house better in blue. Yellow always made me feel like it was rotting inside."

"Where's your coat?" I shivered, wishing I had mine. It was definitely almost December.

Daniel didn't answer. His gaze never left the house that used to be his. I sat next to him in the crusty grass and draped part of my blanket over his legs.

Daniel sniffed. "I can't do this."

"Do what?"

"This. Any of this." He took in a deep breath and rested his chin on his knees. His silhouette was white and soft in the moonlight. "I don't know how to be anything other than what I am." He clutched his necklace, almost like he wanted to rip it off. "I don't want to be this anymore."

"Why?" I resisted the urge to touch his face. "You're amazing. The things you can do are out of this world. You're a hero."

"There's nothing heroic about me, Grace. You should know that. Your brother does. It's why he hates me." His hands shook like they had when he was child and he knew he was in trouble. "What I am . . . It's why no one can ever love me."

My heart sank deep. I hated seeing him this way. I turned my gaze to his house. It did look better now. The new owners had added a porch, put up shutters, and painted it a nice robin's-egg blue. "That's not true. Your mother loves—"

"I don't have a mother."

"What?" I looked at him.

"That *woman* isn't my mother," he said through clenched teeth. His jaw tightened; the veins in his neck bulged. "Even she didn't want me. She chose *him* over me."

"Who?"

"My father."

"I thought he skipped town when the sheriff took you away."

Daniel snorted. "He didn't stay away for long. He started coming around as soon as I moved to Oak Park with my mom. He kept begging her to take him back. At first she told him to get lost because he wasn't allowed to come near me. But he said he loved her, and she believed him. He said *I* made him crazy. I *made* him do the things he did." Daniel rubbed his hand over his head, as if he could still feel the pain of his fractured skull. "One night I overheard her on the phone with my social worker. Mom told him to come get me because she wanted to leave with my dad. She said she didn't want me anymore. She said I was too much for her to handle anyway." Daniel rocked forward and back, smacking his shoulders against the trunk of the tree.

"Daniel, I didn't know." I wanted to sooth his shaking. I put my hand on his chest and smoothed my fingers up his neck. "What did you do?"

"I ran away. I didn't want to go back into foster care."

"But you could have come back to us."

"No, I couldn't," he said. "That beast—my father—was as horrid as they come, and my own mother chose him over me. You wouldn't have wanted me, either. Nobody would have." He cringed, shaking more than ever. "Nobody ever will."

"But *I* want you, Daniel." I brushed my fingers into his hair. "I've always wanted you."

I had to show him that I needed him. I had to do something. I tilted his head toward mine and put my lips on his. He was like stone—stiff and cold—and I wanted to warm him. I moved my lips, and tried to kiss him, but his mouth stayed rigid and he didn't kiss back. I pressed harder.

His lips parted, melting, soft. He wrapped his arm around my waist under the blanket, and pulled me onto his lap. His hands slid up my back, over my shoulder blades. The afghan fell to the ground. Then one of Daniel's hands was in my hair, cradling my head. His mouth became warm and fierce. He pulled me hard against his chest, as if he couldn't get me close enough.

I'd pictured this moment with Daniel when I was younger. I'd shared a couple of awkward doorstep kisses since then with other guys. But the passion in Daniel's kiss—his mouth searching mine, as if seeking an answer that could save his life—was more than anything I could have ever imagined. The shadows and the winter chill melted away around us. I'd never felt so encircled by warmth. I slid my hands across his shoulders, then up his neck. My fingers tangled with the leather strap of his necklace. I leaned my head back as he trailed his lips down my throat. My heart pounded with the truth I'd been trying to deny—the words I couldn't hold in any longer. Maybe it was the answer he'd been searching for in my kiss.

"Daniel, I lo—"

"Don't," he whispered. His breath was so hot on my neck. "Don't say it, please."

But I had to. He needed to know how I felt. *I* needed him to know.

"I love you."

Daniel shuddered. A low, rumbling growl echoed

deep in his throat. "No!" he roared, and pushed me away from him.

I hit the ground, too shocked to speak.

Daniel, on all fours, scurried back a few feet. "No! No!" He clutched at his neck, as if to grab his stone pendant. But it wasn't there. It was in my hand. The leather strap had snapped in my fingers when he thrust me away.

My hands trembled as I held it out to him.

He reached for it, shaking more than I was. Like an earthquake ravaged in his chest. His eyes blazed as bright as two full moons. He grabbed the pendant, squeezing it so tight it would have sliced his hand had it been sharp, and backed away. The light left his eyes. He breathed hard and fast like he'd just run a marathon.

"I can't do this," he panted.

"Daniel?" I crawled toward him.

He backed away even farther. Sweat beaded on his forehead. He jumped as a car pulled up along the curb. He whispered something so low I could barely understand over the sound of the engine. "It can't be you," I thought he said.

Pete Bradshaw said something as Jude and April got out of the car. A girl's laughter followed. It sounded like Jenny Wilson.

"I can't do it." Daniel retreated into the shadows, still watching the car. "I could never ask."

I glanced at Pete as he waved good-bye to Jude and April. When I turned back, Daniel was already gone.

You could never ask what?

ALMOST MIDNIGHT

I hid behind the tree while Jude and April sat on the porch swing and said their good-byes. I pulled my legs to my chest and buried my head in my knees. I tried to stop trembling. I tried to stop thinking about that kiss. I tried to stop thinking about Daniel's reaction to my admission—that frightening look in his eyes. Daniel's words played in reverse in my head. *I could never ask. I can't do this. I'm no hero. Your brother knows that.*

What did my brother know?

That was it. I had to talk to Jude. No more dancing around the subject. No more treating it like *nothing*. I had to know what had happened between the two of them. How could I truly fix Daniel—how could I help him—if I didn't know what plagued his conscience?

Now if only I could get Jude alone. April's car was in the driveway, but it took them a good half hour to even start inching toward it. I squashed the blanket around my ears to block the sounds of their kissing. April made this little purring noise every time they came up for air.

I must have nodded off because the glow-in-the-dark hands on my watch said it was nearly midnight when I heard April's car finally pull out of the driveway. Jude was about to go into the house when I called his name.

He wheeled around. "Grace, how long have you been there?" He wiped his mouth with the back of his hand.

"Not long." I scrunched the blanket closer around my shoulders to hide the pink splotches creeping up my neck. "I was just walking back from the MacArthurs'. I was babysitting."

"Oh." He looked at the blanket. "You okay?"

"I need to ask you . . ." I stepped closer. "I need to ask you about Daniel."

He jangled his keys in his hand. "What about him?"

"I need to know what happened between you two. Why you hate him so much."

Jude grunted. "So you do care about that?" There was a hint of satisfaction in his voice. "It's about time."

"I've asked you a dozen times. You're the one who won't talk." I stepped up on the porch. "I care, Jude. I've always cared about you."

"Not as much as you care about him."

"How can you say that? You're my brother."

"If you cared so much about me, then how did Daniel get that coat?"

"His coat?"

"That coat he was wearing earlier today. The red-and-black North Face. How did he get it?"

"I . . . I gave it to him." I didn't understand why that

coat was important. And then I remembered. "It was yours, wasn't it?"

Jude didn't answer.

"I'm sorry." I dropped the blanket at my feet. "I didn't realize. That night I got stranded on Markham, Daniel came along and fixed the car. I gave him the coat in return. He really needed it. He's been through so many bad things—it just felt like something small I could do to help."

"Yeah, well, bad things happen to bad people. Didn't you think about that? They get what they deserve."

A shiver ran through me. "What about Maryanne Duke? She never did anything bad in her life, and she still froze to death on her porch. Something still mauled her body."

Jude jerked his head up. "Something? Try *someone*. You're so blind you don't even see it, Grace. You're letting Daniel walk all over you—just like Dad."

"We're helping him. He needs us—all of us."

"He's using you. He's using you both. I saw him with you that night on Markham. Do you really think it was a coincidence that he just happened along? April told me what you've done for him." His eyes narrowed as he looked at the fallen blanket around my ankles. "And I can only imagine what you've done *with* him."

"Jude!" *What a hypocrite.* "You don't even know what you're talking about."

"Don't I? Daniel will do anything to get what he

wants." Jude glared at me. "Tell me, whose idea was it to help him get back into your art class? Whose idea was it to invite him to Thanksgiving dinner?"

"Mine. They were *my* ideas."

"Were they really? Think about it, Grace. Daniel didn't somehow plant those ideas in your head? Subtly suggest how you could help him?"

I paused. "None of that matters. He's not manipulating me, and he's not manipulating Dad."

"Ha!" Jude smirked. "How do you think Daniel even got into Holy Trinity? Who do you think brought him back here? He's got Dad under his spell . . . and for all you know, Daniel's the one who stole James. He sure did find him easily, don't you think? It's just the kind of thing someone like him would do. Pretend to find a baby so people will think he's a hero."

"He wasn't pretending. I was with him. He found him so easily because of his abilities. . . ."

Jude fell into the swing. His eyes wide. His mouth open.

Did I say too much?

"So you know." Jude rubbed his hand across his scars. "You know what he is?"

"Yes."

"What did he tell you?"

I wasn't sure how to answer. Daniel hadn't asked me to keep it a secret. He'd know better than that with me. But still, how much could I say if I wasn't sure Jude was just baiting me for answers? But I had to be honest if I wanted Jude to be the same. "Daniel is an Urbat. His people were created to fight demons. He's a Hound of Heaven."

"Urbat? Hound of Heaven?" Jude laughed. It sounded like a harsh, high growl. "Look it up, Grace. Daniel's screwed you over good."

"No, he hasn't. He's lost and frightened and he needs us. I can help him be a hero." I hadn't thought it before I said it. But I realized that's what I had to do—that was my role in all of this. "I can show him that he can use his abilities to help people. They're a blessing; that's what he told me."

Jude shot up from the swing. "Then that monster is a liar as well as a thief and a murderer."

"Murderer?" I backed away and almost fell off the porch. "I don't believe you. You're jealous of him. You're jealous of the way Dad believed him over you. You can't stand that Dad and I want him to be a part of this family again. You're even making crazy accusations against me. How can I believe anything you have to say?"

"Then you ask him," Jude said. "Go ask your precious Daniel about the night he tried to take that coat from me. Ask him what he did with all the money he stole. Ask him what really happened to those stained-glass windows in the parish. Ask him what he *really* is." Jude slammed the swing into the wall. "You ask him what it felt like when he left me for dead."

"What?" I stumbled backward and caught myself with the railing. It felt like the wind had been knocked right out of my chest. "No . . ."

He lunged off the porch and ran down the driveway.

"Jude!" I shouted after him. But he didn't stop. He kept on running—so fast I couldn't follow—until he disappeared into the night.

Chapter Sixteen

Undone

AROUND TWO IN THE MORNING

Once I had this blouse. It was emerald-green with smooth, expensive-looking buttons. Even though it was on sale, Mom said it cost too much. But I wanted it, so I made a deal with Mom and gave up two whole months of Saturday nights for babysitting so I could pay her back. I earned the shirt just in time to wear it to Pete Bradshaw's sixteenth birthday party. I was asked to dance by five different guys. But later that evening, I noticed a thin green thread hanging from the sleeve. I tried to tuck it into to the cuff, but it kept falling out again. It seemed to get longer each time, so I finally pulled at it and tried to break it off for good. But when I yanked, the entire sleeve split up the seam to the shoulder, and I was left with a gaping hole in my favorite new shirt.

I felt that way now about my life. I'd pulled, or

pushed, or picked, or yanked too hard, and everything seemed to be coming apart at the seams. Actually, my brother was the one who was falling apart, and all I knew is that it was my fault—and I didn't know how to fix it. Jude used to be a saint compared to most teenage guys, so what could have possibly caused him to make up such hurtful lies about Daniel?

Jude had *to be lying*, I tried to tell myself over and over again.

He was flinging accusations in every direction, hoping one would stick. The things he said couldn't be anything but lies.

How could I feel the way I did about Daniel otherwise?

I heard Jude tell April that my father knew what Daniel had done. But Dad wouldn't let Daniel anywhere near us if Jude's lies were true. And I knew that he didn't hurt Maryanne—he loved her—and he didn't steal James. I was with Daniel in the woods. He *saved* James. He was a hero. He may not think so. Jude may not think so. But I knew it. And if I could just get to the truth, I could help Daniel become the person I saw in him—the person I loved. And then Jude would see him, too. They could be friends again—brothers. I could still fix them both.

But as I lay in bed, I felt like I was floating in Jude's and Daniel's words.

I'm no hero. No one can love me.

Monster, liar, thief, murderer.

Monster. Jude had called Daniel a monster.

Urbat? Hound of Heaven? Look it up, Grace.

I sprang out of bed and over to my desk, yanked the cord out of the phone, and plugged it into my computer. My parents had given me Dad's old desktop with the stipulation that I wasn't to access the Internet from my room. Web surfing was strictly reserved for the computer in the family room, where Mom could check the browsing history on a regular basis. But tonight was an exception. I had to know something. And I didn't want anyone to see what I was doing.

I waited for the computer to boot up and then logged on to the Internet. I pulled up Google and typed in "Hounds of Heaven." The cursor turned into a little hourglass and I waited more. Finally, the page pulled up several references to the "*Hound* of Heaven"—all were about a poem some now-dead Catholic guy wrote about how the grace of God chased down the souls of sinners. Interesting, but not what I was looking for. Did I really expect there would be a website dedicated to Daniel's secret colony of ancestors?

I was about to log off when I had another idea. I deleted my search. I started to type *U-r* . . . and then the words *Urbat, Sumerian* popped up in the search bar. Someone else had used my computer to look up the Urbat. I clicked on search, and a list of

Sumerian-to-English dictionaries appeared up on the screen. One was highlighted in purple while the others were still blue. I clicked on it and found a list of Sumerian words for all sorts of things from vampires, to destroyers, to evil spirits. I scrolled down farther, scanning the words until I saw one I recognized.

Kalbi. Daniel's last name. English meaning: dogs.

Did that prove Daniel's claim? Dogs were hounds, after all. But then I scanned farther down the list and found another familiar word.

Urbat.

I looked over at the English translation. It wasn't "Hounds of Heaven."

I gasped for air. I wasn't floating in words and accusations anymore. I was sinking. Sinking deep, and I couldn't breathe.

Urbat . . . Dogs of Death.

Daniel had lied. He'd lied, and Jude knew it. It was something so small—just the meaning of a name. But if Daniel had thought he needed to lie about that, then what else wasn't he telling me?

That monster is a liar as well as a thief and a murderer.

Could there be a shard, no matter how tiny, of truth to what Jude had said? Was Daniel really capable of those things? Whatever had happened between Daniel and Jude must have been pretty awful for my brother still to be so hurt and angry after all these years. But attempted murder?

I needed to talk to Daniel myself. I needed to ask him what had really happened. It was the only way I knew how to help them. It was the only way to mend the pieces back together.

CHAPTER SEVENTEEN

Wolf in Sheep's Clothing

SUNDAY EVENING

Two days later, I slipped the key into the lock of the basement apartment door at Maryanne Duke's house. I'd knocked and knocked, but nobody answered. It was better this way. Daniel might not let me in otherwise. The lock turned over, and I nudged open the door.

I glanced back up the narrow set of cement stairs that led down to the apartment. I'd skirted around the front porch—where I'd stood so many times with Maryanne—and gone straight to the apartment's entrance in the back of the house. It felt weird to be so close to where Maryanne had died—almost like she was watching.

Like *something* was watching.

I couldn't help thinking about what Lynn Bishop, who hadn't stopped talking all through Sunday school this morning, had said about three different families' pets going missing over the weekend. All of them lived in Oak Park.

I stepped inside and rebolted the door behind me. *Am I crazy for being here?*

It was the only solution I could think of. Daniel hadn't come to the house again since Friday. I didn't expect he would. Not after what happened when we kissed. And there was no way we could have this conversation at school. But still, it was getting dark, and I'd just let myself into a guy's apartment uninvited. And not just any guy—a superpowered guy my brother accused of being a murderer.

I shook off that thought and put my backpack on the kitchen table. I put the key in my pocket. Maryanne had given it to me two weeks before when I helped her clean the apartment after her last renter had moved out. I hadn't remembered to return it before she died.

I scanned the studio apartment. The only signs of Daniel in this place were the duffel bag and dirty laundry strewn across the powder-blue sofa bed, a couple of dishes in the sink, and an open box of plastic utensils on the kitchenette counter. Everything else about the room was the epitome of *grandmother*: carpet the color Maryanne called "dusty rose" but I always thought of it as "puke pink," and wallpaper dotted with tiny daisies of the same hue. And no matter how hard I'd scrubbed, this apartment always smelled overwhelmingly like old person—like dust and decay.

I opened my backpack and pulled out a brown paper sack and two Tupperware containers. I opened the fridge. It was empty. Hopefully, that would work to my advantage. I pulled a couple of plates from the cupboard over the microwave and wondered how long I should wait before I started to put things together. But then a shadow crossed in front of the window. I sat at the table, trying to look natural—but really trying to hide the fact that my knees had started to wobble.

Maybe this was a mistake. Maybe I should go. I heard a key in the lock. *Too late.*

The door swung open and closed. Daniel threw his keys on the sofa bed and kicked off his shoes. He sloughed off his coat and pulled his shirt up over his head.

I gasped.

Daniel whirled around and crouched, as if ready to pounce. His eyes flashed when he saw me. He dropped his shirt and straightened up. "Grace?"

"Hi." My voice wavered.

His stomach muscles tensed. He brushed the stone pendant that lingered between his defined pecs. I couldn't help noticing the way his long, lean muscles and untamed hair made him look like a wild, powerful animal. For one small second, I wished he *had* pounced on me.

"What are you doing here?" Daniel didn't sound pleased.

I stood up. "I brought supplies." I pointed at the brown paper sack.

He raised one eyebrow.

"Linseed oil and varnish." *Why is my voice so shaky?* "You keep promising to show me that technique, but you never deliver."

"You shouldn't be here." He held his hand over his pendant, pressing it against his chest. "Not after . . . And your parents . . . Does anyone know you're here?"

I swallowed hard. "I brought dinner, too." I pulled the lids off the containers. "I've got pork chops and rice and Mom's turkey à la king."

Daniel stepped closer. "That's nice of you, Grace." He stepped back again. "But you need to go."

"You want one or the other? Or some of each?"

Daniel opened the paper sack on the table and pulled out the bottles. I was surprised he hadn't put his shirt back on, but something fluttered inside of me because he didn't.

"Some of each then?" I scooped out the leftovers. "I thought we could eat and then get started. I've got a couple of Masonite boards in my bag."

Daniel wrapped his long fingers around the neck of the oil bottle—strangling it.

I picked up the plates and backed away to the kitchenette. I put one plate on the counter and turned toward the microwave with the other. But the microwave was something from the dawn of the modern age, with dials instead of buttons. "How do you work this . . . ?" I turned back toward the table, but Daniel was suddenly beside me. My eyes were level with the lean, all-too-capable muscles in his chest.

"You don't have to do this." He grasped my wrist.

I dropped the plate. It crashed between our feet. Shards of glass and grains of rice scattered across the linoleum floor.

"I'm sorry," I said. "I'll clean it up." I tried to pull out of his grip as I bent down, but he didn't let go.

He drew me up. "I can do it."

"No, it's my fault." I trembled in his grasp. "I'll clean it up." I looked around, as if searching for a broom. "And then I'll get out of your way."

Daniel released my arm. "Are you okay?"

"Yeah." I rubbed my wrist. "But it's late, and I should get home." I was being a chicken. I was failing. But at that moment I knew the truth might be more than I could handle. "We can do this another time."

"Grace, what's going on?" He placed his hands on my hips.

I looked down at the mess between our feet. "I forgot that I needed to do something."

"I know you didn't come here to paint. I can see it in your face." He paused for a second. "Is this about the kiss? Grace, did you come here for something else?" He brushed my cheek. "Because I don't think you're ready—"

"No," I practically shouted. "No, not at all. I came here because . . ." But I couldn't say it. I needed to go. I needed to get out of there. I tried to pull away, but he held me tight around the hips.

"Grace?" he asked, his voice sounding hurt. "What's wrong?"

"Nothing." Heat tingled up my neck.

"Look at me then."

I gazed up into his eyes. They were deep and soft and familiar. My brother *had* to be lying.

"I don't think you should be here just as much as you think you should go," he said. "But I can't send you away like this. Tell me what happened."

"Jude."

Daniel's eyes shifted downward. He moved the broken plate with his bare foot.

"I don't know what's wrong with him. He's not himself. He's making all these crazy accusations against you." I bit my lip. "He called you a monster. He said that you were using me. And he said other awful things about you. Things you did."

Daniel moved his hands away from my waist and crossed his arms in front of his naked chest.

"I refused to believe him. I didn't think you could do those things." I paused. "But he said that you were lying about the Urbat. I know it doesn't mean 'Hounds of Heaven.'" I sucked in a breath. "*You* lied to me . . . and now I don't know what to believe anymore."

Daniel looked up at the ceiling. "I'm sorry, Grace. I should have stayed away from you. He told me to keep away from you and Jude, but I couldn't. I saw your name in that art class, and I had to know. I told myself that if you could look me in the eyes . . . then maybe you could still love me. Maybe there was hope for me after all." A tear ran down his face. He wiped at it with his knuckles. "But I was selfish. I didn't care what it would do to you or Jude. All I wanted was your love, and now I know that's the one thing I can never have."

"Yes, you can." I touched his bare, sinewy bicep. "Just be honest with me. I can help you if I know the truth."

"You can't help me." He turned away and gripped the edge of the counter. "I could never ask."

"You don't have to ask. I know what I'm supposed to do."

The muscles in Daniel's shoulders went rigid. "You can't possibly . . ."

"I figured it out. I'm supposed to help you use your abilities to help people. I'm the one who can turn you into a . . . a superhero."

"Damn it, Grace!" he roared. The counter creaked and groaned under his white-knuckled grasp. "Who the hell do you think I am? A superhero? I'm not Peter Parker. I'm not your own damn Clark Kent. Your brother told you right—I am a monster!"

"No, you're not. I can—"

"I'm using you, Grace," he snarled. "You think I can be saved, but I can't. You don't even know what I'm capable of!" He swept the second plate off the counter. It exploded at my feet.

I jumped back, my shoes crunching on broken glass. "I don't care," I yelled at him. "I don't care if you're using me. And I don't care what lies my brother tells about you. That person he's describing isn't you."

He reeled on me, his eyes black and empty. "And who is that person?" he said. "What did Jude say about me? Because I'm pretty damn sure he knows exactly *what* I am."

I looked away at the cat-shaped clock above the stove.

"He said you were a liar and a thief and a murderer," I whispered. "He told me to ask you what it felt like when you left him for dead."

Daniel drew in a deep breath and let it out. "Like every remaining ounce of light and hope was sucked out of the shell I used to call my soul."

"Then it's true?" My voice cracked in my throat. "Tell me what you are. Tell me what you did. I think you at least owe me the truth."

I heard the shifting of broken glass as he moved away. I kept looking at the cat clock. Its eyes swung back and forth with every second that passed until Daniel finally spoke.

"I didn't lie about the 'Hounds of Heaven,'" he said from the kitchen table. "That's what my ancestors were originally called. Everything I told you was true—God's fight against evil, His blessing on my people—I just didn't tell you the ending to that story."

I turned to look at him. He sat in a kitchen chair, leaning over, his elbows on his knees. He looked down at the floor so all I could see was the top of his shaggy head.

"My ancestors fought the forces of hell for many years. They seemed like an unwavering force against evil; only the devil figured out the flaw in their armor—the flaw that's in all of us. The Hounds had been blessed with an animal essence that made them strong and agile, but they were still human, with human emotions. What they didn't realize is that the animal, the wolf that lived inside of them, fed on those emotions. The negative ones particularly: pride, jealousy, *lust*, fear, hate.

"The devil nurtured those feelings. As the Hounds grew more prideful—believing they were superior to all other humans—the wolf inside grew. It influenced their thoughts, their actions, devoured pieces of their souls. Their blessing became their curse.

"They turned their backs on God and his mission. They despised mortals and were hated and feared by them. And then the wolf started to lust for the blood of the ones the Hounds had once sworn to protect. And when a Hound gives in to that bloodlust—as most of them do—and he commits a true predatory act—tries to kill someone—the wolf takes control. It now has the power to take over the Hound's form at will, becoming an embodied wolf. It holds the Hound's mortal soul ransom as it hunts and ravages and kills."

"Is that where the name Urbat comes from?" I asked. "The Dogs of Death?"

He nodded. "There are many names. Hundreds, actually. The Skin-Walkers, *Loup-Garou*, Oik, Varkolak, Varulv. The name you are probably most familiar with is Werewolf."

"Werewolf? Your family are werewolves?" I stepped back. "Are you . . . Are you a . . . ?"

"A wolf in boy's clothing?" He wasn't joking. "I'm a hybrid actually. My mother was full human. My father was the Kalbi. He was the beast." Daniel looked up at me. "What I told you about the Urbat living in packs was true. They live together for protection and kinship." He fingered his necklace. "Many of them try to control the wolf; others like the taste of blood. My father was one of the latter. He challenged the alpha of his pack and lost. The alpha banished him instead of ripping out his throat—that was a big mistake.

"My father wandered for a while. But a wolf's greatest instinct is for a pack, a family. He ended up in Rose Crest, where he chose a woman he could dominate. He tried living as a mortal with her. But then I came into the picture. I think he sensed he wouldn't be able to control me as easily . . . and that made him crazy. I drove him to hunting again."

"Your father"—I could barely bring myself to ask—
"he was the Markham Street Monster, wasn't he?" I
thought about how his father seemed to sleep all day.
How he worked a night shift at a warehouse near the
shelter on Markham. How all those strange things
stopped happening around the time he skipped town.
"He killed all those people."

Daniel lowered his head even more. He didn't need
to answer.

"And you were born with the wolf's essence, too?"

Daniel reached down and scooped up a few shards
of broken plate. He held them in his open palm. "My
wolf wasn't as strong when I was younger—probably
because I wasn't a purebred. Gabriel says there are
some descendants of the Hounds who are so mixed in
breed they probably don't feel it much at all." He closed
his hand over the bits of glass and squeezed. He winced
and opened his bloody palm. "I didn't know the truth
then about my family. All I knew was that there was
something very wrong with my father—which is how I
discovered that I could heal faster than normal people.
That I could heal myself."

He closed his eyes and pursed his lips. It was like the
cuts on his hands sucked the blood back in, then healed
over into thin, jagged scars. All that remained in his
hand were a few pink bits of glass.

"But as I got older, I felt the monster stirring. I fought
it as hard as I could. But I've failed. The wolf took me

over, too—turned me into a beast like my father."

"But if the wolf took you over, that means you've . . ." I thought of Jude, of those scars on his hands and face, of the things he'd accused Daniel of. "That's when it happened. You tried to hurt Jude, and that's when the wolf took you over. That's why he's so afraid of you."

Daniel closed his fist around the glass again. His knuckles went purple, then white. Blood snaked around his wrist. I turned away and studied the puke-pink daisies on the wall.

"The night I ran away from home," he said, "I broke into the parish. It was after the fund-raiser for the fire repairs, and I knew your father always put off taking donations to the bank. I was already quite strong then. It only took a second to break the lock on the outside door to the balcony. The plan was to get in and get out with the money, but as I was leaving, your brother showed up. He saw me with the cash box and told me to put it back. He seemed so self-righteous, and it made me sick. The wolf told me that all of this was his fault. That I wouldn't have even been there if it weren't for him."

"What do you mean?"

"I always felt the wolf drive for a pack. But I wanted a normal family. With a mother who put her child first, and a father who was steady and kind and didn't make me tremble in my bed at night. I wanted a family like yours. I wanted to be Daniel Divine." His voice faltered.

I heard him shift in his chair. "I hated my father. I hated the monster that burned inside of me. Every time I got mad, or jealous, or . . . Something inside of me swelled, grew, eating me alive. It told me to hurt, to hunt. At first I thought I was going insane. I pushed it away. But somehow I *knew* that my father was responsible for what was happening to me. I followed him once. I saw what he would become—the things he did. I knew that was what my future held.

"I thought maybe I could get rid of the monster if I got rid of my father—told someone about what I saw. I wanted to tell. I almost told. But then I thought I had to forgive him. That no matter how bad he hurt me or anyone else, I had to turn the other cheek. You're the one who told me that. Told me my father hurt me because he was desperate."

My knees went numb. I clung to the counter for support. I didn't understand what I'd said back then—still didn't really. But that wasn't what I'd meant. Not at all.

"So I kept my mouth shut," Daniel continued. "Sometimes I tried to paint the things I saw, but that only made my father go ballistic. One day I finally tried to tell Jude about the Urbat—what little I'd learned about them by then—but he thought I was making up stories. So instead I told him how my father hurt me. I thought if I told one person, but made him keep it a secret, it would ease the burning a bit, and I wouldn't be betraying my father. I made Jude promise not to tell.

But he broke that promise. He ruined everything."

"But you got what you wanted." The numbness in my knees spread up my legs. "You became our brother."

"But it didn't last. Before I had only dreamed what it would be like to be in a real family, but if your brother hadn't broken his promise, then I wouldn't have ever *known* what it was like. I wouldn't have known what it felt like to be wanted and then get ripped out of the only warm, loving place I'd ever had. Things would have gone on like in the past, and my own mother wouldn't have had to choose between that monster and me."

Daniel cleared his throat and coughed. "It was easier to control the wolf when I was with your family. But when I left, it started stirring again. But this time I didn't fight it. I sought out other people who had demons inside—other creatures of the night." He made a scoffing laugh. "Although, most of their inner demons weren't quite so literal."

Daniel swallowed so hard I could hear him from across the room. I could tell he wasn't going to make any more jokes.

"The wolf grew stronger," he said after a moment. "It influenced everything I did. And then that night in the parish when I saw your brother standing there and he had everything I ever wanted, the monster finally broke free."

I cringed, imagining Jude alone and frightened.

"I raged and wailed on Jude like my father used to

wail on me. I wanted to make him feel all the pain I had inside. He didn't even try to fight back. He just took it like he was some kind of martyr, and that made the wolf fume. I wanted to strip him of everything he had."

Daniel took in a long breath. "When I told Jude I was taking the money *and* his new coat, you know what he did? He got to his feet in front of those stained-glass pictures of Christ, took off his coat, and offered it to me. 'Take it,' he said. 'It's cold outside, and you need it more than I do.' He put the coat in my hands, and he was so calm and peaceful and I didn't understand. I didn't know this place he was coming from. I didn't know how he could just offer it to me like it was nothing—like I'd done nothing. That's when I thought it—I wanted to kill him. And then something seared through my veins, and I started to shake and scream . . . and I lunged at him.

"All I remember after that is waking up outside on the parish grounds. My clothes were missing and shards of colored glass were scattered all around. There was blood all over me. But none of it was mine. I had no idea what happened—what I'd become. Gabriel says it's like that the first few times; you're not conscious of your actions at all. I was frantic. I didn't know where your brother had gone. But then I saw him, lying, twisted, in the bushes a few feet away. And I knew I was responsible."

I held my hand over my heart. It was racing so fast it

felt like it was going to burst through my ribs. "Was it you or the wolf?"

Daniel was silent for a moment. "The wolf took him through that window. But *I* was the one who left him there. I saw the blood on his face. I knew he needed help. But I ran away. I took the cash box and I left him there."

The chair creaked as he stood up. I heard him moving closer to me. I could see his dark reflection in the cat clock's shifting eyes.

"You want to know what the real kicker is?" he asked, only a few inches from me now.

I didn't answer, but he told me anyway.

"That money only lasted me three weeks," he said. "Five thousand dollars of blood money, and I pissed it away on shit-hole motel rooms and girls who said they loved me until the drugs ran out. And at the end of three weeks, when I'd sobered up enough to remember what I'd done, I started running. But no matter how far or fast I ran, I couldn't get away from the wolf. So I kept running and drinking and using—anything to numb the memories away—and I ran so far, that's probably how I ended up back here."

He moved closer to me—as close as he was when I kissed him in the moonlight. "Do you know me now? Do you still think I'm worth saving?" His breath burned the side of my face. "Can you look me in the eyes and say you love me now?"

I shifted my gaze from the clock to my feet. I picked

my way through the broken glass and grabbed my back-pack, leaving the bottles of linseed oil and varnish on the table, and went straight to the door. My hand was on the doorknob when I stopped.

"Jude didn't break his promise," I choked out. "I was the one who told on your father. I'm the one who turned you into the wolf."

I wrenched the door open and ran up the stairs to the minivan. I drove aimlessly for at least an hour and somehow ended up at home in my bed.

I had no thoughts in my head. No feeling in my skin. There was nothing in me at all.

CHAPTER EIGHTEEN

Book of Secrets

I woke the next morning, tangled in the bedsheets. My shirt clung to my chest, sticky with cold sweat. My head throbbed. It felt like someone was drilling a hole in the base of my skull, the pain radiating up behind my eyes. I squinted at the alarm clock. It was much later than I thought. I pushed myself out of bed and into the shower.

I stood in the stream of hot water and let the heat prick at the numbness under my skin, washing away the shock. That's when the tears came.

I never cried. Not since I was a baby, according to my mother. I didn't get the point. Crying never fixed anything. But as the tears started to roll down my face, mingling with the rain from the showerhead, I couldn't hold it in anymore. I sobbed into the steam, hoping no one could hear me over the somber buzz of the bathroom fan. It was like I finally let out every tear I'd ever held back. I cried for the time Don Mooney held his silver knife to my father's throat. I cried for the times I overheard Daniel's father ripping into him. For the time his mother took him away from us. For when Charity and I were sent to our grandparents for three weeks without any explanation. I cried for Maryanne's death, for James going missing, for Jude.

But mostly I sobbed for what I now knew about myself.

I felt like such a fraud. My father told me my name meant mercy, help, and guidance. But he was wrong. All Grace Divine meant was blundering, meddling, disappointment. Everything I touched—everything I tried to help—fell apart and slipped through my fingers.

Why did I have to press the issue, refuse to stay ignorant? Why couldn't I go back and stop myself from creating this mess?

If I had just stayed out of things, if I had just minded my own business for all these years, would everything be the way it used to? Would Daniel still be the blond-haired boy next door if I had kept my mouth shut about his father? Would Daniel and Jude still be the best of friends? Would my brother be undamaged? Would Daniel be human?

But how could I have not done anything? Daniel would still be living a life of abuse and torture—he might not even be living at all. And how could I have not helped him when he came back?

He still meant so much to me, even now after I knew the truth.

But I couldn't believe I put my need for Daniel over my own brother. I saw the pain in Jude's face the first time I mentioned Daniel's name at dinner. I looked Jude right in the eyes and promised I would leave it alone, that I would keep out of his secrets, but instead I went and dragged the only person who ever hurt him back into our lives. My feelings for Daniel caused the pain, the fear, and the anger that were slowly taking over my brother.

"I hate you," I said into the water. I pounded my wet fist on the shower wall. "I hate you, hate you, hate you," I said as if speaking to Daniel.

But the problem was—I didn't. I didn't hate Daniel at all, and I knew I should.

I had betrayed my brother once again.

I stood in the shower until it turned cold. And then I stood longer, letting the icy water cut paths across my skin, just to feel something other than my guilt. I stumbled out of the shower, shivering and clutching my stomach. I made it to the toilet and heaved out what little liquid was left in my body. I felt withered, drained, and I crawled back into bed, still wrapped in my wet robe.

The house was quiet. Everyone else must have left for the day. The silence pressed in on me, making my head pound even more. I closed my burning eyes and let the silence envelop my body. I slept off and on, trying to make up for too many sleepless nights. But each time my eyes drifted closed and then open, I felt more drained than before.

I stayed in bed for two days.

WEDNESDAY

My family left me alone. I was shocked—but grateful—that Mom didn't try to make me go to school. Every once in a while she sent Charity up with food. Charity would leave it just inside my door, staring at me like I had the plague as she retrieved the untouched plates she'd left hours before. I wondered if my family really thought I was sick, but I feared that they knew what I had done—that they were just as ashamed of me as I was of myself. How could I face my brother again, knowing the pain I'd caused him? How could I show my face to anyone?

It was midafternoon on Wednesday when I heard my father in his study below me. I wondered what he was doing home. Wednesday was one of his busiest days at the parish, and Jude would be there for his independent study. I thought about Dad surrounded by his books, how he'd seemed lost in them for weeks. What *was* he doing?

But then I knew. It suddenly clicked. I wasn't the only one to blame in all of this.

"You knew," I said from the doorway.

Dad looked up from his book.

I thundered into the room, right up to his desk. "You knew what he was, and you still brought him here!" I grabbed one of his books. *Loup-Garou.* "That's what these books are for. You're helping him."

My parents were such hypocrites! All this crap they taught us about not keeping secrets, and here my father was keeping the biggest one of all.

I threw the book on the desk. It skidded across the wood and knocked over the lamp. "You're the one who started all this. Not me."

Dad pushed his glasses up the bridge of his nose. He closed his book and put it on top of one of the stacks. He looked completely unruffled by my behavior. It made me want to scream at him more.

"I wondered when you would come to me," he said. "I hoped that if we left you alone, you eventually would." He sounded like the perfect pastor dealing with a troubled parishioner. "Shut the door and take a seat."

I was itching not to listen to him, but I did what he asked anyway. Once I was sitting, I picked up another book. The words and letters were all unfamiliar, like Arabic.

"So you want to know why I'm helping Daniel," Dad

said. "The answer is simple, Grace. He asked me to."

"When?"

"Daniel contacted me about six weeks ago. I made the arrangements for his return."

"But why would he want to come back here?"

"He hasn't told you?"

I flipped through the pages of the book until I came to an illustration. It was an etching of what looked like a man transforming into a wolf. A full moon hung in the background. "He said something once about art school. He needed Holy Trinity to get into Trenton. But that was just a cover, right? This doesn't have anything to do with art school, does it?"

Daniel just used that to make me feel empathy for him—feel connected in our goals.

"That was the cover story we invented," Dad said. "But that doesn't mean Daniel doesn't want to go to Trenton. He wants to reclaim the life he should have had." Dad leaned forward, his hands clasped together on top of his desk. "Grace, the reason Daniel came back is he's searching for a cure."

Something fluttered in my chest. "Is that even possible?"

Dad looked down at his hands. "While Daniel was gone he sought out the colony that his father came from. He asked them for a place in their pack. However, Urbat who have experienced the change—become werewolves—do not procreate often. It is typically against their nature. And in the pack dynamic, only the alpha is allowed to mate. Daniel's mere existence was an affront to their ways." Dad clasped and unclasped his fingers. "I don't think those ancient wolves had any idea what to do with such a young Urbat—especially one who came from a volatile father who had been banished from their colony. Many of the elders were quite wary of letting Daniel live among them. The alpha granted him a probationary period while they deliberated his future. While there, Daniel met a man—"

"Gabriel?"

Dad nodded. "Gabriel is the beta of their pack. Second in command. He took Daniel under his wing—or paw, as the case may be—and taught him many things about the history of their people. And about the techniques they've developed over the centuries to help control the wolf. The necklace Daniel wears is quite rare. It helps him keep the wolf at bay, and it makes him more sentient—more able to control his actions—while in wolf form. The pendant is many centuries old. I've contacted Gabriel to see if he has another to spare. . . ." Dad rubbed his hand down the side of his face. The dark patches under his eyes had gotten deeper and darker since I last saw him.

"Although Gabriel has a lot of influence with his pack, after the time of probation, he was unable to convince the other elders to let Daniel stay with them permanently. I think the memory of the damage his father caused to the pack was still too fresh. They sent Daniel away."

I bowed my head. Just another set of names to add to the long list of people who had rejected Daniel—a list *my* name was now on after I couldn't look him in the eyes.

"However, before Daniel was removed from the colony, Gabriel told him that there may be a way for him to free his soul from the clutches of the wolf. That there may be a cure. Gabriel said he couldn't tell him the details but that the record of the ritual could be found if he looked hard enough. He told Daniel to enlist the help of a man of God. He told him to return to where someone loved him—he told him to go home."

"And that's why he contacted you. You're the man of God."

"Yes. I've been poring through every text on the subject since. Searching for the cure." He gestured to the scattered books on his desk. "Then I realized that the answer must be something religious in nature—something only a man of God could obtain. I remembered meeting an Orthodox priest many years ago. He told me about a relic they kept in his cathedral. A book that contained translations of letters written by a monk who traveled to Mesopotamia during the Crusades. Although I thought little of it at the time, the priest joked that he had documented proof that God had invented the werewolf."

Dad opened his desk drawer and pulled out a wood box. The lid was inlaid with a golden pattern of alternating suns and moons.

"I drove most of Thursday night to the cathedral. It took quite a bit of convincing, but the priest finally consented to loan the book to the parish. I couldn't rest until I found the answer."

"You found it?" My heart raced. "You can cure Daniel?"

"No." Dad stared down at the box. "I can't help him anymore."

"No, you didn't find it? Or no, you can't cure him?"

Dad took off his glasses, folded in the arms, and placed them neatly on his desk. He leaned back in his chair and squeezed the bridge of his nose. "Tell me something, Grace. Do you love Daniel?"

"How can I?" I studied a hangnail on my thumb. "Not after what he did to Jude. It wouldn't be right. . . ."

"Do you love him?" Dad's voice told me not to consider those other things. "Do you?"

Tears welled behind my eyes. How did I have any more to cry?

"Yes," I whispered.

Dad sighed and picked up the box. "Then it's out of my hands." He placed the box in front of me, something rattled inside it as he did. "I feel you must discover the answer for yourself. I'll be here when you do . . . but the choice is yours to make."

I sat cross-legged on my bed with the box balanced between my knees. I couldn't believe all the answers—the final pieces of the puzzle—could be found in such a narrow box. Could I really hope for such a possibility? Maybe all it held was more disappointment. Maybe there was no cure after all. It would explain how distraught and tired my father seemed. Maybe he thought I needed to discover that for myself . . . become resigned just like him.

But he said I had a choice to make. And choices can't be made without knowledge—without answers.

So why can't I open the box?

The truth was that I was afraid of answers. Ignorance may not be bliss, but it seemed preferable to all the pain that accompanied the answers I'd found already.

I stared at the box until my knees ached in their position. My fingers trembled as I reached for the blackened gold latch. I popped it open and pushed up the lid. Inside, I found a book that looked older and more brittle than any of the ones in Dad's office. The cover was a faded sapphire-blue, with the same gold sun-and-moon inlays as were on the box. I brushed the cover tentatively. I was afraid the book might fall to pieces as I picked it up.

Several slips of paper protruded from the top end of the book. Had Dad marked certain passages to make my reading easier? I turned the delicate tissuelike pages to the first marked entry. The page looked like a handwritten letter, or a copy of one, in faded brown ink. Dad said this was a translation, not the original. I found myself wishing I'd taken Mrs. Miller's calligraphy class, in addition to painting, as I tried to make out the pale, scripted words.

My Dearest Katharine,

Tidings of thy joyous marriage to Simon Saint Moon could not have come at a better time. My encampment has been besieged by despair and many of the foot soldiers and squires cower at the cries of wolves that surround our camp by night. They think God will let them devour us because of our sins.

My squire, Alexius, claims that the wolves are not ordinary animals, but the Dogs of Death of local legend. He tells me they are men who were once blessed by God to be his soldiers, but the devil turned them from their quest, and now they are cursed to roam the earth as savage beasts.

Oh little sister, you would love dear Alexius. I do not regret taking him on as my squire after the fires. Many of the other local boys have not fared as well. I pray we will give up on this campaign and move on to the Holy Land. I did not leave our village behind to aide in the killing of other Christians. Perhaps the devil is trying to sway us from our quest also.

Father Miguel assures us that our mission is true and that God will protect us in our fight against the Greek traitors. . . .

A knock sounded softly against my bedroom door. I covered the box and book with my blanket. "Come in," I said, expecting Charity with dinner.

"Hey." Jude leaned against the door frame. He held a dark green folder in his hands. "This is for you." He crossed the distance to my bed and handed it to me.

"What is it?" I pushed the book farther under the covers with my foot.

"All of your homework." Jude half smiled. "Junior grades are critical for college admissions. I didn't want you to get behind. I got April to copy her notes from English. But Mrs. Howell says you still owe her a parent-signed test."

Crap. I'd forgotten all about that.

"I told her you haven't been feeling like yourself lately, and I talked her into letting you retake the exam instead. She says you can do it after school when you're feeling better."

"Wow. Thank you. That was really . . ." *Just like* the thing my brother always did. It's what made him . . . him. But I'd figured he'd never want to talk to me again. Not after what I'd done. "I really appreciate this."

Jude nodded. "When you're up to it, I'll wait for you after school while you take your test. That way you won't have to walk home alone." He walked to the door, stopped, and looked back at me. "It's time to get out of bed, Gracie."

He knows. I know the truth about what happened to him . . . and he knows.

"I'm sorry I didn't listen to you," I said softly.

Jude nodded slightly and shut the door behind him.

After I heard Jude walk down the hall, I pulled the box and book out from under the blanket. I closed the lid over Katharine and her brother and locked the box in my desk drawer. I couldn't read any further. I couldn't search for answers anymore. I needed to drop the whole issue. Jude was moving on, and so was I.

CHAPTER NINETEEN
Choices

I realized as Jude and I drove the few blocks to school in the numbing cold, that even though there was an understanding between us, we still weren't going to talk about it.

Some things never change.

Maybe it's better that way.

Jude walked me to my locker and then took off to find April before first period. I tried to act natural, like this was just any other day and I was any other girl. But it was hard to pretend that I was normal.

Normal people gossiped—mostly about the strange things that had happened over the weekend. I'd hoped that the rumor mill would have died down during my three-day absence from school, but apparently it was still running full tilt. Word had spread about Jenny Wilson finding her mangled cat in the middle of her cul-de-sac. Other people talked about Daniel rescuing James in the woods. They whispered about Jude's accusations. And I got the distinct feeling people were also talking about me—more than the usual, that is.

Normal people passed the flyers plastered around the school of Jessica Day's class picture from Central High. They'd look at her long blonde hair and her big doelike eyes and shake their heads, saying, "What a shame." But normal people didn't know what danger she may really be in. They didn't know what horrors really existed in this world. They had no idea there was a werewolf in my AP art class.

How would everyone else react if they knew that truth?

Would they accuse Daniel of being the new Markham Street Monster? Would they blame him for all the bad things that had happened lately?

I stopped midstride on my way to fourth-period art. Did *I* believe any of those things? I told myself that it couldn't be true. Daniel had that necklace, so even if he went into wolf mode he'd be able to stop the monster from hurting people. Wouldn't he? There had to be another explanation.

Or maybe that necklace didn't work as well as he and my dad thought. Or perhaps it did work—perhaps Daniel was fully conscious when he did those things. . . .

I stood outside the art room until long after the bell rang. I knew that Daniel was in there. Enough people had been talking about him for me to know he'd shown up for school. I wished he hadn't. I took three deep breaths. Daniel wouldn't hurt those people if he was in his right mind. There was definitely another explanation—and it wasn't my job to figure it out. Someone else could play Velma from now on.

I pushed the door open and went straight for Barlow's desk. I put my tree sketch in front of him and didn't wait for any comment before I went to the back of the room for my supply bucket. Lynn and Jenny stopped talking as I approached. Lynn shot me a sidelong glance and then said something to Jenny behind her hand. I ignored them and pulled my watercolors out of my bucket. I could feel Daniel's presence only a few yards away; I could smell his earthy-almond scent even with all the oil solvents and chalk dust lingering in the air, but I couldn't bring myself to look at him. I grabbed the rest of what I needed and joined April at our table.

"I called you, like, ten times," April said. She didn't look at me as she drew sharp, angled lines in her sketch pad. "You could have at least emailed me back or something."

"You're right." I opened my box of pastels and dumped out the chalk bits on the table. I'd forgotten that most of them were broken. "I'm sorry."

"So are you over it?" April nodded slightly toward Daniel.

"Yeah." I picked up a red pastel bit. It was too

small to draw with effectively. "I think so."

"Good." April put her charcoal pencil down. "Jude says Daniel is a bad influence on you."

"What else does Jude say these days?" I asked.

She sighed. "He's upset that your dad keeps trying to get him to be friends with Daniel. Your dad says Jude should just forgive and forget, and be happy Daniel's back." April shook her head. "I don't get it. I mean, Jude's his *real* son. Why would he even want Daniel here?"

"I don't know," I mumbled. My mind flitted back to that book of letters in my bedroom. "Has Jude said anything else?" I asked, wondering how much April really knew about any of this.

April shrugged. "He invited me to the Monet exhibit at the university tomorrow night."

"That's sweet." I inspected another broken pastel. It was just as useless as the first.

"Yeah, but my mom won't let me go because it's in the city. It's like she suddenly cares about me after what happened to Jessica Day or something." April crinkled her nose. "I think we're just going to have a movie fest at my house. You can come, too, if you want."

"No. But thanks anyway." I'd seen enough of Jude and April snuggling to last me a lifetime.

April pulled her box of pastels from her supply bucket and slid it in front of me. "You can borrow mine if you want." April gave me a small smile. "I really am glad you're better now."

"Thanks," I said. But I glanced back at Daniel. His gaze was shifted away from us, but from the look on his face it seemed like he'd been listening to our entire conversation from across the room.

That didn't make me feel better at all.

LATER THAT SAME DAY

Daniel had asked me to spend my lunch breaks and after school with him and Barlow. I doubted that offer still stood—or that he'd actually expect me to stay now—and I cleared out to the library when the lunch bell rang, refusing April's offer to join her and Jude at the café. I stayed until it was time to go back after lunch. When fifth period was over, I took off as quickly as I could for my next class.

"Wait up, Grace," Pete Bradshaw called as I approached my locker.

"Hey, Pete." I slowed my pace.

"You okay?" he asked. "I said your name three times before you noticed."

"Sorry. I guess I was a little distracted." I put down my backpack and turned the combination to my locker. "Did you need something?"

"Actually, I wanted to give you something." He pulled a package out of a plastic bag. "Donuts." He handed me the box. "They're a little stale, though. I brought them yesterday, but you weren't here."

"Thanks . . . um . . . What are these for?"

"Well, you still owe me a dozen from before Thanksgiving. So I thought if I got you some instead, you'd feel extra indebted to me." Insert "triple threat" smile here.

"Indebted to do what?" I asked coyly.

Pete leaned forward. His voice was low as he spoke. "Is there something really going on between you and that Kalbi guy, or are you just friends?"

Something really going on? Now I was sure people were talking about me.

"Don't worry," I said, "I don't even think we're friends."

"Good." He leaned back on his heels. "So these donuts are supposed to make you feel guilty enough to go to the Christmas dance with me."

"The Christmas dance?" The dance hadn't passed my mind in days. Did people who knew the secrets of the underworld go to dances? "Uh, yes. I would love to go," I said. "On one condition, though."

"What's that?"

"Help me eat these donuts, or I'll never fit into a dress."

Pete laughed. I opened the box and he snagged three donuts.

"Can I walk you to class?" he asked as I shut the box in my locker.

I smiled. It was such a 1950s-perfect-boyfriend thing to ask. "Sure," I said, and hugged my books to my chest and pretended I was wearing a poodle skirt and oxford shoes. Pete wrapped his arm around my waist as we walked down the hall. He nodded to more than a few quizzical-looking people as we went.

Pete seemed so confident, so normal, so good. *He's just what I need,* I thought as I watched him—but I couldn't help noticing there was someone else watching me.

WEDNESDAY OF THE NEXT WEEK,
JUST BEFORE LUNCH

I sat next to April in the art room working on a preliminary sketch from an old snapshot for a portfolio piece. It would eventually be a painting of Jude fishing behind Grandpa Kramer's cabin. I loved the way the light swept in from the side of the photograph and glistened off the top of Jude's bowed head like a halo. But for the moment, I was working with pencils, sketching out the basic lines and defining the negative and positive spaces. There was more shadow in the picture than I had realized, and the graphite of my pencil was worn down to a useless nub, but I was avoiding the pencil sharpener in the back of the room because Daniel's seat was only three feet away from it.

A few minutes before the lunch bell, Mr. Barlow

made his way over to Daniel's desk.

"Look at Lynn fume." April nudged me.

Lynn Bishop glared at Daniel as Mr. Barlow stood beside him, watching him paint. She looked like she was trying to burn a hole in Daniel's back with her eyes.

"Looks like Barlow's got a new favorite. Poor Lynn," April said with mock sympathy. "You're totally better than she is anyway. You should have heard Barlow going on about that sketch of your house you turned in last week." She pointed at my drawing and sighed. "I love this one, too. Jude looks *so* hot in that picture."

"Hmm," I said. I gathered up a couple of spent pencils and made a break for the back of the room while Daniel was occupied.

I put a pencil into the sharpener.

"Stop!" Barlow bellowed.

I jumped and looked behind me but Barlow had been speaking to Daniel.

Daniel held his brush midstroke. He looked up at Barlow.

"Leave it the way it is," Barlow said.

I leaned sideways a bit to get a look at Daniel's painting. It was of himself as a child—a subject Barlow had assigned the rest of us earlier in the year. So far, Daniel had a simple background of red hues and the flesh tones roughed in for his face. His lips were outlined in pale pink. And since Daniel always went about things in the hardest way possible, he'd finished the eyes before anything else. They were dark and deep and confused like I had always remembered them.

"But it isn't finished," Daniel said. "All I've perfected are the eyes."

"I know," Barlow said. "That's what makes it so right. Your eyes—your soul is there, but the rest of you is still so undefined. That's the beauty of childhood. The eyes show everything you've seen so far, but the rest of you is still so open to possibility, to whatever you might become."

Daniel held the brush tightly between his long fingers. He glanced at me. We both knew what he had become.

I turned away.

"Trust me," Barlow said. The Masonite board scraped against the table. I assumed he'd picked it up. "This will make a great portfolio piece."

"Yes, sir," Daniel mumbled.

"Are you done or what?" Lynn Bishop stood next to me with a fistful of colored pencils.

"Sorry," I said, and moved out of her way with my still-dull pencil.

"I hear Pete asked you to the Christmas dance." Lynn shoved a pink pencil into the sharpener.

"I guess word gets around."

I heard Daniel's chair sliding back over the ferocious gnawing of the sharpener.

"Yes, it does," she said in her knowing, "I've got a juicy bit of gossip" tone. "Interesting he still asked *you*."

"What's that supposed to mean? Pete's been friends with my brother for years."

"Hmm." Lynn removed her pencil and inspected the long, pointy pink tip. "I guess that explains it—an act of charity for your brother. Pete must be trying to bring you back to the land of the living."

I was already cranky, and I didn't need crap from the gossip queen of Holy Trinity—kind of an oxymoron if you think about it—but the lunch bell rang, stopping me from telling her what she should do with her pencil.

"Mind your own business," I said, and walked away.

April picked up her backpack as I approached. "Do you think there are CliffsNotes to *Leaves of Grass*?"

"I doubt it." I put my pencils in my supply bucket.

April groaned. "Jude is going to quiz me on it after school, and I kind of told him I already read it." She crinkled her nose and put the book in her bag.

"Nuh-uh!" I teased. "You're so dead. Say good-bye to the Christmas dance. Jude hates liars."

"Oh, no. Do you think he'll be that mad?" She paused. "Wait, you said Christmas dance." She pointed at me. "Did he say something to you? He *is* going to ask me, right? Hey, do you want to go shopping for dresses after school?"

I smiled, but I couldn't help wondering if I should say something to April about Jude. She seemed head over heels for him, but I couldn't help wondering if my brother's sudden interest in her was his way of rebounding—not from another relationship but from his own emotions. Or maybe it was April who was taking advantage of my brother. She sure did get over her shyness around him the second he seemed vulnerable. But the look on April's face was genuinely eager.

"Don't you think you should focus on studying for the English final before dress shopping?" I asked. "Didn't your mother threaten to ground you if you don't pass?"

"Ugh. Seriously, why did she have to start taking an interest in me now?"

"Hey, Grace," a raspy voice said from behind me.

April's eyebrows went up in double arches.

I turned toward the owner of the voice, already knowing whom it belonged to. I looked at his navy-blue sweater with the sleeves pushed up to his elbows, his khaki pants, the slip of paper he held in his hands, the top of his hair that seemed to get lighter with every day that passed—I looked anywhere but his face, anywhere but his eyes. My gaze finally rested on his paint-smudged forearms.

"What do you want?" I asked. My voice came out colder than I expected.

"I need to talk to you," Daniel said.

"I . . . I can't." I placed my drawing on top of my supply bucket and shoved it under my table. "Come on, April. Let's go."

"Grace, please." Daniel held his hand out to me.

I flinched. His hands reminded me of the things he'd done to my brother. Would he have tried to do the same things to me if he'd known I was the one who turned his father in? "Go away." I took April's arm for strength.

"It's important," Daniel said.

I hesitated and let go of April.

"What, are you crazy?" she whispered. "You can't stay with him. People are already talking."

I stared at her. "Talking about what?"

April looked at her shoes.

"Hey, you girls coming?" Pete asked from the art-room doorway. Jude stood next to him, grinning at April. "We've gotta book if we want a booth."

"Coming," April said. She gave me a pointed look and then broke into a huge smile. "Hey, guys," she said as Jude wrapped his arm around her waist.

"You coming, Grace?" Pete held his hand out to me just like Daniel.

I looked at the three of them in the doorway. April tilted her head and gestured for me to come. Jude looked at me and then glanced at Daniel; his smile faded into a thin, tight line.

"Let's go, Gracie," Jude said.

"Please stay," Daniel said from behind me.

I couldn't bring myself to glance at him. All Jude had ever asked me to do was stay away from Daniel. I failed in that promise originally, but I had to keep it now. I couldn't talk to Daniel. I couldn't be with him.

I could not choose Daniel over my brother again.

"Leave me alone," I said. "Go somewhere else. You don't belong here."

I took Pete's outstretched hand. He locked his fingers around mine and pulled me to his side, but his touch didn't make me feel the way I did when I was close to Daniel.

AT THE CAFÉ

I was six bites into my veggie burger, Pete was on reason three of his "Five Ways Hockey Could Change the World" lecture, and April was squealing with delight because Jude had just given her a blueberry muffin with an invitation to the Christmas dance when it fully hit me: I told Daniel to get out of my life. I dropped my burger and ran for the restroom. I barely made it to one of the toilets before garlic and seaweed burned up my throat.

When I came out of the stall, Lynn Bishop was standing at the sink. She stared at her reflection in the mirror, her lips pursed but her eyes wide.

"Bad veggie burger," I mumbled, and stuck my hands under the faucet.

"Whatever." She chucked her paper towel into the trash and left.

CHAPTER TWENTY

Fears

After dinner, I locked myself in my room. Cramming for my retake chem exam had eaten up most of my time last week, and I was still struggling to keep up with my other classes. With finals looming, I knew I was in trouble. I'd tried to study with April and Jude after school, but April had still been so giddy about Jude asking her to the dance, I realized it would be more effective if I worked on my own. But after a few hours of history and calc and a little Ralph Waldo Emerson, my weary gaze kept drifting down from my textbooks to the drawer in my desk.

I took the key out of my music box and unlocked the drawer. I removed the book from the box, curled up in my comforter and pillows, and carefully turned to the second marked page.

A little bedtime reading couldn't hurt anyone, right?

Dear Katharine,

I am increasingly convinced that Alexius's stories of the Death Dogs are not mere myth. I wish to document as much as I can about this phenomenon.

Father Miguel says I am obsessed. But I fear he is the one with the obsession. He has persuaded large numbers of our campaign that they must punish the Greeks for their murder and betrayal. Even many of the Templars and Hospitalars are convinced by his inflammatory words. I find Alexius's stories a welcome distraction in all this plotting and persuasion.

Alexius took me to a blind prophet who taught me more on the subject. While some Urbat, as he called them, are born with the wolf essence, others are created when bitten by an existing Urbat—much like the spreading of some terrible plague.

It may be that an Urbat created through infection, rather than birth, is more susceptible to the influences of the wolf. The curse may progress much more swiftly in the infected party if he is not vigilant in controlling his emotions. . . .

Daniel hadn't mentioned that his wolf condition was contagious. I couldn't believe that I had actually wanted to be like him, and now it made my mind spin to realize that it was as simple as a bite from his teeth—almost as simple as a kiss.

I looked at my hands and couldn't help picturing

them covered in shaggy fur. My fingernails grew long into pointed claws that could rip flesh from bone. My mouth suddenly felt like it was full of razor-sharp teeth and long, tearing fangs. What would my face look like with a long snout and muzzle? What if my eyes turned black, with no inner glow—reflecting only the light around me?

What if I became a monster, too?

I shuddered and pressed my hands to my face. My skin was still smooth and hairless. I was still human.

I picked up the book, hoping to find solace—to find answers. But the letter stretched on for several more pages, and most of it documented how the Dogs of Death had come to exist—how their blessing became their curse. It confirmed what Daniel and my father had told me but didn't teach me anything new. I skimmed until I came to a portion that mentioned moonstones.

It is strange, dear Katharine, but the blind man says that the Urbat have much greater difficulty controlling the wolf possession during the night of the full moon. As if the moon itself has power over them. Because of this, I think there may be a way to manage these beasts. Perhaps if an Urbat were to keep a small piece of the moon close to his body, it would act as a counteragent to the effects of the larger moon, helping him keep the wolf at bay while still retaining its mythical strength. Much like how the ancient

Greeks treated disease with the idea that like cures like.

I have heard tales of rocks that fall in fiery glory from the heavens. What if some of these rocks have fallen from the moon itself? If I were able to fashion a necklace from one of these moonstones — if finding one was possible — perhaps I could help the Death Dogs reclaim their blessings.

However, such a necklace would be no cure. It would only offer control. I fear that these Urbat have lost their souls to the clutches of the wolf, and unless they are freed of it before they die, they will be doomed to the depths of hell as demons of the dark prince.

My eyes no longer felt weary. I hadn't thought of what might happen to Daniel if he died. Would he really be doomed to live in hell as a demon forever? No wonder he was so desperate to find a cure. It would be one thing to live with a monster inside—it was a whole other thing to be damned for all eternity.

I skimmed a few pages farther, looking for anything that might tell me more.

The only things powerful enough to deliver a mortal blow to an Urbat are the teeth or hands of another demon, or if he is punctured through the heart by an object of silver. It is believed that silver is poisonous to the beasts. . . .

I didn't want to think any more about death, so I turned to a new letter.

My Dear Katharine,

I wish to take an expedition into the forest. The blind man says he will find me guides who can get me close enough to observe a pack of Urbat without being discovered. The journey would cost twenty marks — all that I have.

Father Miguel says the winds are shifting in our favor. He thinks tomorrow the armada will be able to move in closer to the city walls. Perhaps the only good that might come from our forces taking the city is that I might be able to search the books of the great library for more texts on the subject of the Urbat. What jewels of knowledge must lie therein.

If not from the library, I must know more about these Hounds of Heaven. I will make preparations for the journey. My dear Alexius is reluctant to join me, but I will persuade him to go, for I need a translator. He seems to fear the Urbat more than any of the local boys. When pressed about the issue, all he utters is, "The wolf seeks to kill what he loves the most. . . ."

I dropped the book. It skittered across the hardwood floor. I leaned out of bed and gingerly picked it up. Little particles of yellowed paper sprinkled from the binding. I opened the book and found that the page I had just been reading and a few others had disintegrated under my absentminded handling. But my guilt for damaging the book was nothing compared to the other thought that crumpled my insides.

The wolf seeks to kill what he loves the most.

Did Daniel love me? He said I was special. He said I "did" things to him. He said he missed me—sort of. But he hadn't said he *loved* me.

But he'd kissed me like no one ever had. He made me want to tell him how I felt.

But I couldn't forget how he shook and the way his eyes glowed when I did. He'd lost his necklace momentarily, and he looked more frightened than I'd felt. Had I been in danger then? Had the wolf wanted to kill me? If Daniel didn't have that necklace, would I already be dead? Or would he have just turned me into a beast like him?

I put the book away. I could not handle any more questions—or answers—for a long time.

Chapter Twenty-one

Hopeless

AVOIDANCE

Trying to steer clear of Daniel became as difficult as running away from my own shadow.

Friday afternoon, he came into Brighton's Art Supplies while I was picking out a new set of hard pastels to replace the ones I'd broken the week before Thanksgiving. I waited until he was finished at the cash register and had gone before I took my box up to the front. When I pulled out my wallet, the girl behind the counter informed me that my "wicked hot friend" had already paid for the pastels.

"What if I don't want them anymore?"

She shrugged and snapped her gum.

I left the box on the counter.

"Are you sure?" she called after me like I was crazy.

"You can keep them."

On Saturday, he was at the parish repairing a broken

pew when I brought the bulletins from the copy shop to my father. I set them on his desk and left through the office door that led into the alley between the school and the parish.

Sunday morning, I saw him staring down at me from the balcony during Dad's sermon. And by Monday, I realized that running any errand seemed to put me in danger.

That afternoon, Dad sent me to Day's Market with a list of groceries. It was his turn to make dinner while Mom took a late shift at the clinic—something she'd been doing more of since Thanksgiving so she wouldn't have to leave James at day care.

I rounded the corner into the canned-goods aisle and literally bumped into Daniel as he crouched over a box of canned peas. He stood up and turned around. He wore a Day's Market apron and held a box cutter—the point of which was smeared with blood. He grimaced, and I noticed the back of his other hand was scraped with a long angry cut.

"Sorry," I mumbled, and tried to move around him.

He stepped in front of me and blocked my path. "Grace." The cut in his skin healed over as he put his hand on my grocery basket, stopping me from stepping away. "We need to talk—alone."

I looked at the bloody box cutter he held against his apron.

The wolf seeks to kill what he loves the most.

"I can't." I let go of my basket, backed away, and ran out of the market.

Dad didn't question why I came home without the ingredients for chicken-fried steak. He made mac and cheese instead. Don, James, and I were the only ones who joined him for dinner anyway. And I wasn't surprised at all when Dad asked Don how Daniel was working out at the market.

"Real great," Don said. "Mr. Day's been so stressed about Jess, he needs all the help he could get. Lucky Daniel needed a job."

Or convenient, I thought—but it was Jude's voice that echoed sarcastically in my head.

I pushed away my plate. Daniel had cared for Maryanne. She made him feel safe and loved. And now that she was gone, he had a comfortable place to live. Daniel had never met James, but he loved this family. "Saving" James had made Daniel a hero in my family's eyes, if only for a moment. Daniel and Jess had been in the same grade for many years. She'd lived in Oak Park while he was there with his mom. And then she had moved to the city and lived there until she disappeared. I knew all too well from Daniel's admissions that I was not the first girl in his life. People always described Jess as "troubled." Wasn't that the kind of person Daniel said he'd sought out for companionship? Was it possible that he could have ever loved Jessica Day?

All I knew was that she was missing, and Daniel

had a good job that let him fulfill the requirements for Barlow's class. Which meant he'd be able to stay in Rose Crest indefinitely.

Convenient. It was all too convenient.

But to what end? Were they random attacks on people he cared about? Or did they serve some purpose? Did they point in some direction?

Did they get him closer to . . . me?

Something deep down in my heart told me my doubts about Daniel had to be wrong. Dad had read those letters. He knew that Daniel's inner wolf would target the people he loved, and still, he kept Daniel here. He helped him get that apartment. He helped him get that job. He wouldn't do these things if he thought Daniel was hurting people, or if he would hurt me.

But the thing was, I'd thought the same thing about Jude's accusations. I'd thought that if Daniel had truly tried to kill my brother, Dad would never let him near our family. But I'd been wrong about that. He helped Daniel, fully knowing what he'd done—what he *was*.

Was Jude right? Did Daniel have Dad under some type of spell?

Or did Dad just know something that I didn't?

GETTING OUT OF THE HOUSE

I didn't know why, but I felt like I couldn't read the book of letters in my bedroom that night. Like the words that echoed off of them would be heard by everyone in the house. I drove to the library. It was almost closing time, but I settled into one of the scratchy orange couches, trying to push down the nerves that rumbled inside of me. I figured that if Dad really knew something that I didn't, then the answer was probably hidden in these letters.

My Sister,
   They have destroyed it. They have destroyed the great library!
   The knights and their footmen have sacked the city. They have looted and plundered the great treasures. They have set fire to the library, destroying all I wished to learn. They call the Greeks heathens, yet our Knights of Christ are the ones who rape the city.
   The smell of smoke and blood permeates my tent. I cannot abide it much longer. My vigor for a journey into the forest is renewed. I fear my writings of the true origins of the Urbat may be the only that exist after the destruction of the library. I must restore the documents of their secrets to atone for the sins of this campaign. Thou may think me foolish, yet I will not be deterred.
   God's love be with thee and Simon,
   Thy brother in blood and faith

Katharine—
   We are betrayed!
   I fear my Alexius is killed.

Our guides led us deep into the woods, and when it was close to nightfall, they took our horses and my twenty marks and left us stranded. Alexius was frightened when the howling encircled us. I do not know what has become of him. I do not recall how I made it back to my tent. My cloak is torn and bloody.

I fear I have been bitten. Something writhes inside of me. I must fight it. I must find the answers before the wolf devours my soul. Before it comes for thee, my most beloved . . .

Even though Daniel was a monster, even though he could infect me, I still loved him.

I wanted him to be innocent.

I wanted him to be mine.

But Dad had given me this book when I told him about that love.

He told me to find the answers for myself.

But is this what he wanted me to know? That Daniel was drawn to kill me like this man to his sister? Did he want me to realize that loving Daniel was impossible?

That any idea of our ever being together was completely hopeless?

Because if that was his plan . . . it had worked.

WEDNESDAY EVENING

Semester finals hit with a vengeance. I never did catch

up with my studies in time. I struggled to push Daniel, Death Dogs, moonstones, and Jessica Day out of my mind. But in my religion and history classes, all I could think of was the Crusades. During my chem final, I wondered if Katharine's brother was ever able to find a moonstone for a necklace. It was nearly impossible to work calculus problems while wondering if Jessica was living or dead. And it wasn't possible for me to paint anything knowing Daniel was watching me from the back of the art room. So not only was my love life in shambles, my chances for college—for Trenton— seemed just as hopeless as I turned in my jumbled English essay test on transcendental poetry.

At least it was the last day of school before Christmas vacation, and I'd have three weeks to recover before I had to face my parents with my report card. The dance was tomorrow, but tonight everyone was headed to the hockcy game to blow off steam. As much as I wanted to be at the ice rink eating candied almonds with April, cheering for Pete, I couldn't bring myself to celebrate like everyone else.

I'd told Pete I was too tired to go out when he invited me to the after-party at Brett Johnson's. He looked so disappointed that I added, "Have to rest up for the dance, you know." He smiled and told me that I "owed him one." But even though I said I'd be spending the night in bed, I couldn't stay home, either. I guess that's how I ended up helping my father with his Wednesday-night Bible-study class at the parish. I figured it would be the place I was least likely to run into Daniel.

I should have known better.

I helped Dad pass out study guides and extra Bibles and then busied myself in the parish kitchen. I arranged Mom's fudge brownies on a silver tray and placed a mini candy cane in each individual mug of hot chocolate. The brownies were for later, but I passed out the cocoa to the cherry-nosed guests as they listened to my father's melodic voice reading from the Bible. His voice sounded like a lullaby, and Don Mooney's eyes looked heavy as I handed him the last steaming mug.

"Thank you, Miss Grace." He blinked, and took a sip.

I sat in the empty chair next to him. I was surprised Dad wasn't reading the story of Christ's birth the way he usually did this close to Christmas. Instead of mangers, and shepherds, and angels, he was reading the different parables of Christ. I found my own eyes getting a bit heavy, too, until I heard the outside doors to the parish creak open. Footsteps came down the hall, and I regretted not making a couple of extra mugs of hot chocolate.

"Let us move on to the prodigal son," my father said.

I flipped the pages of my Bible to Luke 15, and right on cue, the door opened and Daniel slipped inside the classroom. He breathed on his hands as he looked around for a place to sit, and noticed me watching him. I looked down at the open Bible in my lap.

Dad's voice went on without pausing. He read the parable of the father who had two sons. One son was good and steady and hardworking; the other took his father's money and squandered it on whores and riotous living. The latter son's life sank so low he decided to return to his father to beg for help. My dad read on about how the father rejoiced when his prodigal son returned, fed and clothed him, and called their friends together for a celebration. But the good son, who had stayed faithful to his father's teachings, was angry and jealous of his brother, and refused to welcome him home.

When Dad finished the last verse, he asked, "Why was it so hard for the *good* son to forgive his brother?"

His change of tone startled the audience. A few people looked around, probably wondering if the question was supposed to be rhetorical.

"Mrs. Ludwig," Dad said to the elderly woman in the front row, "when your son stole and wrecked your car last winter, why was it so hard to forgive him?"

Mrs. Ludwig colored slightly. "Because he didn't deserve it. He didn't even say he was sorry. But the Bible"—she tapped her worn, monogrammed copy—"says that we must forgive."

"Exactly," Dad said. "We don't forgive people because they deserve it. We forgive them because they need it—because *we* need it. I'm sure you felt much better after forgiving your son."

Mrs. Ludwig pursed her lips and nodded.

My neck felt hot. I knew without looking, Daniel was staring at me.

"But *why* is it so hard to forgive?" Mrs. Connors asked.

Don blinked and snorted, snoring.

"Pride," Dad said. "This person has already wronged you in some way, and now *you* are the one who has to swallow your pride, give something up, in order to forgive him. In fact, the scriptures say that if you remain in your pride and choose not to forgive someone, then you are the one committing the greater sin. The *good* son in this story is actually in much graver danger than his prodigal brother."

"So should the prodigal be loved no matter what?" Daniel asked from his corner.

I shot up out of my chair. This was all just too much.

Dad gave me a quizzical glance.

"Brownies," I said.

There was a collective "mmmmmm" from the audience as I left the room. Dad's lesson was probably cut short when I came back with refreshments, but I didn't really care. I wanted to go home. I cleaned up the napkins and gathered the empty mugs while the others milled around, talking about jolly things like presents and carols. Once the room was tidied enough, I went to my father and asked if I could take off early.

"I don't feel well," I said. "I'd like to get to bed."

"Finals burnout?" Dad chuckled. "You deserve a good night's rest." He leaned over and traced the cross on my forehead. "I promised to drive a couple of the ladies back to Oak Park, so I can't send you with the car. I don't want you walking home alone, though." Dad looked to the back of the room. "Daniel," he called.

"No, Dad. That's stupid." I felt a surge of anger against my father. The cross he traced on my forehead seemed to burn my skin. Why was he making this so hard on me? "It's not even that far."

"You are not walking alone in the dark." Dad turned to Daniel as he came up to us. "Will you be so kind as to walk my daughter home?"

"Yes, Pastor."

It wasn't worth protesting, so I let Daniel walk me into the hall. As the classroom door clicked shut, I stepped away from his side. "That's far enough. I can make it the rest of the way myself."

"We need to talk," Daniel said.

"I can't talk to you anymore. Don't you know that?"

"Why?" he asked. "Give me one good reason, and I'll leave you alone."

"One good reason?!" Was this the same person who'd told me he was a werewolf? Was this the same person who admitted doing those terrible things to my brother?

"Try Jude for one." I threw my arms up and stomped toward the coatrack near the exit.

"Jude's not here," he said, and came after me.

"Stop, Daniel. Just stop." I looked down at my coat buttons. Why wouldn't they go into the right holes? "I can't talk to you, or be with you, or help you, because you scare me. Is that reason enough?"

"Grace?" He reached for one of my shaking hands.

I shoved them into my pockets. "Please let me go."

"Not until I tell you . . . You have to know." He wrapped both hands around his pendant, and said like it would solve every problem in the world, "I love you, Grace."

I stumbled back. His words felt like a knife in my heart. They were everything I desired to hear, and everything I hoped he'd never say. And they couldn't solve a thing. I stepped away farther; my back butted against the large oak doors of the parish. "Don't say that. You can't."

Daniel dropped his hands. "You really are afraid of me."

"Isn't that what you wanted?"

He bowed his head. "Gracie, let me fix what I've done. That's all I want. All I care about is you."

I wanted to be able to forgive Daniel. I really did. But even with everything Dad said, I didn't know how. It's not like I could just flip a switch and forget everything he'd done to my brother. It's not like I could change the fact that loving me meant that something inside of him wanted to kill me. But it's not like I could just stop loving him, either—couldn't stop the aching to kiss him, to be with him.

How could I go on seeing him like this every day? I knew I'd give in eventually—I'd lose everything.

I pushed on the door latch. "If you cared, then you'd leave."

"I told your father I'd walk you home."

"I meant for good, Daniel. You'd leave here for good."

"I won't let you walk alone."

"Then I'll call April or Pete Bradshaw," I said, even though I knew both of them were at the hockey game.

"I can take you," Don Mooney's voice boomed down the hall. He held a large fudge brownie in his fist, and there was a smudge of chocolate frosting on his chin. "I don't mind."

"That would be nice, Don." I pushed open the door. "Good-bye, Daniel."

Chapter Twenty-two
Alpha and Omega

WALKING HOME

I clung to Don's bearlike arm as I stumbled down the street. My breath created a thick, white fog around my face, and a migraine pressed behind my eyes—but that's not why I found it so difficult to see. I once would have never believed that I'd be happy to have him as my escort, but I silently thanked God that Don had been there to see me home.

I could tell he wanted to talk to me by the way he sputtered and sighed, as if trying to get up the courage to speak. We were almost to my front porch when he finally said something.

"Are you gonna come with us on deliveries tomorrow?"

"No." I wiped at my face, trying to hide the tears I used to be able to stop myself from crying. "The Christmas dance is tomorrow evening. I have a date."

"Oh, that's too bad." He kicked at the porch step. "I was hoping you would be there."

"Why?"

"I wanted you to see," he said. "I bought thirty-two Christmas hams to donate for the parish."

"Thirty-two!" Why did that make my tears come faster? "That must have cost a fortune."

"All my Christmas money and then some," he said. "I wanted to help the needy instead of buying presents this year."

"That's great." I smiled because I knew that Don himself technically fit into the "needy" category.

"I have something for you, though." Don dug into his pocket. "Pastor says I should wait till Christmas, but I want you to have it now. I hope it will make you feel better." He opened his giant fist and offered me a small wooden figurine.

"Thank you." I rubbed away the few tears that remained in my eyes and inspected the present. It was crudely carved, like what a child would make, but I could tell that it was an angel with flowing robes and feathered wings. "It's beautiful." It truly was.

"It's an angel like you."

I tried to hide a frown. The last thing I felt like was an angel after what I'd said to Daniel. "Did you make this with your knife?" I asked. "You didn't put it back, did you?"

Don looked around. "You still won't tell, will you? Promise you won't?"

"I promise."

"You are an angel." He hugged me around the middle, squeezing all the air out of my lungs. "I'd do anything for you," he said, and finally let go.

"You're a good man, Don." I tentatively patted him on the arm, afraid of another bear hug. "Thank you for walking me home. You didn't have to."

"Didn't want you going home with that boy." Don grimaced. "He's a mean one. He does bad stuff and calls me 'retard' when no one's around." Don's face flamed red in the lamplight of the porch. "He's not good enough to be with you." He lowered his voice and leaned in like he had a big secret. "Sometimes, I think he might be the monster."

Don's accusation surprised me—but not the monster part. It made it easier to reject Daniel when I thought of his taunting Don.

"I'm sorry he treats you that way. But don't worry, I won't be hanging around Daniel anymore." I tucked the angel figurine into my dress coat pocket.

"Not Daniel. He does good work for your father and Mr. Day." Don shook his head and slumped down the porch. He stopped at the end of the front walk. "I was talking about the other one."

I was rooting around in the pantry for some ibuprofen, or anything that might make my head stop pounding, when I heard a howl from the front room. I ran to see what it was and found Charity watching her wolf documentary. It was the same part from before, with the two wolves savoring a fresh kill. It seemed extra morbid to me now.

"Why are you still watching this?"

"My final report's due on Friday," Charity said. Her middle school didn't get out for Christmas for another two days. "I wanted to get in a wolfy mood before I finished typing it up."

Wolfy mood. She had no idea.

I stood and watched the plight of the little omega wolf, desperate for food but being denied. My heart sank as the alpha lunged at his throat, taking him down into the snow, and snarled into his pleading face. Then the little omega rolled over and exposed his belly and jugular to the alpha—giving up. I wondered how anyone could survive being treated that way his whole life.

I thought of Daniel and his father. The way his dad had screamed and snarled at him for any little thing. I remembered how, when Daniel joined my family for dinner, he would stare reluctantly at his food while the rest of us ate—until my dad, joking, would tell him to stop being shy. I remembered all of his bruises. I remembered what it sounded like when his father beat him into oblivion for disobeying his rules about painting in the house.

How had Daniel ever survived his father's monster?

But then I realized that he hadn't. He'd let the monster overpower him. The pain had been too great, and he had rolled over and given up, too. That he'd lasted so long was a miracle.

And now he faced a lifetime as a monster himself. And even if he died, there was no escape. He'd be damned as a demon for all eternity.

I'd wondered if that was the fate Daniel deserved. But it all seemed different now, like looking at a Seurat painting from a whole new angle. Daniel had done something undeniably wrong. But did he have to live with that mistake forever? Couldn't he be redeemed? Couldn't everyone? That's what Dad taught with every sermon. It's the meaning of my name. *Grace*.

Or was it possible that some souls could not be saved? Isn't that what demons are? Fallen angels—damned to hell forever. Was Daniel's giving in to the bloodlust such an irredeemable act that he was now one of these fallen angels, too? But perhaps he wasn't actually a demon. Maybe the demon was simply inside of him. Was the wolf trapping Daniel's soul in its clutches, in some kind of limbo, keeping him from salvation?

Daniel said it himself: the wolf was holding his soul ransom.

So didn't that mean there was a price that could be paid? Was there something that could be done to free his soul and make him just like the rest of us? So grace could have him instead of the darkness?

Dad had said that he couldn't help Daniel anymore. It was out of his hands. But he didn't say it wasn't possible. He didn't say there wasn't a cure. He'd given me the book. He'd put it in *my* hands. He'd told me I had a choice to make.

I ran up the stairs to my bedroom and pulled open my desk drawer—the book was gone. My heart hammered into my throat. I pushed things off my desk, hoping the book was in among my schoolwork. I threw the pillows and blankets off my bed. It had to be here somewhere! Then I felt ultimately stupid and grabbed my backpack. The book had been in there since I went to the library. I pulled it out, more brittle bits of pages sprinkling from the binding.

I carefully turned to the last letter I'd read. Half of it was missing—disintegrated in the hostile environment of my school bag. My dad and that priest were so going to kill me. I flipped to the second to last marked letter, one I hadn't read yet. Katharine's brother had come up with the idea of the moonstones. Had he found one in time to stop himself from going after his sister? Had he bought himself enough time to find the cure?

> Oh, Katharine,
>   I am lost.
>   The wolf has me in its clutches.

My fingers curled around the book. I wanted to throw it away, but I forced myself to read on.

> I smell the rage and the blood wafting from the city, and I feel drawn to it. What has repulsed me in the past now whets my appetite.
>
> The wolf preys on my love for thee. It tells me to return home. I am enclosing this letter with a silver dagger. If I come to thee as a wolf, I ask that Saint Moon try to kill me. I do not have the courage to dispatch myself. But Simon must not hesitate. He must thrust the dagger straight and true into the wolf's heart. It is the only way to keep thee safe. Saint Moon must protect our people from this curse.
>
> Oh, Katharine! I know I should not ask, but alas, I must. If thou hast the courage, then let it be thee who plunges the knife into my wolf's heart. For I have learned from the blind prophet that the only way to free my soul from the demon's clutches is to be killed by thee. My inner wolf seeks to destroy the one I love for reasons of self-preservation. For the only cure to free my soul is to be killed, in an act of true love, by the one who loves me most. . . .

And there it was—scrawled in faded brown ink across a yellowed page—the reason that everything had changed when I told Daniel I loved him. It was the thing Daniel said he could never ask. The reason he said all those awful things the way he had—the reason he'd tried to scare me away.

He'd known the truth that night under the walnut tree. My father must have told him that afternoon. It's why Daniel was so distraught. He feared that there was no cure for him because he thought no one could love him. But I think what he really feared was that *I* did.

I was the one.

And he could never ask me to kill him.

CHAPTER TWENTY-THREE

Truth

THIRTY MINUTES LATER

I sat with the book open in my lap until a small brown spider crawled across the brittle yellow pages. The spider paused for a moment and then climbed up onto the back of my hand. I didn't flinch. I didn't brush it away. Its tiny legs pricked my skin as I let it wind up my arm.

The spider perched on my shoulder—only inches from my face. I scooped it up and cupped it in my hand. It would only take a slight flexing of my fist to smash it.

I imagined it squished in my palm: all brown and gooey and warm.

I shuddered and opened my hand a bit. The spider tried to scurry out of my grasp. I cupped it again, blocking its escape.

Killing was wrong. Isn't that one of those basic

truths? *Thou shall not kill*, and all that commandment stuff. But that only pertained to people, right?

I thought of Mr. MacArthur and his spaniel's spring litter. I thought of Daisy, all runty with only three legs. She'd been so tiny, so helpless. Mr. MacArthur had wanted to put her down—for her own good. That had seemed so wrong to me. But maybe he was right. Maybe she would have been better off going out that way. Better than being ripped to pieces by my next-door neighbor. By the Markham Street Monster.

But then she wouldn't have been *my* Daisy.

The spider twitched inside my hand. Wasn't it okay to kill a pest? To kill something dangerous? A beast? A monster? That was the real difference here, wasn't it? Daniel had a demon inside of him. And the only way to kill the monster was to kill him. It was the only way to save his soul.

But would I be the one who went to hell instead?

Would I lose myself?

I shook my head. Katharine's brother wouldn't have asked his sister to do such a thing if that were the case. He wouldn't trade her soul for his.

At least, I wouldn't think.

I walked to the window and pushed it open with one hand. I pulled out the loose screen, climbed through the window, and crouched on the eave of the roof in the bitter night wind.

The spider was restless in my hand, twitching and

fluttering its legs against my skin. I felt a sudden sting in the middle of my palm. My fingers flinched inward. I *wanted* to smash it. But then I hesitated and opened my hand and dropped the spider. I watched it scuttle across the shingles and out of my reach.

A small red lump rose in the middle of my hand. The stinging was only slight compared to what I felt inside. I loved Daniel. I was probably the only person who had ever loved him so much. And that made me the only person who could save him. But what he needed me to do was impossible. I'd lived without him before, and I thought I was prepared to do it again when I told him to leave town.

But how could I let him *die*? How could I be the one who killed him?

I looked up at the almost-full moon that hung over the walnut tree. Through my blurry eyes, it seemed too bright and strangely colored—a blood-red moon. I wished on it then like I had when I was kid. I wished this responsibility could pass to someone else. I wished for another way. I wished for a world free of darkness.

But I knew those wishes couldn't come true. So I wished for something different.

I wished for time.

Chapter Twenty-four

Always

As terrible as the truth was, there was something restful about it. Like knowing the answers finally calmed my brain enough for me to sleep peacefully for the first time in weeks. I woke up to a rustling sound. I assumed it was the wind and rolled over on my blanketless bed and saw the book lying open next to me. I wondered why, if the clock said it was only 2:00 a.m., it was so light out. I got out of bed and pulled my blinds open. The sun glinted off the walnut tree, and I realized it was afternoon.

Something rested inside my windowsill—a white cardboard box, like something you'd put a present in. My name was written across the top. I picked it up and was surprised by its weight. I backed away from the window and pulled off the lid. There was a note on top of a large paper-wrapped bundle. I recognized the handwriting from my childhood.

Gracie,

You are right. If I love you, then I should leave. I have already caused so much damage to your family. Staying only puts you all in greater danger. I do love you, so I will go.

But I wanted you to see that I've been trying to make things right. I didn't just come here to ruin your life. Will you please give this to your father? If I tried to give it to him in person, he wouldn't take it. I wanted it to be the full amount. I wanted to fulfill my obligation. But it would be wrong to stay until I had it all. I've kept only a small amount to buy supplies. I'll send more when I earn it.

Please tell Jude that I am gone. Tell him I will never return—for his sake, and yours.

I'll love you always,
Daniel

I dropped the note and unwrapped the bundle. It was stacks of bills—thousands of dollars to replace the money he'd stolen from the parish. This was Daniel's mysterious "obligation."

How long must it have taken him to earn it back?

But more important, how long had this been in my room? Was Daniel gone already?

I ran down the stairs to Dad's study, hoping he would know where Daniel might go. The room was empty. I realized that even though I didn't have school, it was still a weekday. I bounded to the kitchen, where Mom was paying bills at the table.

"Where's Dad?" I practically shouted. "Is he at the parish?"

Mom raised her eyebrows. "He and Don went out to the shelter."

"What? I thought that was tonight."

"Don got called for an extra shift at the market tonight. He didn't want to miss delivering his hams, so Dad took him early."

"When did they leave?"

"Ten minutes ago."

Urrgghh! I wouldn't be able to reach him for at least another twenty minutes. "Would it kill us to buy a couple of cell phones?!" I shouted, and threw up my hands.

"Grace!" Mom dropped her checkbook.

"Seriously. Life would be so much easier." I grabbed the minivan keys off the hook and went to the garage door.

"I need to pick up Charity from school," she called. But I didn't stop.

I drove in the direction of Oak Park. Too bad I didn't have a superhuman sense of smell—I could just follow Daniel's scent. I was halfway to Maryanne Duke's when something told me he wouldn't still be at his apartment. I flipped an illegal U-turn and headed toward Main Street. He said he needed supplies. Maybe he'd be at the market.

I parked the van behind a motorcycle in the lot. Was that the same bike we rode into the city that night? If so, it meant Daniel was planning on taking off to somewhere far away—far enough that he wouldn't just run on his own two feet. Far enough that I wouldn't be able to find him.

I ran into the store, passed several kids from my school picking up their dance flowers at the floral counter, and went straight up to Mr. Day at the cash register.

"Have you seen Daniel?" I asked, interrupting Lynn Bishop, who was purchasing a red rose boutonniere and bottle of hairspray.

Mr. Day looked up from the register. "He just quit, dear. I think he's headed out of town."

I swore—not quite under my breath.

Mr. Day cleared his throat. "He may still be in the back. I asked him to—"

But I was already headed for the door marked EMPLOYEES ONLY. No one was in the back room, but I noticed a door that led out to the parking lot. I bolted outside just in time to see a helmeted driver cruise by on the motorcycle.

"Daniel!" I shrieked, but my voice was nothing against the roar of the engine as the bike sped away. "Don't leave."

The world closed in on me, spinning. I had no more breath in my chest. My knees felt soft. I wished for something to grab on to—to keep me from falling.

But then I was being pulled up instead of sinking to the pavement. Strong arms wrapped around me. Warm breath tangled with my hair.

"Don't leave," I said.

"I'm here, Grace," he said. "I'm here."

A FEW MINUTES LATER

Daniel held me until I could breathe again. The only thing obscuring us from the full view of everyone on Main was a stinking Dumpster, but I didn't care. I wrapped my arms around his neck and kissed him.

He kissed me back. His lips firm but yielding, hard yet soft. He was holding back—keeping me safe.

I cupped my hand over the warm stone pendant of his necklace, holding it tight against the nape of his neck as I looked him straight in his dark brown eyes and said, "I love you."

Daniel's hands pressed against the small of my back, pulling me hard against his body. He kissed me deep and strong. My knees melted softer than before.

He pulled back slightly, his eyebrows furrowed. "Do you know what that means?"

"Yes. It means I'm the one who can cure you."

He pulled away. "No, Grace. I'll never ask you to do that. I can't possibly ask you to kill . . ." He shook his head. "And it's too dangerous."

"I don't care. I'll do it."

"Grace, we're not talking about a little prick with a knife and a little blood on your end. You'd have to *kill* me."

"Don't act like I haven't thought this through."

"Have you, Grace? Do you realize it's not just me you'd have to kill? The letter said to plunge the knife into the *wolf's* heart. I'd have to be in full wolf form, and that would be too dangerous for you. I'd rather go to hell than ask you to do that."

I stepped back for a second, creating a gap between us. I hadn't thought *that* through. I hadn't even considered any physical dangers on my end—staring down a werewolf that knew I wanted to kill it.

I stepped closer to him again. "You won't have to ask." I took his hand in mine. "I'd do anything to save you."

"Anything?"

"Yes."

"I won't let you. I can't. . . ."

"Then why did you stay? Why didn't you leave as soon as you knew what the cure was?"

"Because . . ."

"Because this is what you really want. You hoped I'd come to realize that this is what you need."

All this time, I'd been trying to fix Daniel—save him—but you can't save someone unless he wants to be saved. I understood that now. Like I understood a lot of things.

I squeezed his hand. "If this is what you want, then let me do it for you."

Daniel looked up at the sky and scratched behind his ear. "You really are one of a kind. I mean, it's not every day my girlfriend offers to kill me."

"Girlfriend?"

That wry grin slid across his face. "That's the part you question? Man, I *should* leave town before I really screw you up."

"You can't go anywhere."

"Right, 'cause we've got to go find a nice quiet place where I can turn into a werewolf, and you can run a knife through my heart."

"Don't say it that way."

Daniel looked down at our entwined hands. "And it doesn't bother you? You'd be perfectly fine with ending my life?" His voice became bitter. "You'd go on with *your* life as normal? Keep dating guys like Pete, go to Trenton without me, become some famous artist and never give me a second thought. You'd be fine with all that?"

"Yes," I said.

He pulled out of my grasp.

"I mean, no . . . I mean, of course it bothers me. It will bother me when the time comes. But the rest of it doesn't have to be like that. You can do all those things with me—not the date Pete part, of course. But it's not like I need to kill you right now. We can—"

"You don't understand." He wouldn't look at me. "I either need to die, or I need to leave—today. Before tonight. Before I cause any more damage . . ."

I brushed my hand down his cheek.

He flinched away.

"You didn't hurt those people," I said. "Maryanne, James, Jessica Day. It wasn't you, right?"

Daniel fingered his necklace. "No. It wasn't me."

"You've got that moonstone necklace. You can live a . . . seminormal life. You can even use your abilities to help people if you want. We don't have to do it today. Eventually, yes . . . but not right now." Putting it off, not really having to face the reality of it all, was the only thing keeping me sane. "That's why you can't leave me. We need to stick together so I'll be there when it needs to be done. Just give me more time, and then I'll free your soul before you die."

"Grace, I wish it were that simple. Time is exactly what we don't have. We can't put this off indefinitely. There's more than one person out there who wants me dead. And if anyone other than you kills me . . ."

"Who? Who wants you dead?" I felt like I could wring that person's neck with my own bare hands—moral consequences be damned.

"My father, for one." Daniel's eyes were wide like a frightened child.

"Is he here? Is he back? Is he the one who—?"

"No," Daniel said. "Last I heard, he was in South

America somewhere. I'd know if he were anywhere close."

"Then why are you so worried? We can deal with all of this when the time comes. All I'm asking for is more time. Can't we just *live* for today?"

Daniel sighed, sounding resigned. He pulled me into his arms and leaned my head against his chest. I listened to his two heartbeats thrumming under his skin. The slower pulse seemed closer to my ear, the faster one fluttering behind it.

"Is your human heart in front of the wolf's heart?" I asked.

Daniel made a noise like he was surprised that I'd noticed the fact that he had more than one heart. "Yes, but only when I'm in human form. When I'm the wolf, then its heart takes the dominant position. But it's always with me—part of me."

That must be why I needed to stab him while he was in wolf form—to guarantee that the wolf's heart took the brunt of the blow.

"What did the letter mean when it said 'In an act of true love'?" I asked. If I was going to do this—kill him—someday, I wanted to make sure I understood exactly how to do it right. "The letter said the cure would only work if you were killed 'in an act of true love' by the person who loved you most."

"I think it means the intent has to be pure," Daniel said into my hair. "Not something done out of fear or hate or coercion. It has to be an act of pure, unwavering love."

"No fear." I pictured myself alone with a monstrous wolf. Was that something I was capable of? I'd have to be. "Just love," I said, and buried those other thoughts.

"Yes," Daniel snorted. "True love's first kill."

He held me tight against him. The parking lot had emptied and filled with a new set of cars by the time he let me go. He brushed his hands through my hair and kissed my forehead.

"You can so do better than that." I stretched up on my toes for a real kiss.

Daniel turned his head away. "What about your brother?"

"I don't want to kiss *him*," I said, and pecked my lips along Daniel's jaw.

"He's here, you know." Daniel swallowed air. "I can taste him."

"Okay, let's put that on our 'Top Ten Things Not to Say While Making Out' list. Supersenses are cool and all, but kinda not romantic. Besides, Jude's probably just picking up April's corsage for the dance. . . . Oh, crap."

Daniel stiffened. "What is it?"

"I'm supposed to go to the dance with Pete tonight. We're sharing a car with April and Jude."

"No." Daniel let go of me. "You can't go out tonight. You have to cancel."

"You know I can't do that. Pete's probably already spent a ton of money. He's a nice guy. I can't just bail—"

"Pete's not as nice as you think," Daniel grumbled.

I laughed. "Are you jealous? Pete's just a friend—"

Daniel grabbed me by the hips. "Of course I'm jealous, Gracie. You just told me that you love me but you are going out with another guy. But this is more important than my jealousy. If I'm staying here, then you have to stay in. I've got enough to keep my eye on. I can't have you out there. Not *tonight*."

"What's with tonight?"

He looked down. "The full moon."

"The full moon?" I looked at the little crescent carved in his necklace. "You're afraid of the—"

"Even with this moonstone necklace, the wolf is hard to control under the light of the full moon. It's when the wolf has the most draw on the emotions." He bit his lip. "I try my hardest to never go into wolf form. Even though I can control my actions now, it scares me to give the wolf that much leeway. I've only gone wolf twice since I've been back. The last was when I was looking for James. The moon was waning, so I felt safer letting the wolf have a little freedom. But the first time . . . it was the last full moon. That time scared me. I'd turned and was miles from my place on Markham before I realized it." Daniel looked at me. "Do you remember the last full moon?"

"No." Where had the last month gone?

"It was the day I first saw you again." Daniel dropped his hands from my hips, but he didn't step away. "Your dad had asked me to stay away from you and Jude until we figured things out, but I couldn't. I think he knew I wouldn't be able to, either; he was just doing the fatherly thing." Daniel studied the back of his hands. "I've always *liked* you, Grace. I don't know if you knew that?"

My heart fluttered. "Really?"

"Ever since the day you marched home with that three-legged runt of a puppy, I knew that there was no one else quite like you. Gabriel told me to find someone who loved me—and I hoped if there was anyone in this world who could, it would be you.

"So when I saw your name in that art class, I was so curious. . . . I remembered you as this spunky, unbelievably caring, totally bossy *kid*, and I couldn't help teasing you a bit. But then when I looked at you and saw how beautiful and amazing and strong you had become—it was like something woke up inside of me."

He stepped back now. As if he needed to put distance between us. "I'd never felt that way before. I didn't know I was capable of feeling that way . . . but the wolf felt it, too. And when the full moon came out, it told me to go find you. It told me I *couldn't* stay away. I even tried locking myself in my room, but that didn't work. Like I said, I was almost to your house before I came to my senses. I had more control, but I still couldn't leave—not until I saw you again."

I gasped. "I saw you. You were that dog, that *wolf*, that sat under the walnut tree. The one that was watching me."

I don't know why that surprised me—that I'd seen him as a wolf. I guess I'd pictured some kind of grotesque mix of man and beast. But that dog had been beautiful, large—larger, I realized now, than any dog I'd ever seen before—and sleek, majestic. Like the sculpture of the wolf with Gabriel in the Garden of Angels.

"So you're afraid that now that you know—and the wolf knows—that I'm the *one*, the wolf will come for me?" I smiled, trying to lighten the mood. "At least I know I'll have one free night to myself a month."

"Three," Daniel said. "You'll have three nights to worry about."

"Huh?"

"The moon is technically full for three nights. I came looking for you on the third night of the last full moon. Tonight is the first of this month."

"Three nights to myself then? All the better, I guess. New relationships can be so time-consuming." I shrugged and tried to laugh.

Daniel didn't. "I wish making you lonely was the only thing I had to worry about. If I'm staying here, if we're going to be together, then I have other things to take care of tonight. That's why you need to stay in. Please, Gracie. Don't go to the dance, or dinner, or anywhere with Pete and your group. I can't be distracted tonight. I need you to be safe."

"I can't just cancel."

"I've never been more serious, Grace. Please, do this for me." He engulfed me in his arms, pressing me to him with such urgency. "Promise me you'll stay out of harm's way." He kissed me then like he had under the walnut tree—like his life depended on it.

"Okay," I said, and sank into his arms.

CHAPTER TWENTY-FIVE
The Other One

BEFORE THE DANCE

What is it about promises? They should just be out-lawed. *Seriously, I'm going to hell for this one*, I thought as April slipped one last bobby pin into my upswept hair.

"You look amazing," she said.

I'd tried to keep my promise to Daniel. I really did. I'd called April first thing when I got home. I thought I could soften the blow on Pete if I convinced her to call him for me and tell him I had the chicken pox or something equally contagious. But no, that had been a mistake.

"Don't do this to me!" April yelped over the line. I could hear the din of the Apple Valley Mall behind her. She'd just left Nails 18 and was fumbling with the phone, trying not to ruin her manicure. "I will never forgive you," she said, more than half meaning it. "Do you have any idea what this means to me? You will ruin my entire life if you don't go."

April's used-to-be-absent mother was keeping her on a tighter and tighter leash as more and more days passed without the police finding Jessica Day. She would only let Jude come over for "studying," and she'd agreed to the dance only if April shared a car with Pete and me. April was to go straight to dinner, then to the dance, and then back home, with absolutely no unplanned stops in between.

"But I'm sick. I can't go."

"No, you're not. You just told me that was your excuse for Pete."

Crap.

"Please, please, please. You have to do this for me. I'll just *die* if I don't go to the dance with Jude."

I laughed. "Well, if it's a life-and-death situation . . ."

"Thank you, Grace. You will never regret this!"

I really hoped I wouldn't.

It was just dinner, the dance, with no unplanned stops in between. Daniel wouldn't know I wasn't locked up in my room for the night. He wouldn't be distracted. I wouldn't be in danger.

Seriously, why did I never learn?

April strategically situated a lone, curling tendril down the side of my cheek. "Pete is going to flip when he sees you."

I hope not, I thought, but smiled and thanked her anyway.

April had almost gagged when she came over early and saw the hairspray-mates-with-mousse mess I'd made out of my hair. I don't know why my hands shook so much—it's not like I was nervous for my date with Pete.

"You look like a 1980s beauty queen," she'd said, and sat me back down at the bathroom vanity.

"Isn't that look *in* this year?"

I could see April roll her eyes in the mirror as she set to work fixing the disaster. And I have to admit that I ended up looking pretty darn good. It was a good thing the guys were totally late, or I would have looked scary instead.

I stood up and inspected myself in the full-length mirror. Sometime during finals, April had dragged me to a dress boutique in Apple Valley. I hadn't been in the right frame of mind for shopping, so I'd let April pick out my dress—and I'd bought it without even trying it on. But I have to say: once again, she'd done a stellar job. I loved the way the white satin dress felt against my skin, and I loved even more the way it looked with my violet eyes and flawlessly coifed dark hair. The tight, sculpted bodice actually made it look like I had breasts, but my favorite parts were the pop of color in the purple sash around the middle that made my waist appear impossibly small, and the quick coat of matching purpley toenail polish that April had picked up for me at the mall.

I did a girly little twirl in front of the mirror. Too bad

Daniel wasn't the one who was going to see me in this.

The only thing I wasn't sure about were the thin spaghetti straps. Mom was pretty strict about sleeves when it came to my clothing. She'd been so busy with her late shifts at the clinic that she hadn't even asked to see my dress after I bought it.

I brushed my bare shoulders and shivered.

"Don't worry," April said. "I brought a wrap for you. I just strategically left it downstairs so you wouldn't have to put it on until after Pete sees you."

"I don't know if that's such a good idea—"

The doorbell rang.

"Showtime." April plumped her pink lips that matched the shade of her rosy pink dress. She took my hand and led me to the staircase where we could make our "grand entrance."

Jude, who had agreed to get ready over at Pete's house so April and I could get ready here, looked sullen but dashingly brooding in his black suit. He held a pink five-rose corsage for April. Pete, in a navy-blue blazer and tan dress pants, put his fingers in his lips and let out a long whistle of approval when he saw us.

My bare shoulders felt warm and itchy. I could see the stern look on my mother's face.

"Tell me you have a wrap," she said as Pete greeted me with a peck on the cheek.

"It's in the front room with my purse," April said.

When Mom went to get it, Pete leaned in slipped a

corsage of pale purple roses on my wrist. "Don't you look *divine*," he whispered in my ear, and then he kissed me on the cheek again, so low it was almost my neck. He smelled of an extra dose of spicy deodorant and something strangely sweet that I couldn't place.

I stepped away from him and let my mom securely wrap the length of purple chiffon around my shoulders.

"Be glad your father isn't back yet, young lady," Mom said in my ear. "Or you wouldn't be going out at all."

Part of me wished he was here then. I felt *wrong* for being on this date—and not just because of my broken promise. I wasn't the slightest bit uncomfortable when *Daniel* kissed me like that, but Pete was different. There was this look in his eye that made me shiver as he watched me while Mom snapped pictures of us—it was the same look I noticed him wear when I played street hockey with the guys in the cul-de-sac, like he was determined to win no matter what.

We paraded out the door. Pete squeezed me to his side and waved good-bye to my mom. I was glad we were all going together in the Corolla.

"Wow, is that really the time?" I said when I noticed the clock in the dash. "Are we going to make it to the dance after dinner?" It was almost seven, and the guys had chosen a restaurant in the business district of the city. Our group would be nearly done eating by the time we got there. The prospect of being out late made my broken promise seem even worse.

"Yeah," April said. "You guys are way late."

"I'm starving," I groaned, trying to cover my real reason for being concerned about the time.

"Don't blame me," Pete said. "Jude here suddenly forgot how to get home from the florist or something. It took him three hours to pick up your corsages."

April stared at Jude. He didn't say anything in his defense. I didn't complain anymore. I just hoped he wouldn't stay in his shell all night.

Pete draped his arm across my back.

Goose bumps ran up my arms even though it was a surprisingly warm evening. The air was still, and it wasn't even cold enough to need a coat—the weatherman called today the "warm before the storm," and I knew our annual white-Christmas blizzard was just around the corner. Despite the unseasonable warmth, Jude had the heaters blasting, and I kept my shawl around my shoulders and held it closed in front of my chest.

Maybe it was Jude's sullenness, April's sudden silence, Pete's occasional sidelong glances, or the light of the full moon shining through the windows that made the air in the car seem too thick, too solid. My arms pricked with nervousness, my heart beat too fast—like I was anxiously waiting for something to happen.

I was glad for the fresh air when we got out of the car. I wanted to linger in the lot, but the others hurried off to join our group. I breathed in the night, letting it wash over me until I saw something move in the moonlit shadows beyond the restaurant's marquee. I didn't wait to see what it was and dashed inside the restaurant.

My anxiety grew as dinner went on. Before I joined the group, Pete had ordered me a steak, medium rare, even though Jude could have told him I liked my steak cooked so well done it was practically burned.

"It just felt like a red-meat kind of night," Pete said with a wink and a "triple threat" smile. He turned that smile on our waitress, whom he then tried to coax into bringing him a glass of wine.

But when she gave him a "nice try, buddy" grin and suggested she bring him another Coke, he called her something quite unfavorable under his breath.

I blinked at him, not sure if I'd heard right.

"Don't worry, man," Brett Johnson said from beside Lynn Bishop, "I've got you covered." Brett passed a waded cloth napkin down to Pete.

Pete smiled with approval when he unwrapped a golden flask.

As he poured what seemed like half the bottle's contents into his Coke, I found myself wondering how well I knew Pete. He'd been my lab partner and study buddy since August, and Jude had been friends with him for a couple of years—a fact that usually gave a guy automatic approval in my mind. But Daniel had tried more than once to tell me Pete wasn't as nice as he seemed, and Don hadn't wanted a certain boy to walk me home. Someone he called "the other one." Hadn't I mentioned

Pete's name before Don offered to walk with me?

Pete offered me the acrid-smelling flask.

I waved it away.

Pete just shrugged.

But Lynn Bishop made a snarky-sounding snort. "Figures," she said.

I was about to ask her what her problem was when Pete passed the flask to Jude—and instead of waving it away like I expected, Jude drizzled a bit over his Sprite. It took every ounce of self-control not to shout at him in front of his friends. I didn't want to ruin the night for April. Good thing she'd gone off to the bathroom with a pack of girls so she wouldn't know what Jude had done.

The others had finished with dessert by the time our appetizers came—except for Brett and Lynn, who'd shown up as late as we had. The ones who were done said their good-byes, promising to wait for the rest of us before they did group pictures, and left. Pete talked louder and louder as the meal went on. He swung his arms, smacking me in the shoulder as he recounted the previous night's hockey game with gruesome detail. Although Jude had the same alcoholic beverage in his drink, he didn't relax the way Pete did. He seemed to get stiffer and harder like a statue with every sip.

After paying his bill, Jude got up and headed toward the back of the restaurant. I got up to follow him.

Pete grabbed my arm. He trailed his hand up to my

elbow. "Don't be long, angel." He bared his teeth in a huge, hungry grin.

Sometimes I think he might be the monster, Don's voice whispered inside my head.

I shook it off. That was completely crazy. Pete was proving to be a jerk, but not a monster. But Daniel had been afraid of something—something that might happen tonight during the full moon—when he didn't want me out with Pete. . . .

I almost laughed in spite of my nerves. What were the odds that two werewolves had the hots for me? Like I was some gigantic monster magnet. Was there a sign on my back that said, BITE ME, I'M AVAILABLE!? I gave myself another shake and told Pete I'd be back in a minute.

His eyes didn't flash when he looked at me. He didn't seem crazed by any wolf. Anything that burned inside of him was purely testosterone-based.

The hall toward the restrooms was dimly lit, and I could hear angry voices at the end of it. Actually, one of the voices sounded irritated and very distinctly like my brother's, but the other was softer, cowering, and definitely female. I quickened my pace to see what was going on and found Jude with Lynn Bishop backed into a corner. He was practically shouting, waving his finger in front of her face.

"If you have a problem with Grace," he said, "then you come to me first before you start spreading your venom around school."

Lynn nodded, speechless for once.

My hands went into fists. "If she has a problem with me, then she should come to *me* first."

Jude turned. His stance softened. "It's okay, Grace. I'm taking care of this. Go back to your date."

I put my hands on my hips. "What gives you the right to 'take care' of things for me? I can 'take care' of myself."

"Well, you're doing a terrible job of it yourself."

"What is that supposed to mean?" I asked. I watched Lynn slink away, no doubt wanting to text our conversation to everyone she knew from a safe distance. "You know what? Never mind." I swung my purse over my shoulder and turned to walk away.

"You don't want to know what she said about you?" Jude called after me. "You don't want to know what the entire school is talking about behind your back?"

I turned. "No, I don't. At least not from you—not right now—because I'm pretty sure this has something to do with Daniel. And no matter what I say, you won't believe it because you made up your mind about him a long time ago, didn't you?" I pursed my lips. "You keep pretending everything will be fine if *I* stay away from him, but it won't be until you deal with all this hate yourself."

"You're siding with him? Maybe the rumors are true."

"And so what if they are? I love Daniel. I tried not

to for your sake. But I can't stop loving someone just because you can't forgive him." I lowered my voice. My lips trembled. "You think you're the good one, but Dad says the *good* son is the one who's in the greatest danger."

Jude stumbled like I'd punched him in the gut. My nerve failed, and I ran into the ladies' room before he could say anything back.

IN THE CAR

I stayed in the bathroom until April came to collect me. She seemed more concerned than mad, and I was glad she didn't tell me that I'd ruined her night—I felt guilty enough already. We piled into the Corolla. I insisted on driving, and Jude relented without a fight. We headed back to Rose Crest for the dance, even though it was the last place I felt like going. All I wanted now was to curl up in bed and wait for the full moon to be swallowed by the day—and I could be with Daniel again.

No one spoke as we drove, except for Pete, who yammered on and on about being overcharged for his drink refills—not exactly the concerns of someone fighting an inner demon. I tried to forget any thoughts of monsters and wolves and focused on surviving the torturous evening ahead of me. At least we were going to get to the dance at the tail end, and then we could go straight home.

But as I turned down Main Street on our way to the school, I saw a line of police cars in front of Day's Market. Their blue and red lights cast sinister shadows on the green awnings of the shop.

"Those are cops from the city," April said. She stuck her head out the window like an anxious pup. "I wonder what's going on."

I pulled the car over in front of Brighton's, across the street and kitty-corner to Day's. It was as close as we could get. A uniformed officer was stringing a line of police tape across the entrance to the market's parking lot, and a few bystanders had gathered to gawk. Word must not have gotten out yet, or half the town would be here.

"There's Don." I pointed at him.

He wrung his Day's Market apron in his giant hands as he spoke to a dark-haired man in a suit. The man patted Don on the shoulder and then went inside the shop.

"Where's Mr. Day?" April asked.

Where's Daniel? He'd told me he was going to finish up a late-afternoon shift since Mr. Day had promised him time and half if he wouldn't quit before Christmas. But he'd said he wanted to be done by nightfall. He'd be gone by now—but to where, I couldn't guess.

Is this what he had been worried about? Is this what he'd wanted to prevent? Did my going out cause this to happen?

I pulled the keys out of the ignition.

Pete grabbed my hand. "Let's just go to the dance. We'll miss the whole thing if we stop."

"Yeah," April said. "Maybe we should just go." Her voice had a high, doglike whine to it. "I told my mom I wouldn't stop anywhere else."

I opened the door and got out. "Don!"

He looked up. His face was distorted by shadows. He crossed the street and as he came closer, I saw that his eyes were puffy and blotched with red. "Miss Grace?" He came up to the car. "You shouldn't be here. It isn't safe."

"What's going on?" I lowered my voice, hoping the others wouldn't hear.

Don looked back at the market. "He was here."

"Who was here?" Jude asked, suddenly beside me.

April got out of the car and stood behind him.

"The monster." Don groaned. "The Markham Street Monster. He . . . he . . ." Don wrung his already crumpled apron.

"What is it, Don?" I put my hand on his arm. "You can tell me. It'll be okay."

"He killed her."

"Who?" Jude asked.

"Jessica," Don sobbed. "I was taking out the trash . . . and I found her body. She was behind the Dumpster."

I covered a gasp. *Where is Daniel?* Did he know a body had been found right next to where we'd been kissing only a few hours before?

"And you're sure it was Jessica?" Jude asked.

Don nodded. "Her face was so clawed up, I wouldn't have known it was her if it weren't for her hair. When the cops came by to tell Mr. Day she was missin'—they'd said she had green hair."

"Green hair?" That girl! The one who rammed into me at the party. The one with all the piercings, and the huge eyes, and the green hair. No wonder it seemed like I knew her from somewhere. "Oh, my . . . I saw her . . . I saw her the night she disappeared."

"Where?" April asked.

"At Da—" I stopped when I saw Jude staring at me. "Just somewhere in the city."

"At Daniel's?" Jude grabbed my arm. "She was at Daniel's apartment on Markham Street. She was at that filthy party."

"What? How did you know—?"

"Then it's true?" Jude twisted my wrist. "She was there, wasn't she?"

"Yes," I said. "But Daniel didn't have anything to do with this. He told me—"

"He told you? And you just believed him?" Jude sank his fingers into my arm like they were teeth. "Of course you do. You'd believe anything he said."

"Stop this now," I tried to say to him like my father would, but Jude's fingers only bit harder.

"I don't understand," Pete said from the other side of the car. "You think Kalbi did this?"

"It wasn't Daniel," Don said. He lowered his voice as if he wanted to say something only to me, but his whisper was an echoing shout. "It was the monster, Miss Grace." He glanced over my head at Pete. "The monster was the one who took James, too. Your dad and I stopped at the police station in the city. Your dad asked for the blood-test results—but they said they didn't have none. They said they couldn't even figure out if the blood was from a human or an animal. It had to be the monster."

"You see." Jude's hand trembled. He dropped my arm. "You see. This is him."

"No," I said. "It can't be. There must be someone else."

Jude reeled on me and grabbed me by both shoulders. "Where is he?"

"Jude, stop," I said quietly, all too aware of the cops across the street.

"Calm down, you guys." April yanked at Jude's arms, but he didn't budge.

"Where is Daniel?" Jude clenched my shoulders through my chiffon wrap and shook me.

"I don't know," I said. "I don't."

Jude let go. He backed away to the driver's side of the car.

How did he get the car keys?

"Jude, stop. This is insane. You've been drinking." I looked at Don for help, but he cowered away into the street.

"Please," April yelped.

"Hey." Pete stepped in front of Jude. "If you think this is Kalbi, then go tell the cops."

"No," Jude said. "They can't stop him."

"Then what are you going to do?"

"I'm going to find him."

"Then I'm coming with you." Pete opened one of the back doors.

"No!" I tried to grab the keys, but Jude shoved me away.

"Hey," someone called from the police line. "What's going on over there?"

Jude jumped into the driver's seat. As he gunned the engine I scrambled into the backseat next to Pete.

"Hey, stop!" someone shouted.

But Jude shifted the car into drive, and we went flying down Main Street, leaving April and Don behind.

We didn't go far. Jude floored it a couple of blocks and then skidded down Crescent Street. We flew past the high school, and just when I thought we were going to pass it, Jude whipped the car around and into the crowded lot. He drove up and down the parking lot, searching between every car.

"Turn the car around, Jude," I said softly. "Let's go home and talk to Dad. He can help."

Jude pulled the car to a stop in the alley between the parish and the school. He opened his door and got out.

"What are you doing?" Pete asked.

"He's here," Jude said. "I know he is." He stood still for a moment, as if listening. All I could hear was the echo of the music in the gym.

"Jude, please, listen to reason." I started to get out of the car.

"Stop her!" Jude said.

Pete grabbed my arm.

"Keep her here. Do whatever it takes." Jude took a couple of steps into the alley.

A police siren whirred past the school and continued on down Crescent.

"What are you going to do?" I asked.

"I'm finishing this." Jude turned toward me. And that's when I saw it: his eyes, once mirror images of mine, were twin tornadoes. Black, silver, sharp, twisted—glinting with the light of the full moon.

Human eyes don't glow in the dark. Only animal eyes do.

"No." I gasped. I tried to pry myself from Pete's viselike hands.

"I'm going to find Daniel and finish this," Jude said.

And then he was gone.

Chapter Twenty-six
Hero

IN THE ALLEY

"Let me go!" I pushed against Pete's chest. I had to find Daniel before Jude did.

This was what he'd been afraid would happen tonight!

"Please, Pete. You have to let me go."

"So you can warn Kalbi?" Pete didn't look me in the eyes. "Why can't you just stay away from him?"

"I have to stop Jude. I have to stop this from happening. I'd do the same if he was after you."

Pete looked up at me, but he didn't loosen his grasp. "Relax, Grace. This is Jude you're talking about. He's just going to find out what's going on."

"He isn't *Jude* anymore," I said. "Can't you see that?"

Pete shook his head, confused.

"You have no idea what this is about, do you?" I

asked. "You're in danger. We're all in danger. You have to let me go."

Pete's grasp weakened. I pulled away from him and grabbed the door handle. He snatched at me, but all he got was a fistful of my satin shawl. It trailed behind me like a purple banner as I jutted out of the car and down the alley. Pete bolted after me.

I stumbled in my heels and almost fell in a pothole. Pete grabbed me by the shoulder and swung me around.

"I'm trying to save you!" He slammed me against the outside wall of the parish. "Jude told me to keep you away from Kalbi. But you make it impossible. Why won't you stay away from him?"

"Stop, please." I tried to shove him away, but he was heavy and unmovable.

"I'm supposed to be your hero," he said. "*I* was supposed to save you on Markham Street."

"What?" But then I realized. "You were the one outside my car." No wonder he'd insisted I stay behind. "You tried to scare me just so you could *play* hero?"

"Jude said we had to keep you away from Daniel. He said all you needed was a good scare. The car broke down, so I used the opportunity." Pete clenched my shoulder. "I would have been your hero if . . ."

That noise. It was a howl. It was Daniel. "If something hadn't scared you away?"

"I ran," Pete said. "And then Kalbi came along

before I got back." His fingers dug into my shoulder. "You're supposed to want me, not him!" Pete pressed his body against mine, grinding my bare back into the rough brick. His hot breath was a vile mixture of breath mints and alcohol.

"You're drunk, Pete. You don't really want to do this."

"You owe me this," he said. "I've wanted this for a long time. But you told me to be patient—so I was. And then you went off and did it with *him*."

"What—?"

"Don't deny it. Everybody knows. Lynn saw you leaving his place. She saw him follow you out half naked." Pete gritted his teeth. "So if you'll give it up for that piece of filth, then what's wrong with me? Am I not dark enough? Am I not bad enough for you?" His body crushed me against the wall. "I *can* be if that's what you want."

Pete smashed his lips over my mouth. The strap of my dress snapped in his clawing grasp. I slammed my fists into his back. He grabbed my arms and pinned them against the wall. I grated the heel of my shoe down his leg.

Pete wrenched back his head. "I knew you'd like it rough."

I sucked in a breath and called for help. Pete laughed and smothered my mouth with his. I felt completely trapped under his weight.

Pete's body suddenly lurched sideways, and he

released me. He sputtered and grabbed his side. His lips made a perfect *O* shape as his hand came up. Blood painted his fingers. He stumbled back. "Monstrrrr . . ." he said, and fell to the ground.

"Oh, my . . ." I cast about in the dark and saw it—a great, hulking, bearlike thing—crouching in the shadows of the school's side entrance. Moonlight reflected off the bloody knife in its giant hand.

I screamed. It was such a shrill, foreign noise I didn't realize it was coming from me at first. But I couldn't stop.

The hulking shadow lunged at me.

I turned to run, but I tripped over something lying in the street.

The bear man caught me, crushing me around the middle as it wrenched me up away from Pete's crumpled body. The beast held my back to its chest, its ragged breath in my ear. I kicked at its tree-stump legs. I screamed louder, even though I knew no one in the school would hear me over the thumping music. A huge hand clamped over my face, covering my mouth and nose—silencing me.

"Don't scream." His voice was trilling, almost crying. He was afraid. "Please don't scream, Miss Grace." He wasn't a monster at all.

"Don?" I tried to say, but his hand pressed so hard over my mouth, no sound came out.

"I didn't mean it. He was hurting you. I thought he

was the monster. I had to stop him. I'm supposed to be a hero just like my granddaddy taught me." Don's knife scraped my arm as he held me. It was sticky and wet with Pete's blood. "But he's not the monster, is he?" Don's voice grew shriller. "He's . . . just a boy." His hand tightened over my face. "I didn't mean to do it."

I couldn't breathe. I tried to tell him to let go, but I had no voice. I clawed at his hand.

"You can't scream, Miss Grace. You can't tell nobody. Pastor will be mad. He'll send me away like he almost did after the fire. I didn't mean it. I was trying to help."

Blood dripped off the knife—it slithered down my arm.

"You can't tell nobody!" Don bawled. A hot tear landed on my shoulder.

Stop! You're hurting me. I can't breathe!

"I didn't mean it. I didn't mean it," Don cried over and over again. His hand tightened around my face as he sobbed, almost as if he didn't realize I was there anymore.

I blinked, fighting the long wispy fingers of darkness that slipped in behind my eyes. My body felt limp, uncontrollable. I couldn't fight the dark any longer.

THREE YEARS AGO

I stared into the still, quiet darkness from the front-room window. Watching. Waiting.

Mom paced behind me. "I don't know where he could be," she said, more to herself than to anyone else. "The Nagamatsus said he left Scouts two hours ago."

Dad said good-bye to the person on the phone and came out of the study.

"Who was it?" Mom practically sprang on him. "What did they say?"

"Don," Dad said. "There's a problem at the parish."

Mom's breath caught. "Jude?"

"No. Something with the remodeling."

"This late?"

The keys jangled as Dad took them off the hook. "I'll be back soon."

"But what about Jude?"

Dad sighed. "He's a good kid. If he isn't home by the time I get back, *then* we'll start to worry."

Mom made a noise like she didn't agree with that plan.

My gaze didn't leave the blackness of the night. The storm clouds parted, and I thought I saw something moving near the walnut tree. I leaned into the window.

"Jude," I said. "I see him."

"Thank goodness," Mom said, but her voice had that edge to it like she was preparing a lecture.

"You could always get him a cell. . . ." I started in on my favorite topic, but then I noticed that Jude wasn't walking toward the house from the side yard—he was stumbling.

And why was his face smeared with chocolate syrup?

Jude grabbed the porch railing. His legs folded under him, and he crumpled onto the porch steps.

"Jude!" I ran to the front door, but Dad was already there.

"No, Gracie," Mom shouted.

I couldn't see over their bodies that filled the doorway. "What happened?" I tried to squeeze between them.

"Da—" I heard Jude sputter. He coughed like he was choking. "Dan—"

Dad pushed me back. "Get away, Gracie."

"But—"

"Go to your room!"

And suddenly I was being pushed up the stairs. I couldn't see anything beyond my mother's body and her shoving hands.

"Room, now. Stay there."

I ran to my bedroom and pushed up the blinds. I couldn't see the porch or anything that was going on with Jude. But something else caught my eye. It was something white yet shadowed in the full moon's glow, crouching under the walnut tree, watching what I couldn't see on the porch. I squinted, trying to make out what it was, but it receded into the shadows and vanished.

"I'm sorry," the darkness whispered, cutting off the forgotten memory in my head. It was one of those phantom voices from so long ago. It was too far away and I tried to reach for it, but something bound me tight—I couldn't remember what.

"I'm sorry, Don," the phantom said.

The voice was followed by a *thump*, a metallic *clink*, and half a gasp. The bands that held me fell away, and I felt the rushing of wind, then hardness under my back, and warmth pressing over my lips.

Sweet air filled my mouth, my lungs. The misty darkness retreated from my brain. My eyelids felt heavy as I forced them open.

Daniel stared back at me, his eyes black with anger.

"You didn't stay home," he growled.

I coughed and tried to push myself up off of what felt like a table. But my head was as big as a semitruck, so I rolled on my side instead to look at him. He seemed more afraid than angry.

"You didn't tell me you bit my brother," I replied.

A FEW MINUTES LATER

"Is Don okay?" I rubbed the sides of my sore jaw as I lay on an art-room table. The pulsing of the music from the gym mingled with the pounding inside my head.

Daniel paced in front of the window behind Barlow's desk. He hadn't looked at me since I'd asked about my brother. "I only knocked him out. He'll be fine soon."

"*Only* knocked him out?" I said. "And what about Pete? Did he look dead to you?"

"Pete?" Daniel looked back at me. "Pete wasn't there."

"Oh. That's good, I guess." Pete may have run off and left me to fend for myself, but I was still glad he wasn't dead. I fingered the broken strap of my dress. Bruises formed under my skin. "Pete attacked me. . . . He did this to me."

Daniel's hands locked into fists. "I thought I could smell him all over you." His eyes went blacker than before. "Good thing he wasn't there, I would have—"

"Don beat you to it. Stabbed him in the side with his silver knife. He thought Pete was the monster and kind of lost it when he realized what he'd done."

Daniel nodded like the scene he'd come upon finally clicked. "I sensed more anguish in him than malice."

I sat up. Little flashes of light swam in front of my eyes. "Why didn't you tell me my brother is the monster?"

Daniel turned to the window. "Because I wasn't sure myself. I don't remember biting him. I tried to deny that I could have done anything like that until the day James went missing. That was Jude's blood on the porch—but it didn't smell normal, his scent was confused."

"Because he's a werewolf?"

Daniel gazed out the window at the full moon hanging

over the parish next door. He brushed his moonstone pendant. "He's not a werewolf. Not yet anyway."

"But he hurt those people. That was him, wasn't it? Wouldn't that turn him into a full-blown werewolf? A predatory act?"

"Not if they were already dead when he found them. Maryanne froze to death. Jessica must have died from something else—overdose, maybe. He must have mutilated their bodies somehow, making it look like a wolf attack. Violence against common animals doesn't count. That cat that turned up dead was just for show. And he didn't intend to kill James. He just wanted to scare people."

"But how could *he* do those things? How could he take Baby James? Didn't he know James could have gotten hurt or worse? James would have died if it weren't for you."

"It was the wolf, Grace. The wolf hasn't taken him completely over yet, but it has enough control to influence his actions. It feeds off his emotions. The stronger the emotion, the more hold it has. Each time he did something was after we were together. . . ."

"He knew that you fixed my car on Markham," I said. "And somehow he knew I was at that party at your place. He knew that Jess was there, too. Do you think he followed me, followed my scent?" I rubbed my eyes—they still didn't want to focus quite right.

"Jess was so wasted," I went on. "Maybe he found

340

her. Maybe the wolf made him do something to her body and then he planted it somewhere, but no one found it." My stomach churned when I pictured my brother with her mutilated corpse. "And he was at the market today. He must have seen us together, and with all those rumors Lynn was spreading . . . Pete said it took Jude three hours to pick up the corsages." My throat closed in an involuntary gag. "Do you think he went to the city to retrieve the body—to plant it where you work?"

Daniel nodded. "Here's the crazy thing, Grace. He probably doesn't remember doing any of those things. He's probably only aware that he's been losing minutes, even hours of his life. But he doesn't know what he's done. He really believes *I'm* the monster."

"And he thinks he has to stop you."

Daniel stiffened. He stared far out the window. After a moment, I heard it, too: police sirens blaring toward the school.

"Jude wants to kill you," I said.

Daniel backed away from the window. "Then the police are the least of our worries."

"We have to find Jude." I swung my legs over the side of the table. "He's here looking for you. We need to go find him first." I felt stronger now so I tried to stand.

Daniel pushed me down. "*We* aren't going anywhere. You are staying here while I go look for Jude."

"Like hell I am." I got right back up. "Stop telling me what to do."

"Grace, this isn't a game. Just stay here."

"But what if he finds me first?" I asked, trying a new tactic. "What if he goes home? Charity's babysitting James. They have no idea what's happening to Jude. What if he tries to hurt them, too?"

Daniel rubbed his hand across his face. "So what do you think we should do?"

"Take me with you. We have to find Jude. We have to get him away from all these people. If he sees us together, then we can lead him away from here." Then what, I had no idea. "Maybe I can calm him down. If only we had another moonstone." I looked at his pendant. "Could you . . . ?"

"No, Grace. Not tonight. Not under the full moon. I don't know if I could control it—not with you even in the same county." He gripped the pendant between his fingers. "I might destroy everyone."

"Then there has to be another way."

Multiple sirens blared into the parking lot. There was more than the sheriff and deputy on their way. The city police from the crime scene must be coming, too.

"We need a plan," Daniel said.

Car doors slammed outside the window.

"There's no time." I grabbed his hand, and we ran out of the room.

The echoes of our footsteps were lost in the music as we got closer to the gym. The dance seemed like the most logical place to start looking for Jude. I didn't know who had called the police—Pete? Don?—or who exactly they'd be looking for; all I knew is once they entered the dance, we'd lose our chance to get Jude away from everyone else.

Daniel pushed open the gym doors. Red and green streamers reached across the room in a zigzag pattern. Balloons bobbled in the air. A strobe light bounced off the dancers, who twirled and swayed to the music— completely oblivious to what was going on. How we'd be able to pick out one person in this din seemed impossible.

We slipped inside the gym, and I hugged Daniel to me, linking my arms around his neck so it looked like we were dancing, quite intimately.

Daniel stared down at me. He raised one eyebrow.

"My dress is a mess."

Daniel, clad in jeans and a white shirt, stood out enough in a room full of suits and slacks, but we definitely wouldn't be able to search for my brother incognito if anyone noticed my bruises or Pete's blood smeared across my white dress.

Daniel wrapped his arms around my waist. And for a fleeting moment, I felt safe to be in his strong embrace— like it was a promise that everything would turn out the way it should.

Daniel rested his chin on my shoulder. I heard him inhale deeply, holding the breath in the back of his throat, mulling it for tastes. The room wafted with so much sweat and perfume, could he really pick out one person's scent? Daniel lifted me off my feet and twirled us toward the center of the crowd. His movements were lithe and graceful, navigating us through the other dancers without disturbing anyone. For a second I forgot to breathe—forgot why we were even here.

"There," Daniel whispered into my ear.

I followed his gaze. I could see the top of a dark, disheveled head moving beyond the wall of dancers, following Daniel and me as we glided across the room toward the locker-room doors.

"We just need to keep him following us," Daniel said. "Get him out of here before—"

The music stopped and the lights flipped on. We halted as the crowd came to a standstill.

"May I have your attention?" Principle Conway said from a microphone near the DJ. "Please, stay where you are. Stay calm. There's been a crime near the school. The police are locking us down until they have the situation under control. No one will be allowed to leave. . . ."

Cries of concern went up in the crowd as uniformed officers moved toward all the exits. Someone shouted and stumbled, as if she'd been knocked aside. Her cry was followed by the clanking of one of the metal exit doors as it swung open and shut. Three officers ran to the door, shouting. The dark head that had been following us was no longer in the crowd.

Daniel cursed. "That was an outside exit."

He looked at the door to the men's locker room. The guard there was distracted by the commotion. Daniel swept me up in his arms. He flew at the door and knocked the officer flat before he even knew we were there. Daniel whipped the door open and lunged into the locker room.

"Stop!" someone shouted behind us. "Freeze!"

Daniel jumped on top of a bench. He grabbed an open locker door, used it to launch us up on top of the row of lockers, slid across, and landed on a bench on the other side. He bolted down its length, and jumped to an exit that led us into a long corridor. He ran, holding me to his chest. Shouts filled the corridor behind us, and then ahead of us around the corner. I heard the buzzing of police radio static. Daniel skidded into a stairwell entrance and lunged up the stairs. Up and up we went until we made it to a heavy-looking door marked ROOF ACCESS. Daniel kicked it, the lock crunched, and we burst through the doorway into the night.

Daniel took in a deep breath. The air had chilled since I was last outside. Clouds smothered the moonlight. A storm was coming.

Voices echoed way down in the stairwell. Daniel hitched me up in his arms.

"What are we going to do?"

"Hang on!" He squeezed me tight and sprinted toward the edge of the roof—running at his full speed toward open air. Before I could cry out, he jumped off the edge, sailed over the alley where Don had stabbed Pete, and landed with a thud on the parish roof. Daniel wrapped his arms around me, protecting me as we rolled on impact across the sloping roof. He scrambled to his feet and pulled me with him up and over the apex of the roof. We crouched behind the steeple.

I started to speak.

Daniel held up his hand. He waited, listening. "They think we doubled back," he whispered.

"You can hear them?"

Daniel gave me a *duh* kind of look. He listened for another moment. "They've lost Jude, too. Someone saw him running toward Day's. They're sending a squad car back there."

"Or is he heading home?" My heart pounded so hard I thought it might burst. "We have to find a phone. We have to call them. My dad calmed Jude before . . . maybe . . . I don't even know if Dad's home yet. I haven't seen him all day."

"He's not home." Daniel ducked back, pulling me with him. A second later, an officer walked through the alley below us. "He's probably somewhere over Pennsylvania by now," he whispered.

I stared at Daniel.

"Your father is on an airplane." Daniel stood when the officer was out of sight. "You were right. We do need another moonstone. Your father is trying to get one."

"From where?"

"From Gabriel. Your father tried to contact him after Thanksgiving, but the colony doesn't exactly welcome intrusions from the outside world. They don't own cell phones or anything like that."

"Welcome to the club," I mumbled.

"Your dad sent several letters, but there was no reply. When he got those blood-test results, he took the first flight he could get."

"So my father knows about Jude?" That made sense. "Why didn't he tell me? Why didn't he tell Jude?"

"He wanted to wait until we had another moonstone. He thought if Jude knew what was happening, he would only change faster. Your father came to see me before my shift ended at the market. He asked me to keep an eye on things while he was gone." Daniel bowed his head. "That was a mistake. I should have been the one to leave."

I grabbed his hand. *Here* was exactly where I needed him to be. "Jude might be headed home. Charity and James are in danger, and if Dad's not here, then I don't know what—"

"We can run there."

"No. If I'm wrong, we could lead him right to them." I slumped my shoulders. "I don't know what the right thing to do is. I don't know where we go from here."

"Jude's scent is in the air. It's more confused, though. I can't tell where he is. I don't know if he's just been here or if he's nearby." He squeezed my hand. "There's a phone in your dad's office. We can call Charity. Tell her to get to a neighbor's house or something. Maybe we can call the airport, too. Leave a message for your father as soon as he lands."

The clouds parted slightly, and a sliver of moonlight shone down on us. Daniel inspected the scrapes across my knuckles. I was scraped all over from tumbling across the wood roof shingles. His eyes glinted too bright as he kissed my wounded hand.

He shuddered and backed away against the base of the steeple. He held his moonstone against the hollow of his neck. "Just give me a minute," he said softly, and closed his shimmering eyes. "It'll be okay."

"That's what you think," a voice snarled behind me.

CHAPTER TWENTY-SEVEN

Fall from Grace

SECONDS LATER

"I knew you were here." Jude teetered on the apex of the roof. He walked across it like it was a balance beam, closing the distance between us. "I don't know how. I just did." His eyes seemed so black yet bright in the dim moonlight. "Kind of a fortuitous place to end this, don't you think? It's like God led me here."

"*God* isn't what led you here," Daniel said. "Think about it, Jude. Think about what you taste and smell. Think about what you feel writhing inside of you."

Jude laughed. "God led me to this, too." He pulled something from behind him. It was Don's knife, still stained with blood. "It was just lying in the alley, waiting for me." He turned it in his hand and watched the moon glint off its tip. "Do you know what this is made of? It's silver. It's what can kill you."

"Jude, please." I moved in front of Daniel, balancing

myself with the base of the steeple. "Please stop."

Jude looked at me, stumbled, and almost fell. He took in the sight of my bruises, my torn and bloody dress, and his hard expression crumpled into a look of concern. "Gracie, what happened?" His voice was soft and childlike. He took a step toward me, his hand held out. "Gracie, what's going on?" He sounded so frightened, so confused.

"Jude?" I reached for him.

Daniel grabbed my shoulder. "Don't."

My fingertips brushed Jude's. "I'm here," I said, and took his hand.

Jude's eyes shot with silver light. He wrenched me out of his way and flew at Daniel.

I fell against the shingles. I steadied myself and looked up just as Jude grabbed the front of Daniel's shirt.

"What did you do to my sister?!" Jude roared into Daniel's face.

Daniel bowed his head.

"Nothing," I said. "Daniel did nothing."

"Don't lie for him." Jude's body heaved with heavy breaths, but he kept the knife at his side like he was afraid to lift it.

"*Pete* did this to me . . . because you told him to do whatever it takes."

"What?" Jude turned slightly. "No . . . that's a lie. He's confusing you. He's getting you to lie for him even though he hurts you. The Bible warns about people like him—ungodly men who feast on your charity and turn grace into lust. That's what he's done to you, and I'm the only one who can see it. He's a monster."

"No," I said. "You're not a saint, Jude. You're the monster here."

Jude shook his head. "How can you defend him? How can you love him? You know what he did." He shifted closer to Daniel. "You left me," he said to him. "You were my best friend. You were my brother—and you left me there to die!"

Daniel's head bowed lower, resigned.

"No, he didn't," I said. "I saw him."

Daniel glanced up. The moon was bright in his eyes, and it illuminated his pale skin. I imagined it setting off his once white-blond hair like it did when he crouched under the walnut tree in my memory of three years ago.

"I saw you that night," I said to Daniel. "You brought Jude home."

Daniel opened his mouth a bit. He closed his eyes and breathed out a tiny sigh. "I did?"

"Yes."

Daniel looked up at the night sky. "Oh, God," he whispered, like it was a prayer of thanks.

Jude stepped back. He loosened his grip on the knife.

"Jude," I said. "It's okay. Daniel helped you get home—"

"No!" Jude clenched the dagger. "No more lies! He's a monster, not my savior. He hurt Maryanne. He killed that girl. He tried to steal James. He's defiled you. I have to stop him before he destroys our entire family." He lifted the knife.

"*You* hurt those people," Daniel said. "You did it. And if you don't stop right now, then you'll turn into the wolf just like me."

"Shut up!" Jude smacked him across the face with the butt of the knife, leaving a long, burnlike welt on Daniel's cheek.

Daniel grunted. "I will not fight you."

"Then you'll die like a coward."

Jude tried to yank him forward by the front of his shirt, but all that came with him was the leather strap of Daniel's necklace—and the moonstone.

Daniel stumbled back. He wrapped his arms around the steeple. A deep rumbling echoed from his body, making him quake. He looked up at the moon and then to Jude.

My brother held the moonstone, looking momentarily stunned.

"Put it on," Daniel said to Jude. "Put it on now . . . before . . ." He grunted and licked his lips.

"Daniel." I crawled toward him. "Daniel, you need it. . . ."

Daniel shook his head. "I need to do this," he said through gritted teeth. He looked at Jude. "I'm sorry.

I'm sorry I did this to you." His face twisted with pain. The rumbling behind his voice got deeper. "Take it, Jude. You need it more than I do."

Jude startled. He clutched the leather strap tighter in his fist and pulled the necklace closer to him. "Is it important to you?"

Daniel panted. "Yes."

"Good." Jude wrenched his hand back and pitched the necklace as far as he could—to somewhere in the void beyond the parish roof.

"No!" I shrieked.

Daniel howled.

Jude grabbed him by the throat. He raised the knife and plunged it at Daniel's heart. But then he screamed and dropped the knife like it seared his hand. It slipped down the roof and stopped in front of me. Jude lurched back. He fell onto all fours. His body shook and rumbled. He howled with pain.

Daniel picked up the knife and pulled me into his arms. He ran to the edge of the roof and jumped. We landed on the fire escape a few feet below. Daniel rammed the door with his shoulder and pushed me inside the balcony of the sanctuary. He followed and slammed the door closed behind him. He slumped down against it, sat on the floor, and dropped the knife. His hand was red and blistered like he'd held a hot iron in his fist.

"Are you okay?"

He grimaced, closing his eyes, concentrating. He looked down at his wound. It was only slightly less red and just as blistered. "That knife must be very old." He nodded to the blade that sat at his side. "It's much purer silver than what I've come across before."

"There's a first-aid kit in my dad's office." It felt like a lame thing to offer, but I didn't know what else to do.

"Go," he said. "Lock yourself in the office. Call the police, whoever."

"I won't leave you."

"Please." He slowly stood, still panting. "This isn't over." His eyes reflected everything he feared.

I turned to go.

"I'll love you always," he said.

"I lo—"

Out of the corner of my eye I saw Daniel jut forward. The door behind him burst open, pushing him out of the way. A massive silver-gray wolf filled the doorway. It growled and snapped and lunged at me.

"No!" Daniel tried to grab its hindquarters.

He missed, and the wolf sank its teeth into my arm, piercing my skin. I fell, knocked my head on the side of a pew, and bit my tongue. The wolf stood over me, snapping and growling like the alpha in that movie. My blood dripped from its teeth. It reared back, about to lunge for my throat.

Then it squealed, and another wolf was on top of it. It was black and sleek, with a diamond patch of white fur across its sternum. *Daniel.* The black wolf snapped and nipped at the other—almost like it was trying not to truly hurt it.

The gray wolf bucked the black one off. Its eyes looked positively feral as it sprang at the black one, biting and tearing. It ripped at its legs, its sides. The black wolf rolled away, yelping and whining. Its white patch of fur was slashed with red. The gray wolf licked its teeth. Black fur fell from its mouth.

I could taste my own blood. It slipped down my dry throat. The wound in my arm pulsed and flamed. It took everything I had to choke back my screams. The gray wolf slinked toward me, its teeth bared, its eyes hungry.

The knife was just out of reach, next to what looked like scraps of Daniel's clothes on the floor near the door. I scrambled for the dagger, but the gray wolf chomped down on my foot, wrenching off my shoe. The wolf shook it in its massive jaws until the shoe snapped and fell to the floor. The wolf snarled and bore down on me.

The black wolf pushed itself up. It growled, its lips pulled back from its long sharp fangs and jagged teeth, and crept toward me. I stretched for the knife and wrapped my fingers around the hilt. The two wolves circled around me. Their eyes locked on each other like they were partners in some horrible dance—and I was caught in the middle. Spit rained on my skin as they snapped and snarled. The heat of their collective breath made it impossible for me to think. Their claws scraped my legs. They danced, weaving back and forth, anticipating each other's attacks. Then the gray one feigned to the left, and when the black one countered, the gray wolf lunged over me. It ensnared the black one by the throat and knocked it to the ground. The two rolled across the floor.

They slammed into the balcony's railing, which overlooked the rest of the chapel. The old wood creaked with the impact. The black wolf lay on its back under the gray one's feet. It whimpered. The sound was pained. Desperate. Afraid.

It knew it was going to lose.

The hilt of the knife slipped in my sweaty hand. I'd told Daniel I would be there when he needed me. I'd be there to save him before he died. I'd free his soul. But I'd thought that would be years away. Not today.

Not now.

Pain seared from the gash in my arm—like fire spreading through my entire body—engulfing me. This was no ordinary wound. It was the bite of a werewolf, the bite of my brother. I was infected.

I carried the wolf curse now.

The same curse that dictated that if I ever tried to kill someone—if I killed Daniel now—the wolf would take me over, too.

I would lose myself.

The choice is yours to make, my father had told me.

But he had no idea what an impossible choice it would be. I could save Daniel's soul or preserve my own. I could be his angel and become a demon.

The black wolf's chest sank. It lay so limp. The gray wolf backed up across the balcony, readying itself to deal the ultimate killing blow.

I could not break this promise.

I am grace.

I flew at the black wolf, raised the knife, and plunged it into the diamond patch of fur on his chest.

I will be the monster for you.

The gray wolf came barreling right behind me. It rammed its head at the black wolf's body, and the two crashed through the balcony railing. A gruesome smacking noise echoed through the empty sanctuary below.

"No!" I ran down the ancient stairs and tripped at the bottom. My knees slammed into the stone tile of the chapel floor. I scrambled on hands and knees to the prostrate body of the black wolf—to Daniel. I laid his furry head in my lap, and stroked behind his ears. They felt too cold. The knife was still stuck in his chest. Blood spattered the floor all around us.

Where's Jude?

My gaze followed a smear of blood across the stone floor. Jude—human, naked—stood trembling behind the altar in the shadows of the sanctuary.

"Don't just stand there," I shouted at him. "Go for help."

But he didn't move. He stood like a pillar of salt in the dark.

I couldn't leave Daniel. I told him I'd be there when he died. I slid down on the floor and lay next to his furry body.

Why didn't he turn human? Did I fail? Did I hesitate too long? Was I too late to save his soul before . . . ? Did I trade myself for nothing?

A cold wind blew over me. Snowflakes encircled us. One landed on the wolf's nose and melted. *When did it start to snow?* I thought as I laid my head on Daniel's bloodstained chest. I listened to a solitary heartbeat grow softer and softer until it was nothing, and waited for my wolf to come—to take me over for what I'd done.

CHAPTER TWENTY-EIGHT

Redemption

IN THE SANCTUARY

I heard a yelp from somewhere beside me. I looked up and saw April quavering in her pink dress in the open chapel doors. The snow blew in from behind her.

"What hap—?"

"Don't ask questions." I sat up. "Please, just go call an ambulance."

I looked at the Daniel wolf. It lay too still, lifeless. The silver knife protruded from his chest. Maybe I didn't ram it in hard enough? Maybe I didn't pierce his heart? Or maybe I needed to take it out. The book had said silver was poison.

I tentatively wrapped my hand around the hilt. It didn't burn my skin.

"What on earth are you doing?" April asked, still in the doorway.

"Go. Please get help."

I gripped the knife tighter, and pulled with all my might. The blade slid out with a sickening sucking sound. Blood spurted from the wound, spreading across his chest, staining the white patch of his fur. But then, instead of flowing out, the blood stopped. It curled, rolling back into the wound. The puncture matted over in scabs, then healed into white flesh.

White skin that matched the rest of his body—his human body. Daniel was with me now, not some furry beast. He lay on his side in a fetal huddle like he'd just been reborn. His naked body was ripped and bloody in several places, including his neck. But he was human, mortal. I'd saved his soul before he died. And that's all I thought mattered . . . until he coughed.

"Grace," he rasped.

I slid my hand down his arm and entwined my fingers with his. "I'm here," I said. "I'm here."

"Um . . ." April said with more than a hint of shock. "I think I'll go for help now."

Moonlight spilled in from the doorway when she moved, casting its ghostly paleness onto Daniel. His hair looked almost white.

"Daniel, I'm so sorry." I cupped his face in my hands. "But you better the hell not die on me!"

His wry smile slid across his face. He opened his eyes. They were dark as mud pies and more familiar than ever. "Bossy as ever," he said. He coughed and closed his eyes again.

"I'll love you always," I whispered. I kissed him on his cold lips and held his hand until I heard the sirens, and someone pulled me away from him.

LIFE AS I KNOW IT

It snowed for seven days straight. After the first day, the police released Jude and me into my parents' custody. They couldn't find any witnesses who could ID us as the ones who ran from the school. And since none of us seemed to "remember" what exactly had happened, all they could determine within any sort of reason was that we had been attacked by a pack of wild dogs—the same elusive pack they were blaming for what happened to Maryanne and Jessica—and had run into the parish for safety.

Daniel's wounds were consistent with a wolf attack— no one could explain the no-clothing part, though—but Jude and I looked untouched by the next morning. My bruises were gone, and the bite mark in my arm had healed over into a pink, crescent-shaped scar.

Jude was just as unharmed physically. But the doctor reported that he was suffering from some sort of post-traumatic stress or something, and prescribed a heavy sedative after Jude had a violent episode when Dad finally got to the station from the airport early in the morning. I realized now that the only thing that probably kept Daniel from coming after my family when he first became a werewolf was all the drugs he was using.

My feigned amnesia faltered only with the details of what happened in the alley. Strategically, I remembered how Pete had attacked me, and how Don had saved me. Pete was the one who went to the police after he stumbled from the alley—leaving me behind—but the police decided to hold him, and his thirteen stitches, for further questioning. I'd forgiven him for what he'd done to me, but that didn't mean there shouldn't be consequences for his actions.

The second and third day I spent in the hospital, pacing up and down the corridor outside Daniel's ICU room until the nurses told me I had to leave. "Go home," they said. "Get some rest, child. We'll call if there's any change."

On the fourth day, my father's phone calls finally paid off, and we found out what had happened to Don Mooney. He was discovered on a park bench near a bus station in Manhattan. The police said his heart had just stopped beating. He had no money or ID, and from the way he looked, they decided he was homeless. So Don had been buried in a trench, three pine boxes deep, in a place called Potter's Field, two days before Christmas.

The fifth day, I went back to the hospital. I spent all of Christmas Eve standing outside the glass window, praying. Dad came to collect me late that evening. "The storm's getting worse," he said. "Your mother doesn't want you to get stranded here."

The sixth day was Christmas. Nobody was in the mood to be festive except for Baby James, who played merrily with bubble wrap and curling ribbons. My parents gave me a cell phone. Dad gave Jude a gold ring inlaid with a large black stone.

"It just came last night," Dad said. "I'm sorry. I tried to get it before . . ." Dad balled up the wrapping paper. "I thought I had to wait until I had it. . . . I'm sorry."

"What is it?" Charity asked.

"A graduation ring," I said.

Jude's eyes were like glass, sedated. He didn't speak. He hadn't said a thing in almost a week.

Later that evening, the phone rang. I listened for a minute until the nurse's voice on the other line said, "He's gone. There was nothing we could do to stop him from leaving. . . ."

I dropped the phone, left it dangling in midair, and ran to my room.

Early in the morning of the seventh day, I awoke at my desk with a paintbrush stuck to my arm. There had been another note in the box Daniel left in my room. He'd written out instructions on how to use linseed oil and varnish with my oil paints. I'd fallen asleep at my desk while finishing my portfolio piece of Jude fishing at Kramer's pond.

It was the brightness from the window that awoke me. I peered through the blinds. The early-morning moon reflected off the six inches of snow that had fallen during the night. It looked so different outside than it had a few days before. Now the crusty brown lawn, the leaf-gunky gutters, the neighbors' houses, and the ghostly walnut tree were all covered with a thick layer of pure, white, undisturbed snow. No cars or plows had been down the street yet to throw mud on the curbs or leave black tracks in its perfection. It looked like someone had come along with a brush and painted the world white, making it a giant blank canvas.

Then I saw him. A large wolf that looked almost black in the shadow of the walnut tree. It stared straight up at my bedroom window.

"Daniel?" I gasped, even though I knew it couldn't be. I drew open the blinds, but the wolf was gone.

I must have drifted off to sleep again because I awoke, several hours later, to my mother's screams. Dad and I finally got her to calm down enough to tell us that Jude had left during the night, leaving behind only his bottle of prescription sedatives and a note on the kitchen table.

I can't stay. I don't know who I am anymore. I need to go.

But I knew Jude had been gone long before he ran away.

Mom was practically catatonic—expressionlessly rocking Baby James in the front room—when I slipped out of the house. I knew where I had to go, and I was glad she didn't stop me. I drove for miles down the newly plowed streets and parked the car a little ways off from my destination. I trudged up to the open gate. A man with silver-streaked red hair nodded as I passed him.

"Nice to have a visitor on a day like this."

I tried to smile and returned his wish for a happy new year.

A narrow path had been dug out along the walks, but I preferred to walk in the snow. I let my feet sink in the icy cold, leaving my tracks in the perfect whiteness. I held my dress coat closed over the wooden box, protecting it from the drifting snow and the nipping wind. I sat on a stone bench in the memorial and pulled the book of letters from the box. I opened it to the last marked page and read the letter again.

To Simon Saint Moon,

I found these letters, sealed and addressed to thy wife, among her brother's effects after his disappearance. I have carried them with me these last two years, in hopes of giving them to Katharine in person.

I am saddened by the news of her death. To leave such a young son motherless is a tragedy. I would say it is strange for a wolf to travel so far into a village, yet there have been several other attacks in populated cities such as Amiens, Dijon, and, most strangely, Venice. Alas, all the cities that sent men on our ill-fated campaign have been plagued by these vicious killings. Perhaps God punishes us for our sins where the Pope fails to fulfill his threats of excommunication.

I do not know what these letters contain. I have left them sealed out of respect. I must warn thee, however, thy brother-in-law went mad before he was lost to the forest. His writings may reflect the illness of his mind.

The dagger was found with his letters. It is a valuable relic. Perhaps young Doni can inherit it when he comes of age. He should have something to know his uncle by. Brother Gabriel was a good man. He was one of the few voices of reason against the bloodshed—until the madness took him.

Regards,
Brother Jonathan de Paign
Knight of the Templar

I closed the book and held it to my chest. Katharine had no idea what killed her. She hadn't known it was her own beloved brother. I walked up to the statue standing in the garden in front of me. It was the tall angel who stood with the wolf entwined in his robes. I brushed the snow from the wolf's head, from the angel's wings.

"This was you," I said to the angel. He was the man who helped Daniel—the one who gave him his moonstone necklace and sent the ring for Jude. "You wrote these letters. You are Brother Gabriel." I looked up into his eyes, almost expecting him to answer.

Brother Gabriel was still alive after all these centuries.

Would Daniel have lived for as long if none of this had happened?

I felt like I'd lost everything. Daniel and Jude were gone. My mother was lost in her sorrow. My dad blamed himself. Even April avoided me, like she was too freaked out by everything she'd seen in the sanctuary.

I took off my gloves and knelt in the snow. I undid the button of my coat pocket and pulled out the little carved-wood angel Don had made for me. I brushed its crudely shaped face and the words I'd scratched into the bottom of the figurine: *Donald Saint Moon.*

I imagined Simon Saint Moon getting those letters and the silver dagger possibly only a few weeks after his wife had died—a few weeks too late. I imagined his sorrow at discovering that Katharine's own brother had killed her, his anger at knowing he could have prevented her death—if only they'd gotten that package sooner. I pictured Katharine's son, Doni, growing up with the legacy of his mother's death.

Was it Simon or Doni who took up the quest to destroy werewolves first?

For some reason, I think it was Doni. He must have passed that silver dagger and his mission on to his own son, who then passed it to his, and then on and on through the years, until it came to Don Mooney—the last of the Saint Moons. But Don was different from the others: mentally challenged and alone in the world, with only that knife and his grandfather's stories. He died trying to be a hero like his ancestors. He died before I had a chance to thank him for trying to save me—before I ever told him I forgave him for hurting my father all those years before.

"You belong here, too," I said, and placed the tiny wood angel next to Gabriel in the snow. It seemed a far better memorial for my friend than being planted in a field like a rutabaga or a tulip bulb. "You are a hero."

"People will think you're nuts if you keep talking to inanimate objects."

I almost fell over as I turned to the voice behind me.

And there he sat, on the stone bench where I'd first held his hand, balancing a crutch between his knees.

"Daniel!" I ran to him and threw my arms around his neck.

"Whoa." He winced.

I noticed the bandage across his throat, and I loosened my grip.

"They said you left. They said you got up and walked out in the middle of a shift change. I thought I'd never see you again."

"But you came here?"

"I hoped . . . I hoped you'd come here, too."

Daniel kissed my forehead. "I told you I'd stick around as long as you'd have me." He smiled, all crooked and devious. "Or should I have taken you stabbing me through the heart as a sign you wanted to break up?"

"Shut up!" I punched him in the shoulder.

"Ow."

"I'm sorry." I took his hands in mine. "I didn't do it to hurt you," I said, referring to that night in the parish. "I did it because I promised to save you."

"I know." He squeezed my hand. "And you did."

I looked at the bandage on his neck, the bruises down his jaw—the wounds he couldn't heal on his own anymore. I kissed a scrape on his hand. The smell of his dried blood didn't make me writhe like I thought it would.

"There's one thing I don't understand." I leaned my head against his shoulder. "Why didn't the wolf take me over when I stabbed you?"

Daniel turned my face toward his. He stared down into my eyes. His were so rich and deep, filled with his own personal light, not just a mere reflection like the moon. "Is that what you thought? That you'd become a werewolf if you saved me?" His eyes glistened, but only from tears.

"Yes. I'd been bitten. The wolf was in me. I thought if I killed you—that would give it control. You said a predatory act would do it. . . ."

"Grace." Daniel cupped my face. "What you did

wasn't predatory. It was an act of love. It's why I'm still alive." He smiled. "I went to see Gabriel. That's why I left the hospital. He came here to bring a moonstone for your brother, and I had to see him before he left. I needed to know why I lived. Gracie, Gabriel said that I am the first—the only—Urbat who has ever received the cure and lived. He said only the ultimate gift of love could have freed my soul . . . and granted me back my life." He kissed my cheek. "I understand now. *You* gave me that ultimate gift. You thought you would become a werewolf if you saved me, and you still did it. You were willing to trade yourself for me. There is no greater gift. . . ." He leaned in to kiss my lips.

I pulled away.

"What is it? What's wrong?"

"But the wolf *is* in me. My wounds healed so fast . . . and I feel stronger. I feel like all I want to do is run." I bit my lip. "It will take me over someday. Doesn't it eventually take everyone?"

"No, Grace. Not everyone."

"But Gabriel, he wrote that people who were bitten turned faster. I mean, he was a monk, and he changed within a matter of days. How do I even stand a chance?"

"He was surrounded by the carnage of war. You're not. You're surrounded by people who love you. People who can keep you grounded."

"But Jude had those things, too. He was one of the

best people I've ever known, but he turned so fast. I'm not nearly as good as him."

"Jude *was* good. But he let his fear and jealousy get to him." Daniel shrugged. "'Fear leads to anger. Anger leads to hate. Hate leads to the dark side.'"

I raised an eyebrow and held back the urge to punch him in his injured arm.

"What?" Daniel held up his hands. "Like you weren't there when we watched the *Star Wars* movies fifty-three times that one summer."

"Fifty-four. Jude and I stayed up until two a.m. to finish *Return of the Jedi* after you fell asleep one night. I tried to make caramel popcorn and almost burned the house down. Jude took the blame for me. . . ."

My voice cracked. It hurt so much to think about Jude the way he used to be. "I hope Jude knows that if he . . . when he returns . . . I'll be here for him."

"Then let that be your anchor," Daniel said. "Stay strong so you'll be *Grace* when he needs you." He brushed his fingers down my cheek, wiping away a stray tear. "And you don't have to go through this alone. You have me." He reached into his coat pocket and pulled something out. "And you have this." He opened his hand and held out a jagged black rock. It was his moonstone pendant, broken in half.

I took it from him. It was warmer than the last time I touched it, pulsing with a power I'd never noticed before. It was hope.

"I thought I'd never find it in the snow," he said. "It's been a long time since I had to search for something without my abilities."

"Are you sure you want me to have this? It's yours."

"I don't need it anymore," he said, and tipped up my chin.

He kissed me softly on the lips, with warmth and love. Then his lips parted, and he kissed me in a way that was so complete—giving me everything he'd held back before. I melted into him, letting go, feeling as free and light as I did when we ran in the forest.

"So what do we do now?" I said as Daniel held me to his chest.

He cleared his throat. "There are a lot of bad things out there. Things the Hounds of Heaven were created to destroy." He trailed his finger down the side of my face. "I can't be the hero you want me to be—at least not in that way. But you can, Grace. You don't have to become one of the dark ones. You can fight it. You can turn this curse into a blessing. You can become the hero. You can become truly divine."

Acknowledgments

I owe my undying gratitude and appreciation to the many people who helped mold this book into what it is, and who also helped shape the writer and person I am today. These people include:

My fabulous agent, Ted Malawer, who couldn't have been more enthusiastic about this book. Thanks for being my champion.

All the amazing people at Egmont USA who decided to take a chance on me. Special thanks to Regina Griffin, Elizabeth Law, Mary Albi, Nico Medina, and (of course) my brilliant and patient editor, Greg Ferguson.

My copyeditor, Nora Reichard, whose painstaking work makes it look like I actually know how to use a comma.

Joel Tippie, who designed the breathtaking cover. I couldn't be happier with it.

My wonderful writing teachers over the years, including: Dean Hughes, Louise Plummer, Virginia Euwer Wolff, John H. Ritter, Martine Leavitt, Randall Wright, and A. E. Cannon.

My critique friends: Gaylene Wilson, Kim Woodruff, Julie Hughes, Elena Jube, and Jamie Wood, who forced me to finally rewrite the whole book—and then told me to make it even better. Thanks for all of your advice and suggestions.

My writing posse: Emily Wing Smith, Kimberly Webb Reid, Sara Bolton, Valynne Maetani Nagamatsu, and Brodi Ashton. Some people claim that writing is a solitary and lonely endeavor, but you guys make it a blast. Thank you for always being willing to read, brainstorm, help rewrite that @$&% scene (you know the one) over and over again, and for making me laugh all the time. Here's to many more years of friendship and writing together!

My supportive, loving, and always-willing-to-bend-over-backwards-to-help-out parents: Nancy and Tai Biesinger. And for the record, the mother in this book is in *no way* my own mother (except for the ability to make divine turkey à la king), who is truly one of my best friends.

My enthusiastic and helpful friends, neighbors, in-laws, immediate and extended family, especially my siblings: Noreen, Tai, Brooke, and Quinn. Special thanks to Noreen for the many early-morning walking/brainstorming sessions and for many more hours of babysitting. Additional thanks to my niece Whitney for being my mother's helper, my friend Rachel Headrick for letting my boys play at her house and for letting me talk her ear off (I miss you already, dang it!), Matt Kirby for his many words of wisdom, and James Dashner for showing this newbie the author ropes.

My amazingly adorable (most of the time) children, who put up with my many hours of being glued to the computer—and who aren't afraid to whack me in the head with lightsabers when it's time for me to stop working. Thanks for loving this crazy mom. I love you, too!!!

Last, but never ever least: my practically superhuman husband, Brick, who is my faithful reader, editor, motivator, sounding board, fan, web designer, marketing guru, pseudo-psychiatrist, best friend, and true love. Thank you for always believing in me, even in those moments when I don't believe in myself. I will love you always.

Turn the page for a sneak peek at the second book
in the DARK DIVINE trilogy

The Lost Saint

A
DARK DIVINE
NOVEL

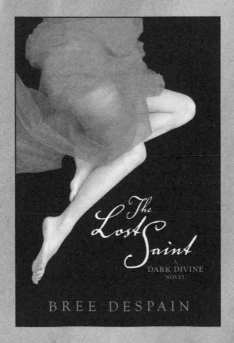

Consequence

"Do what he wants, and you might survive," a harsh voice said into the boy's ear before he felt a sharp blow to the kidneys. He fell forward onto the concrete, his arms splayed out in front of him.

"So this is the one who tried to get away?" another voice asked from the shadows. It was a deeper, older, more guttural voice. Almost like a growl. "This isn't a clubhouse, boy. You can't just decide to stop playing and go home."

The boy coughed. Bloodstained saliva dribbled from his mouth. "I wasn't . . . I didn't . . ." He tried to push himself up onto his knees, but a kick from behind sent him sprawling forward again on the ground. His mind raced, replaying what he'd done to get him to this place.

This place.

They'd said he could call this place home. They'd

said they were his friends. They'd called him their brother.

And that's all it took. That's all he'd wanted.

But this place wasn't home. . . .

"You belong to me," the man said as he stepped out of the shadowed alcove. "And that's why you'll tell me what I want to know."

This place was a prison. And these people were not his family. . . .

The man the others called Father towered over the boy, glaring down at him with glowing, yellow, murderous eyes. "Tell me!" the man roared, and slammed his booted foot down on the ring on the boy's extended hand, grinding into it with his heel.

The boy screamed—but not because of the searing pain he felt as the fragments of the ring sliced into his flesh, and his tendons ripped away from the splintering bones in his fingers. He screamed because he knew that for what he'd done, everyone he'd ever loved, everything he'd left behind, was going to die.

CHAPTER ONE
The Sky Is Falling

THURSDAY NIGHT, SESSION #82

"You can do this, Grace," Daniel said between sharp breaths. "You know you can."

"I'm trying." My fingers trembled as I tightened them into fists.

It was the pain of the transition that always surprised me—no matter how prepared I thought I was. It started as an aching sensation deep inside my body. Pooling in my muscles, making my shoulders shake and my legs throb. My biceps felt like they were on fire.

"Come on, Grace. Don't quit on me now."

"Shut up!" I said, and took another swing.

Daniel laughed and countered to the left. My blow missed his mitt entirely.

"Agh!" I stumbled forward, but Daniel caught me before I fell and pushed me back up. I gritted my teeth and rocked back on my heels in the grass. I was *supposed* to be more agile than this. "Stop moving around."

"Your opponent"—Daniel panted—"isn't going to stand still and just let you hit him." He held his boxing mitts out in front of him, welcoming a new attack.

"He would if he knew what was good for him." I jutted forward with a combination of a hook and a jab that Daniel deflected with his mitts. He spun out of my way, and my next swing went wildly into the air.

"Gah." I shook my head. My moonstone necklace bounced against my chest. It felt warm against my already flushed skin, pulsing with heat.

"You're pushing your punches too much. Save your energy. Quick jabs. Send your arm out with a snap and then bring it back immediately."

"I'm *trying*." The pain in my muscles mounted. But it wasn't from fatigue. It was my powers. My "abilities," as Daniel called them. They were always lingering there, just out of reach, whenever we trained. And if I could just push through the wall of fire that stood between them and me, I could grab on to my powers and use them. Own them.

I cringed as the crescent-shaped scar on my arm pulsed and flared. I dropped my arm and tried to shake out the pain.

"Arms up," Daniel said. "Rule number one: Never drop your guard." He smacked me lightly on the shoulder. It was meant to be a playful hit, but the pain in my scar shot through my arm like electricity.

I glared at him.

"You're getting annoyed," Daniel said. That wry grin of his played on his lips.

"You think?" I sent another combination into his mitts. Three jabs and a hook. I felt a surge of power through my body—finally—and the last punch flew faster and harder than I expected. Daniel missed deflecting it, and my fist slammed into his shoulder.

"Whoa!" He jumped back and shook out his shoulders. "Rein it in, Grace. Don't let your emotions have too much control."

"Then why are you *trying* to annoy me?"

His smile edged from wry to devious. "So you can practice balance." He smacked his mitts together and gestured for me to attack him again.

I could feel my powers pulsing through me—finally in my grasp. I laughed and bounced back several feet. "How's this for balance?" I asked with a smile, and faster than I could think, my body went into a spin kick that landed squarely in one of Daniel's outstretched mitts.

Daniel grunted and stumbled back. His knee wobbled and gave out from under him, and he went flying backward toward the ground.

"Oh no!" I lunged for him and caught him by the arm. But it was too late to stop him from falling, and I toppled with him onto the grass.

We landed side by side on the lawn. I was momentarily stunned—hitting the ground had knocked the wind, and my powers, right out of me. Daniel rolled onto his side and moaned, startling me back into reality.

"Oh no, I'm sorry!" I sat up. "I wasn't thinking. My powers kicked in and I . . . Are you okay?"

Daniel's moan turned into a half laugh. "That's not the kind of balance I was talking about." He winced and pulled off his mitts and tossed them aside.

"Seriously, are you okay?"

"Yeah." Daniel leaned forward and rubbed his knee. He'd trashed it pretty badly when he fell from the parish's balcony a little less than ten months ago. And since I'd cured him of the werewolf curse right after he fell, he'd lost his superhuman powers and had to wait for it to heal like any other regular person. Even after spending weeks on crutches and doing a regiment of physical therapy, his knee still gave him a lot of trouble. "Beatin' up on a gimp. What would your daddy say?"

"Ha-ha." I made a face at him.

"Seriously, though. You're getting good." He groaned and lay back into the grass, tucking his arms behind his head.

"Not good enough."

It took almost an hour of intense sparring before my powers even started to manifest, and once they kicked in, they lasted only, what, like thirty seconds? That was the thing about my *abilities*. They came in spurts whenever *they* felt like it—totally uncontrolled by me. My wounds healed over more quickly than those of a normal human, but I still couldn't draw on that power the way Daniel used to be able to. I couldn't heal myself on my own terms. I'd get bursts of speed or agility, like my body had a mind of its own—like when I kicked Daniel just now—but I usually couldn't control *when* it happened.

After Daniel's doctor gave him the go-ahead to be active again, we started training together three nights a week—when I wasn't grounded, that is. We'd go running, try out some parkour moves, box with mitts like we did tonight, practice trying to hear and see long distances. But even though I was notably faster and stronger than I had been even a few months ago, it was beginning to seem like, no matter how much I tried, I'd never be able to use my powers the way I wanted— instead of them using me.

Daniel sighed. He pointed up in the sky. "Looks like we quit just in time. Meteor shower's started."

I looked up as a shooting star streaked through the dark, clear night above us. "Oh yeah. I almost forgot about that."

Daniel and I had planned on tracking the meteor shower after tonight's training session. We were supposed to count how many meteors we saw in a thirty-minute period for an extra-credit science project at school.

I knew it bothered Daniel that Principal Conway wouldn't even consider letting him graduate last year— he'd missed way too much school during the years he'd spent on the run from the curse that used to plague his every thought. But I, for one, was happy he hadn't left for college yet. And with his attending summer school, doing some extra credit, and testing out of a few classes, we'd get to graduate *together* next spring.

"I'll get the light," I said after I pulled off my glove wraps. I flexed my fingers, stretching out my sore knuckles as I crossed the yard behind Maryanne Duke's old house. I flipped off the porch light, grabbed my hoodie, and headed back over to the lawn. With my sweatshirt draped over my chest like a blanket, I took in a deep breath of autumn air and melted into the cool leaves of grass next to Daniel.

"That's six," I said after a long moment.

Daniel grunted in agreement.

"Oh! Did you see that one?" I pointed above my head at an especially bright star that glistened through the sky until it fizzled into nothing.

"Yeah," Daniel said softly. "Beautiful."

I glanced at him. He was lying on his side, staring at me.

"You weren't even watching," I teased.

"Yes, I was." Daniel flashed me another one of his wry smiles. "I could see it reflecting in your eyes." He reached out and brushed my cheek with his fingers.

"One of the most beautiful things I've ever seen." He hooked one of his fingers under my chin, drawing my face closer to his.

I looked away from his deep, dark brown eyes, surveyed the curves of his muscles under the thin running shirt he'd worn for our training session. Then my gaze flitted to his shaggy hair that had settled into a nice golden blond over the summer—all the dark had finally washed out. I followed the lines of his jaw, and then rested my gaze on the curve of his smiling lips. It wasn't his devious smile anymore. But the one he saved for moments like this—the one that meant he was truly happy.

He was still warm from our sparring match, and I could feel the heat radiating off his body only a few inches away. Drawing me to him. Willing me to close the gap between us. I looked back at his eyes, loving the feeling that I could get lost in them forever.

It was moments like these when I still couldn't believe that he was even here.

That he was still alive.

That he was *mine*.

I'd watched him die once. Held him in my arms and listened to his heartbeat fade away into nothing.

It happened the night my brother Jude lost himself to the werewolf curse—just days before he left a note on the kitchen table, walked out into a snowstorm, and disappeared. The same night Jude infected me with the powers that taunted me now.

The night I almost lost everything.

"There goes another one." Daniel leaned in and touched a kiss just beside my eye. He trailed his lips across my cheek and down my jaw, sending a tingling sensation through my body with the deliciousness of his touch.

Daniel's lips came to my mouth. He brushed them softly there at first, and then pressed gently. His lips parted, and he mingled them with mine.

My legs ached as I pulled him closer—finally closing the distance between us.

I didn't care that we were out in the yard behind Maryanne Duke's old house. I didn't care that we were supposed to be tracking the meteor shower for class. Nothing existed outside his touch. There was nothing under the falling stars except Daniel and me and the blanket of grass underneath us.

Daniel jerked his head back slightly. "You're buzzing," he whispered against my lips.

"Huh?" I asked, and kissed him.

He pulled away. "I think it's your phone."

I noticed the buzzing, too. My cell phone in my sweatshirt pocket.

"So what?" I grabbed the front of his shirt playfully and pulled him closer. "They can leave a message."

"It could be your mom," Daniel said. "I just got you back. I don't want to lose you for another two weeks."

"Damn it."

Daniel smirked. He always thought it was hilarious when I swore. But he did have a point—about my mom, that is. She had only two modes since Jude left: Zombie Queen or Crazed Mother Bear. It was like her own personal brand of bipolar disorder.

I'd left for the evening before she got back from seeing Aunt Carol off at the train station, so I wasn't sure what mode she would be in, but if it was of the overbearing sort, I could possibly be grounded again just for the act of not answering my phone on the second ring.

I sat up and dug into the pocket of my hoodie, but I'd already taken too much time, and the call ended before I pulled out my phone.

"Crap." I couldn't take another two weeks of not seeing Daniel outside of school. I flipped open my phone to check the missed call info, mentally crossing my fingers that it hadn't been my mother, but what I saw made me cock my head in confusion. "Where's your phone?" I asked Daniel.

"I left it inside. On my bed." Daniel yawned. "Why?"

I stood up, still staring at the display on my phone. A dark feeling crept under my skin. My hair stood up on the back of my neck, and my muscles tensed in that way they did when my body sensed danger. The phone started ringing again in my hand. I almost dropped it.

"Who's calling you?"

"You are."

I fumbled with the phone and almost dropped it again. I pushed the Answer button. "Hello?" I asked tentatively, as I put it to my ear.

Silence.

I looked at the screen on my phone to make sure I hadn't missed the call, or accidentally hit the Disconnect button. I returned the phone to my ear. "Um, hello?"

Still nothing.

I looked at Daniel and shrugged. "It must be some weird kind of flyaway." I was about to hang up when I heard something on the line. It sounded almost like a hand covering the receiver.

"Hello?" My skin tingled. Goose bumps pricked up my arms. "Who's there?"

"They're coming for you," a muffled voice said over the phone. "You're in danger. You're all in danger. You can't stop them."

"Who is this?" I asked, panic rising with the tension in my muscles. "How did you get Daniel's phone?"

"Don't trust him," the trembling voice said. "He makes you think you can trust him, but you can't."

Daniel reached for the phone, but I shook him off.

"What are you talking about?" I asked.

"You can't trust him." The voice on the phone seemed suddenly clearer—like the hand muffling the receiver had moved out of the way—and the familiarity of it made my heart almost stop. "Please, Gracie, *listen* to me this time. You're all in danger. You have to know that—" The voice cut off with a clatter, like the phone had been dropped, and the line went dead.

"Jude!" I shouted into my phone.

ABOUT TEN SECONDS LATER

"Wait!" Daniel called after me as he tried to push himself up from the ground.

But I'd hit the button to call back Daniel's phone, and was off the grass and across the back patio before it even started ringing. I could hear his phone faintly playing a metal guitar version of "Moonlight Sonata" from his basement apartment. I felt a burst of supernatural speed and, in a matter of seconds, flew around the house and down the cement stairs that led to the apartment.

The old yellow door was slightly ajar. My palms suddenly went sweaty. Daniel was normally a bit compulsive about keeping his door locked. The hinges groaned as I pushed the door open a little farther.

"Jude?" I called into the studio apartment. The phone had stopped ringing, and the apartment was dark, but I could see a pair of Daniel's Converse lying on the ground next to the crumpled pile of laundry. The sofa bed was pulled out but the blanket was missing, and the sheets were halfway off the thin mattress.

"Gracie, wait." Daniel appeared at the top of the

stairs. "That may not have been your brother on the phone."

"It was him. I'd know his voice anywhere." I was absolutely, upon threat of death from my father, not allowed to enter Daniel's apartment with him alone— but I took a step into the doorway, anyway. "Jude, are you here?"

"That's not what I mean." Daniel limped down the steps. "I mean, Jude may not have been *your brother* when he was calling. He may have been under the influences of the wolf."

Once again, Daniel had a point, and I shivered at the reminder of the things my brother had done before while under the control of the wolf. The crescent-shaped scar in my arm twinged, as if to punctuate the memories. But still, if Jude *was* here, I needed to know. My heart sped up as I took a step inside the apartment.

"Jude?" I flicked the light switch a couple of times. Nothing happened.

My footsteps kept time with my heartbeat as I walked deeper into the dark room. Apprehension tightened in my muscles. Tingling pain spread through my tendons. My body was preparing for something—flight or fight.

I passed the sofa bed, inspecting the crumpled sheets for the phone Daniel said he'd left there. Daniel opened the bathroom door and cautiously eased inside the tiny room. I heard the opening and closing of cabinets, and then the rustling of the shower curtain.

The tingling pain spread to my fingertips, and I tightened my hand around my cell phone. I hit the Redial button once more. I could hear the ringing through my phone before the metal tone of Daniel's phone began. The noise was soft at first, but then it rapidly got louder and closer.

My body whirled on instinct toward the sound. I landed in a crouching position, ready to pounce. A small growl escaped from my lips.

"Whoa, Gracie!" Daniel said. He stood in front of me, his hands up in a defensive position, and his cell phone clutched in one of his fists. "It's just me. I found my phone in the shower."

I lunged at him and threw my arms around his neck. "Holy crap, I thought you were . . . were . . ." I held my breath and pressed my moonstone necklace to my chest, letting anxiety slowly drain out of my body. I don't know exactly what I'd thought was behind me. A werewolf with a phone in its jaws? I felt positively ridiculous now.

"It's okay." Daniel brushed his fingers through my hair. "Nobody's here."

"But someone *was* here," I said. "Unless you have a habit of talking on the phone in the shower."

"Try using your powers to tell if it was Jude," Daniel said. "Use your senses like I taught you."

I didn't have much hope that it would actually work, but I took a deep breath, held the air in the back of my mouth, and tried to let it fill my senses like Daniel had explained it to me at least two dozen times in the last few months. I was supposed to be testing the air for hints of my brother, trying to sift out a faint familiar taste or smell beyond Daniel's almondy scent and the tang of oil paint that always filled his apartment. I let my breath out in a long, frustrated hiss.

Daniel gave me a hopeful look.

I shook my head. I'd failed again.

"It's okay," Daniel said. "It'll come. It just takes time." That's what he *always* said.

"Yeah, I know." I hoped he wasn't going to launch into his usual speech about how it takes balance, and how I'm doing great so far, and how most Urbat take *years* to develop their powers. "Besides, I don't even know if I remember what my brother smells like, and I certainly haven't ever tasted him before."

Daniel smiled. *Lecture averted.*

I took his cell phone from him and used my *human* eyes to inspect it for clues. The face was cracked, like it had been dropped, and I was surprised it still worked. I checked the time and the number of the last call made from the phone. "He definitely called me from this." I shuddered. "He was right in here while we were just outside."

"What did he say?" Daniel asked.

"He said I was in danger. That we were all in danger.

He said, 'They're coming for you,' and that I couldn't stop them. And he said that I couldn't trust someone else . . ." I bit my lip and hesitated. "I don't know, but I think he meant you."

Daniel crossed his arms in front of his chest. "Sounds like his feelings toward me haven't changed." A look of concern settled in his dark brown eyes.

I wondered if he was thinking the same thing as me—that maybe Jude had other intentions for breaking into the apartment. Maybe Jude had thought Daniel would be here alone and vulnerable? But that didn't make any sense. If he had wanted to attack Daniel, my presence certainly wouldn't have stopped him. It hadn't stopped him before.

"Did he say anything else?" Daniel asked.

"No. The call cut off. I think he dropped the phone. He seemed nervous. Maybe his hand was shaking." *Or maybe he'd been about to go through the change.*

"Do you think he was messing with you?" Daniel asked. "Maybe this is just some kind of twisted game to him. He never wanted us to be together in the first place."

"I don't know." I looked down at the phone in my hands. "I guess it's possible. But it doesn't make sense that he'd come back here just for a practical joke. I think he's got some other motivation."

Maybe it was my new wolf instincts taking over

again, or maybe it was just some kind of sibling connection, but something deep down told me that Jude was right . . . we were all in danger. I just didn't know if *he* was the one we were all in danger from.